TO WIN A DEMON'S LOVE

A Novel of Love and Magic

NADINE MUTAS

Nadine Mutas
PO Box 94
New Almaden, CA 95042
nadine@nadinemutas.com
www.nadinemutas.com

This is a work of fiction. Names, characters, places and incidents either are
products of the author's imagination or are used fictitiously. Any
resemblance to actual events or locales or persons, living or dead, is entirely
coincidental.

Cover Design by Najla Qamber Designs
www.najlaqamberdesigns.com
Editing by Faith Freewoman, Demon for Details Manuscript Editing

ISBN-13: 978-1545127186
ISBN-10: 1545127182

❀ Created with Vellum

For Jessica,
I'm so glad that you're my BEAST

And, always, for Sergej

ACKNOWLEDGMENTS

Writing and publishing a book is always at once a solitary endeavor and a team effort. My thanks for sticking with me during the various, crazy stages of producing this story, and for supporting me and just generally being awesome:

To Sergej, because without you, none of this would be possible. You hold my heart and keep me going, and you mean the world to me.

To my mom, for your generous babysitting help during those insane first draft writing days.

To my little demon spawn, for being as understanding as only a toddler can be when Mom stared off into space plotting the next scene during playtime.

To Jessica Hofmann, for believing in me and my writing, and just being the very bestest friend I could wish for.

To Dawn Linse, for all those encouraging, commiserating, inspiring, and deep conversations and brainstorming sessions. Good crit partners are hard to find, and I'm so happy I snatched you right up.

To my Panera girls, for keeping me going and providing that safe, cozy environment of shared creativity.

To my beta readers, Wendy, Debbie, and Jackson, who so enthusiastically read TWADL and gave me valuable feedback. I cherish you guys.

To Faith Freewoman, for a fun and awesome edit, and for catching all those mashed-potato-brain mistakes.

To Erin Hanson, for being so kind to let me quote her poem in my story, and who has so, so many more wonderful pieces of poetry on her blog: www.thepoeticunderground.com. You're an amazing artist, and you inspire me.

And last but not least, to all my readers who loved *To Seduce a Witch's Heart*, and kept asking for the next book. You're everything.

P.S.: Grant, this is what you get when you speak bad about romance novels. You dared me. I delivered.

CHAPTER 1

N *ote to self: Stalking demons while wearing a thong is worse than having a crotch itch while giving a speech to your Elders.*

Shifting from one foot to the other, Lily Murray adjusted the sorry excuse for underwear for what felt like the hundredth time in five minutes.

"I don't know why I let you talk me into this," she muttered to the witch next to her, who didn't seem to have the same ass-eats-slinky-panties problem as Lily. Must be a thong-wearing natural.

Lenora Jones peeked over the metal fence they were hiding behind to check on the *morbus* demon loitering on the other side of the street. "Hey, wasn't my idea to play stakeout in the rain," she whispered back. "I was all in favor of letting that demon go."

Not an option. No way could Lily keep on partying when she knew one of those disease-spreading creatures was skulking in the vicinity. "Pfft, it's not the traipsing or rain I mind. It's the fact that my underwear seems to be hell-bent on disappearing into the place where the sun don't shine." Grimacing, she tugged at the thong again. "How do you put up with these pesky things every damn day?"

"You get used to it."

"You know," Lily said, keeping her voice hushed despite the fact they were far enough away that the demon wouldn't hear them, "I've never really been a fan of that statement. You can get used to a lot of things, and it doesn't make them good. Lack of indoor plumbing, for example. Or a missing limb. Or Pierce Brosnan as James Bond."

Lenora huffed a low laugh, her tawny brown skin shimmering golden in the dim street light when she glanced over at Lily again. "Are you still sore about that? That was like forever ago."

"You gotta draw the line somewhere. And speaking of line..." She adjusted that useless scrap of fabric *again*. "I am never going to wear one of these again. Ever."

"You will if you don't want to have an ugly panty line ruining the look of your sexy dress. No way am I going to let any friend of mine walk around like that." Lenora gave her a playful wink.

"That's assuming I'll ever put on another skin-tight dress. Which I won't."

Lily rose on her tiptoes and peered over the fence. The *morbus* demon—inconspicuous-looking to human eyes due to glamour, though its real form was covered with putrid pus and leaking sores—kept leaning against the wall of the old brewery, staying dry and puffing on its cigarette while the rain pelted down on the overhang. And the demon was still too close to the group of human patrons enjoying a smoke outside the brew pub that had just closed for the night.

2

Dammit. Lily and Lenora couldn't take the bastard down in front of so many witnesses. They had to wait until either it wandered off or the human group disbanded. Of course, if the demon made a move toward the group, Lily would hex its ass in a heartbeat, before it could touch anyone and spread more disease. Until then, they'd have to keep their distance, lest the demon pick up their witch auras and high-tail it out of there.

"You should, though," Lenora said.

"Hmm?"

"Wear a sexy dress more often." She tugged at the hem of the striking blue slip of a club dress Lily had on, now plas-tered even tighter to her skin due to the incessant Portland rain. "You've got a killer body, hon. Flaunt it. It'll help you get in touch with your feminine side and get more dates."

Lily shot her a look. "I am in touch with my feminine side. I always paint my toenails."

For a moment they stared at each other. Then they burst into choked laughter. The rain swallowed the sound, but still Lily clamped her mouth shut and checked on the demon again. *All good.* Hunkering down behind the fence again, she turned to Lenora.

"And just for the record, I don't need help in the dating department. I'm very happy with the status quo."

"You mean moping around for months secretly pining for a good lay that will break your headboard?"

Lily raised her brows. "I like my headboard just fine, thank you very much. It's sturdy. Reliable. And it doesn't ask too much of me, no 'come meet my parents,' or 'please move in with me.' Nope, just straightforwardly doing its job, sitting at the top of my bed and propping up my pillows."

"Lil." Such admonishment in her tone. *Pfft.* "You

wouldn't have let me talk you into going out in a dress that screams 'available' if you didn't need some between-the-sheets action." Lenora checked on the demon again.

"Fine." Lily puffed out a sigh. "You're right."

It had been months since she'd broken up with Jeff—or rather, run screaming in the other direction—and she hadn't been on a date since. The thought of starting another serious relationship was as enticing as using chili paste for a douche, but a little no-strings-attached sex sure sounded good.

Well, not gonna happen tonight. Finding an uncomplicated hookup had to wait for now. Demon-blasting duty came first.

She was about to suggest they go out again tomorrow —*not* in another dress, but maybe slacks and a shoulder-baring shirt, which she found much more comfortable— when something or someone scraped on the concrete behind her. She whipped around. The shadows between the containers in the warehouse yard shifted. Not just the rain playing tricks on her vision. Something was coming.

"Lenora," she snapped, a second before a pack of hellrats broke from the dark and poured out into the yard.

Her powers already primed and ready, buzzing under-neath her skin, Lily struck out. "*Kālam kuru!*"

With a surge of heat, her magic rushed through her body, her hand, shot out toward the advancing horde and hit the first two hellrats straight on. They squeaked and collapsed. Immediately, several other demonic rodents fell upon their dead and ripped into the bodies. *Yikes.* So much for pack loyalty.

She spared a glance to the side while throwing a fire spell at the wave of hellrats closest to her. "Len, you okay?"

Lenora grunted, kicking a rat into the side of the

container, her hand curled around a magically enhanced *shuriken* that she'd pulled out of the gods knew where. She hurled the throwing star at another rat, slicing off the rodent's head. *Neat.*

Assured her friend had it under control, Lily focused on the nasty critter currently lunging at her ankles. She whipped out the dagger she'd hidden in a sheath high up her inner thigh, went down in a crouch, and slashed at the fucker. Using the momentum, she turned in a semi-circle and let her blade slice half a dozen more hellrats who weren't fast enough to evade her maneuver. She remained in the crouch, her calf muscles flexing as she turned in a new angle and struck out again at the newest wave of revolting rodents. Another half dozen down.

She stood and retreated a step to block an incoming rat-missile. Her high-heel slipped on a rain-slick hellrat body. The world tilted in a lurch as she crashed down, barely able to break the fall with her hands. Pain exploded in her palms, her wrists, and, oh just about all the joints in her body.

"Mother. Fuck."

That second of cursive expression was all she got. The next instant, a wave of hellrats swarmed her. No choice but to roll. Gritting her teeth against the yucky feel of rolling over the cold, wet ground in a dress that bared more than it covered, she managed to kick and elbow and slash off most of the hellrats before they had a chance to bite.

"*Skeit!*" The shield charm exploded outward, shoving off the remaining critters. Another killing spell made short work of the rest of the horde.

Breath coming in puffs, Lily flipped over. She'd rolled to the entrance to the warehouse yard in the scuffle, and was now in clear sight of the other side of the street. *Crap on a stick.* Had the demon spotted her? She scooted back behind the fence and peered out.

Her stomach clenched. The group of humans had left— but the *morbus* demon wasn't alone.

"What the—?" She leaned out farther, trying to catch a better view.

Another male approached the demon, though she couldn't make out his features in the semi-darkness and drizzle of rain. Was he human? If yes, she had to act. She couldn't risk him catching a disease.

A quick glance to the side confirmed Lenora was almost done blasting the last of the hellrats. "Len, join me when you can. I'm going for the demon." And with that she was off.

She'd sprinted halfway across the deserted street, her high-heels making wet, clicking sounds on the rain-covered asphalt, when the scene in front of her made her stop dead in her tracks.

The new male punched the demon, kneed it in the guts and grabbed it by the throat. The *morbus* grunted and flailed. To no avail. The other male overpowered it with astonishing ease. Hoisting it up against the wall, the man brought its head level with his and leaned in, almost as if... Was he kissing the thing?

Lily reared back, her mouth falling open. Who'd want to kiss a *morbus* demon? Before she could dwell on that particular question of morbid insanity, the air around the man shimmered. His aura, which had been too faint for her to get a read on, brightened, and a telltale trace of demon magic pulsed off him.

The male was a demon, too.

Rooted to the spot, she could only stare while the *morbus's* aura lit up as well, then flickered like a candle in a gust of wind. The *morbus's* power signature faded, and judging by the flare in the unknown demon's aura, whatever he was doing to the *morbus* fed his powers. The new demon let go of the *morbus*, and the now lifeless form of the contagious bastard sank to the ground.

The male hadn't been kissing the *morbus* demon. He'd *killed* it.

Power curled around the remaining demon. Suddenly, he whipped his head around, homing in on Lily. A sharp buzz zinged through her, as if every one of her cells had been charged with a dizzying bolt of electricity. Those eyes... Swirling red and black, magnetic in the way they locked on to her.

A life leech, a demon who fed off others' life force.

With a gasp, she snapped out of whatever trance she'd been in. This was a demon. A lethal one. She couldn't let him get away.

Summoning her power to her fingertips, she ran toward him. Hand raised, she was about to hurl a spell at him when he was suddenly in front of her. She stumbled from the abrupt stop, and he gripped her wrist, squeezing just hard enough to numb the flow of magic to her hand. What the ever-loving—?

He leaned in, his features illuminated by the street lights. Human-looking, his skin a nice golden summer tan, he was a handsome son of a bitch. His eyes—now silver gray rimmed with amber—held her spellbound.

"Don't," he murmured.

Droplets of rain fell from the hair hanging over his face, caressed her nose. His thumb stroked over the inside of her wrist, and a tingle traveled up her arm.

The next second, he was gone. She staggered from the

sudden loss of his hold, her mind reeling. Turning in a circle, she scanned the street for him. A block down, she barely caught a glimpse of a dark figure disappearing round the corner at incredible speed.

"Lil!" Lenora ran up to her, panting, a hellrat's bloody tail hanging from her voluminous hair. "Are you okay?"

Lily nodded, her heart thundering in her chest. "You've got rat on you." She picked the tail out of Lenora's hair and tossed it away.

"Thanks." Lenora studied the slowly disintegrating shape of the *morbus* demon. "What the hell happened here?"

Lily frowned while images of the scene she'd witnessed replayed in her head. "Somebody just did our job for us."

But the memory that surfaced again and again, refused to release her from its spell, was one of silver-gold eyes and a voice of pure sin.

CHAPTER 2

S omeone was following Lily. That prickly feeling in the
nape of her neck was a dead giveaway.

Unbidden, the image of the life leech flashed through her
mind, rain-slick hair framing his face, his eyes holding her
captive, his hand tight around her wrist in a grasp that had
felt more like a caress. Was her skin still tingling from his
touch? She rubbed her wrist, shook off the memory.

After Lenora had hopped onto the MAX Light Rail to her
family's house in Gresham, Lily had taken the MAX in the
opposite direction, and was now walking the last stretch
from the station to the high-class address of the Murray
family mansion. Since the rain had stopped some time
earlier, it was a beautiful stroll along the streets, which led
through the outskirts of Forest Park, the September night
unusually warm, kissing her damp skin.

Her senses on alert, she unobtrusively scanned the area.
The two-lane street lay quiet, and the huge houses loomed
dark and silent, half hidden behind trees in their generous
front yards. The rustling of leaves in the wind and Lily's

high heels clicking away on the pavement were the only sounds. She deliberately dropped her keys, and while crouching down to pick them up, she managed to sneak the dagger out of its thigh sheath. Straightening again, she pretended to hug herself for warmth and hid the blade between the inside of her forearm and her chest.

If that life leech had indeed followed her here, she'd give him one hell of a welcome.

Or it might not be him, but some other creep. There had been a couple of unexpected disappearances of witches throughout the larger Portland area in recent weeks, with three bodies turning up some time later in different parts of the city. Though the deaths, and thus the disappearances, didn't seem connected—with one witch having bled dry, one having died of some unidentifiable disease, the third little more than a piece of rotten meat—something was in the air.

A hiss broke the quiet, and the next second something sharp stung her butt. She twisted to get a look at her behind. A dart was sticking out from her right butt cheek. What the actual fuck? Someone had shot her. With a dart gun. In the ass. Like some wild animal.

She ripped out the dart while surveying the street. Nothing but shadows. Still, she went into fighting stance, prepared for an attack, her fingers curled into a fist around the dart. Was it a sedative? Meant to knock her out? *Fuckity fuck.* Anger bubbled up in her bloodstream, its heat rising to her face. What kind of sick, disturbed—

The air changed. The split-second warning was enough to prepare her for the attack, and she ducked and slid to the side. The club meant for her head whooshed through empty air instead. She used the momentum of the demon's lunge and her evasive maneuver to slice his ribcage open with the dagger. While the demon cried out, she followed up by ramming her elbow into his spine.

Coughing, the demon stumbled down. She was about to blast him with a spell that would choke him unconscious when her powers fizzled out like a burnt fuse. Her heart lurched. Pinpricks of light danced in her vision. She swayed as a wave of nausea swamped her. *No.* Whatever the bastard had shot her with was kicking in.

She had to get home. It wasn't that far. She only needed to incapacitate him enough to give her a head start—and hope to the gods that she could still run.

With a grunt, the demon jumped to his feet. Eyes blazing with red and black leered at her. Another life leech? This was not the one she'd run into before. Where were they coming from all of a sudden? Was there a convention going on?

Cold sweat broke out all over her. The mad thump of her heart pounded in her head, the sound off somehow. Like a huge machine working against pressure, stuttering. A milky film glided over her eyes. She shook her head and blinked to clear her vision.

The demon charged, his movements a blur. She slid to the side, evading him. Or that was what she wanted to do. Her muscles had a different idea, turning to rubber on her. Those traitors.

She crumpled to the ground, the life leech on top of her. His hands pressed down on her shoulders, grinding her back against the concrete. Maybe if she tried her powers again—reaching deep, she searched for the familiar spark of magic, for the glow that had lit up her soul since she'd turned six and came into her powers.

Empty. Throbbing. Nothingness.

Duck a fuck. This couldn't be happening.

The demon grinned, looming over her. "We're gonna have a lot of fun together, you and me. Can't wait until I get you home." He reached for the club again.

Ugh. He wanted to abduct her? Images of her stuck in a pit while the creep lowered down lotion in a basket flashed through her mind, made her shudder. *Focus, Lily.*

She spat in his face and used the second he reared back and loosened his hold to knock her forehead against his nose. The bolt of pain from the impact was so worth it.

"You bitch!" The demon's voice came out garbled through the blood spouting from his broken nose.

"You're not putting *me* into a pit," Lily muttered while kneeing him in the ribs right where she'd cut him before.

Her muscles were cooperative enough to let her elbow and kick her way out from under the life leech. He was so busy trying to breathe past the pain from her knee jab that he couldn't even hold her back. The fountain of blood gushing from his broken nose and the reflexive flood of tears impairing his vision didn't make things easier for him, not that she gave a fuck.

Somewhere in the scuffle, she'd lost her dagger and the dart. Well, a good old kick to the head would have to do to buy her time to escape. Lying on her side on the ground, she drew back her leg and slammed the heel of her stiletto straight against the demon's temple. He grunted and fell over.

There. That ought to give her a fighting chance to get home.

Muscles spasming, her vision flickering in and out, she scrambled to her feet and swayed for a second. Shit, that drug got her bad. She gulped in a lungful of pine-scented night air and ran.

Throwing a glance over her shoulder while she raced toward the Murray mansion, she checked on the demon. He was on his feet, but wasn't following. Stumbling, holding his sliced side, he fled in the other direction. *Good riddance.* She'd still sic her mom and Baz on the bastard once she made it home, even though chances were slim they'd catch him or find out where he ran.

She maintained her pace as well as possible with rebellious muscles and bones that seemed to be disintegrating. No reason to risk that demon coming back, or some other creature deciding she was snack material.

Through her wobbly vision, she finally spotted the high, wrought-iron fence of her family's grand house. Just a few more feet and she'd be past the magical wards cast around the property. Once she was inside the guarded perimeter, she could crawl the rest of the way. Yeah, crawling sounded good.

Air sawed in and out of her lungs, leaving painful tingles in its wake. Every nerve in her body ached. She felt crappier than the half-digested squirrel the neighbors' dog had upchucked on the sidewalk last week.

She halted in front of the gate and fumbled for her keys in the tiny black purse that had miraculously survived the hellrat fight plus the demon attack. Her hand shook as she unlocked the gate. The air felt heavy, thick, charged with a buzz, as if she was close to a power line.

Just inside the perimeter, the wards shimmered translucent, invisible to human eyes. To a witch or otherworld creature, they appeared as a colorless, fluid shift in the air, like a desert mirage. And they'd strike down any unwelcome visitor—demon or anyone meaning harm to the Murrays—

with enough force to fling the intruder across the street. While possibly frying every hair on their body.

She pushed the gate open with one hand and was about to step on the property when an electric tingle shot up her arm—the one touching the wards. Frowning, she paused. She glanced around, scanned the deserted street behind her.

No time to dwell on peculiarities. She had to get inside. Who knew what the demon had shot her with and how long she had until it made her pass out. Her mom could run some magical tests and check what kind of date rape drug coursed through her system, and then she could administer an antidote...or Lily could simply sleep it off.

She stepped over the ward line. Power zinged over her skin, through her body. Her heart stuttered, then hopped like a cat on hot asphalt. She stumbled, catching her breath. Another step—which felt like walking against a strong air current—and she was inside the perimeter. She laid a hand on her chest, her pulse a flutter in her throat.

What in the gods' name was going on? This had never happened before. It was almost as if...the wards were reacting to her. Which was a load of bullshit. As a Murray witch, she was of course cleared to pass the magical protection, and until this time, it had never felt like more than a pleasant breeze.

There had to be a glitch in the wards. Maybe it was time to recast them and her mom had just forgotten to do it in time, and now the spells acted all wonky.

Shaking her head, she trudged toward the flight of steps to the front entrance. When she passed the rose bushes, which were still in full bloom thanks to the lingering Oregon summer, she did a double take at the intensity of their fragrance. It was like walking through one of those clouds of perfume the sales reps liked to spray-chase you with at Macy's. Whoa. Definite olfactory overload.

"I think it's time to call it a night," she muttered to herself while she unlocked the front door. "Too much weird stuff happening."

The trembling and aching of her muscles had subsided, only to be replaced with such intense hunger it felt like she was digesting herself. That figurative hole in her stomach had to be the size of the Grand Canyon. Was this what coming down from drugs felt like? She'd never taken any, so she had no clue whether it was a side effect of whatever was in that dart.

All right, she had to wolf down something before she woke her mom and had her poke and prod her magically to counter the drug. She passed through the foyer, sticking to the walls to avoid walking underneath the massive chandelier, as she'd done ever since she was a kid—who knew when that suspicious thing would decide to crash down?— and barged into the kitchen.

"Damn, Lil, you look like something not even the cat would drag in."

She shot a dark glance at Basil, who was sitting at the kitchen island, clad in pajama pants and a loose T-shirt. Just peeled himself out of bed apparently.

"Charming as ever, bro," she muttered as she walked past him, opened the fridge, perused it for a minute, and growled. "What happened to the leftover tacos?"

"Ate 'em."

"And the tamales?"

"Made their final journey into my stomach."

"The salad?" Was there a hitch of despair in her voice?

"Had to be finished before it went all squashy."

With a groan of frustration, she turned and glared at him. "I swear you eat like a horse. On steroids!"

An easy shrug of his shoulder. "That's rich coming from the woman who gobbles up whole Thanksgiving turkeys by herself."

"That was *once*. And I'd been starved for a week."

She'd gotten all four of her wisdom teeth pulled at once, and since her aunt Isabel had allowed no one to magically heal her afterwards—saying it would spoil the Murray children if they never experienced the fragility of health—Lily had lived off soup for days on end until she could finally eat something solid again. Which unfortunately happened to be on the day of Thanksgiving, and...well, she hadn't been able stop herself with the turkey.

"And you barfed for about a week afterwards," Baz pointed out kindly.

It had been a bad judgment call.

He grinned, and as always, it was so damn infectious that she snorted into laughter after trying to fight her amusement for a minute. She could never really stay serious around him for long, his calm but serene nature dispelling even her foulest moods. Being twins, they'd always been close, even if their tempers differed as much as their appearances—put next to each other, people never guessed they were related at all. Her eyes were blue, his brown, her hair was inky black, his was dark blond, and the only gene they seemed to share was for height. They used to make jokes about not having the same father—until their mom got so upset about it that they stopped.

"All right, sis," Baz said, his brown eyes sparking. "If I make you a sandwich, will you stop your whining?"

She started to salivate. Baz's sandwiches were famous,

not just in their family, but throughout the entire witch community. Friends dropped by at random times, casually mentioning how they hadn't had the time for lunch, and Baz —being the caring fool he was—whipped up something taste-buds-seducing delicious in no time. He might be without powers as a rare male descendant of a witch line, but, oh boy, it sure seemed like he was magically gifted when it came to preparing food.

Baz opened the fridge, got out the toppings, and laid them out on the table. An unholy growl rose up from her stomach, which was well on its way to transforming into the Hulk. She watched Basil move, her attention caught by the soft glow around him. She squinted. What was that? His normally faint human aura became brighter, sharper, and...yummy.

Her hands shook. The trembling spread, took over her body, until every muscle vibrated with the urgent need to...what?

"So," Baz said as he was slathering cream cheese on the bread, "I take it your night out with Len ended in some kind of fun fight?"

She inched closer, drawn by an invisible force, her eyes locked on his broad back, his heartbeat an enchanting rhythm to her ears—wait, his heartbeat? How on earth was she able to hear that? She blinked, sucked in a breath, and tried to shake the sense of driving need pounding through her veins.

"And is that blood on your forehead, or did you have an especially shaky hand when you applied your lipstick?"

Hunger clawed at her insides. Her vision narrowed, focused on the vibrant, strong human life in front of her, and her breathing went hunting quiet. *Kill.*

"Lily?" The male turned. His pulse stuttered, his face paling. "Your eyes…"

She crouched, flexed her muscles—and lunged. A blur of movements, and then she had the human on the floor, her hands around his throat, claws digging into his skin. His life force pulsed, so bright, so delicious, so strong.

"Lil, stop…" A pained rasp, his hands pawing at her wrists, trying to break her hold.

To no avail. His human strength was no match for her power. His feeble attempts to fight her only incited the predator within.

Darkness curled in the deep, permeated her mind. Her every fiber ached, craving new energy. The kind of energy that flowed through the human's veins, shimmered warm around him, curled into golden puffs with every breath leaving his mouth.

Take. She just needed to take it.

She frowned, ground her teeth, her claws pricking his skin. Thin streaks of blood trickled down his throat. Her insides knotted together. Sweat broke out on her forehead, her back. His life force glowed, mocking her with its enticing potency. She was so close. So close. She leaned in. All she had to do—

A crash outside the French doors to the backyard startled her. Gasping, she loosened her hold on the man—Basil, her *brother*—and scrambled off him. She stumbled to her feet, her hand pressed against her chest. The floor fell out from under her. What had she done?

Baz coughed, massaged his throat, and scooted away from her. His bloodshot eyes found hers, and there was *terror* in them. His neck was red from the wounds her claws had ripped—*claws*. Fucking claws.

What kind of monster have I become?

Footsteps sounded outside the kitchen door. Magic stirred the air, seeping in from the foyer, announcing the powerful witch about to enter the room. Lily's pulse kicked up. *Mom.* Ice-cold fear gripped her chest. *No, no, no. I can't let her see me like this.*

She glanced toward Baz, who was still clutching his blood-streaked throat, his face red from her lethal choke-hold, then raced toward the huge French windows leading onto the back deck. The door to the kitchen opened.

Lily was out the French doors before her mom set foot in the room. The chill of the night hugged her, cooling her sweat-slick skin. Heart pumping in overdrive, panic freezing her mind, she ran. Across the deck, down to the lawn, to the other side of the yard. Her bare feet hit the wet grass, then the mulch at the edge of the property.

Without thinking, she scaled the fence, barely registering that she managed to jump over the six-foot enclosure with the ease of a pole vaulter when she'd always sucked at anything jumping-related in PE. She landed on the other side with the grace of a feline predator—just before she stumbled over her own feet and crashed face-first into a brick wall.

The wall moved.

Strong hands grabbed her arms, and she jerked at the tell-tale trace of demon aura touching her senses. It was him. That life leech bastard who'd shot her was back. Adrenaline powered through her. Panic made a comeback, and she kicked and punched to get away.

"Stop." The guttural growl made her heart stutter, set her instincts on edge.

She bit the next best part of exposed skin she could reach.

His curse colored the air, and he loosened his grip enough for her to twist out of his hold. Her heart beat so fast and hard, it hurt her chest, made her dizzy. Every mouthful of inhaled air stung her lungs. *Run.*

She made it three panicked steps before a freight train of male strength hit her back, and her face hit the mulch.

Well, crap.

CHAPTER 3

A lek eased through the opening in the fence that allowed access to the property bordering the Murrays' backyard. The rain had let up some time earlier, but the ground remained wet and slippery, so he took care maneuvering through the undergrowth, even though he could have found his way blindfolded. After coming down this path several nights a week for months, he'd all but memorized every pebble and root.

He stopped underneath an old fir whose canopy always provided excellent cover from rain showers. The spot also offered an unobstructed view of the Murrays' backyard, as well as the mansion, which was why it was popular with the sentinels sent here to watch the witch home.

Only now the spot was empty. He scanned the shadows, his demon vision sharp enough to see even small details without additional light. Where was he?

"What took you so long?"

Alek turned toward the male voice drifting out of the shadows. A few feet away, the air shimmered like a desert mirage, then a dark silhouette peeled itself from the night, solidified into the shape of a burly man. If the other demon hadn't chosen to reveal his form, Alek wouldn't have been able to spot him, even with his heightened senses, courtesy of the concealing spell of Arawn's dark making. The Demon Lord made sure to keep his people hidden from prying witch eyes.

Alek nodded a greeting at Lachlan, the sentinel on duty. "Got held up." It had taken much longer than he'd planned to get the *morbus* alone, and then Lily showed up and his world stopped for a minute. As it always did when he saw her.

"Mhmhm. I was getting worried there. Not like you to be runnin' late." Lachlan's grin slashed white through the night. "Your female keep you?"

Alek scoffed. *I wish.* There was only one female he'd want to have keeping him, and she didn't even know he existed. Or rather, hadn't known. Tonight that had changed. After Lily saw him taking *prana* from that *morbus*, and he'd just barely stopped her from blasting his ass, she sure knew he existed. Not that it would change anything else.

Besides providing more fodder for his pathetic fantasies about a witch he could never have, that is. The way she looked in that tight dress, the way her wet hair clung to her shoulders, skin glistening from the rain, the electric warmth of her touch when he held her wrist. And she'd seen him, really *seen* him, their eyes meeting for the first time. For a second there, the briefest moment, her face softened when she looked at him, her lips parting... Yep, that mental image would definitely star in his dreams.

Alek rubbed his hand over his face, then nodded toward the mansion. "Anything interesting happen tonight?"

Lachlan shrugged. "Nope. The MacKenna girl came downstairs for a while, but she's mostly been in her room. The Elder witch is sleeping, the younger one's gone out, and the male is in the kitchen." He shook his head, gaze on the sprawling house. "That human can *eat*."

Just another night, then. "Okay, I'll take it from here." Alek clapped the other demon on the shoulder.

"Have fun." Lachlan handed over the bespelled necklace that held Arawn's concealing charm and left.

"Don't I always?" Alek muttered, donning the necklace and turning toward the Murray mansion.

The lights were on in the kitchen, allowing him to see right into the room, his enhanced eyesight able to make out Basil Murray sitting at the kitchen island...eating. Alek checked his phone. Shortly after two. If Lily took the last train, she should be home any minute now.

As always, his stomach coiled and knotted with conflicting feelings at the prospect of seeing her. Part of him hoped she'd show up, allowing him to catch another glimpse of her. The highlight of watch duty. As much as he was looking forward to seeing her, though, he dreaded it at the same time. Being forced to watch someone he'd fallen for against all reason and sense, knowing he could never have her the way he craved, it chafed at him. If only she were a *pranagraha* demon, like him...

As if on cue, Lily entered the kitchen. He could see her clearly through the huge French doors, and his heart did its usual flip at the sight of her. She walked past her twin brother and opened the fridge. He frowned. Was that blood on her forehead? Had she been injured? He shifted against the tree, his hand balling into a fist.

Lily and her brother talked a little, and then Basil started making a sandwich, from the looks of it. Lily's stance changed. Subtle, and he wouldn't have noticed if his senses weren't so attuned to her every move. A prickling sensation swept over his skin, raising the hairs on his arms and neck. Even from this distance, he could make out Lily's eyes—and how they blazed with red.

What the hell was—?

Lily charged. She was on top of Basil a split second later, toppling him to the ground. Basil flailed, trying to dislodge Lily's hands from his throat, his face a mask of panic.

Alek stalked as close to the perimeter of the wards as he dared. The air buzzed with the magical protection, pushing against him. Pulse racing, he stared at the scene in the kitchen.

This wasn't one of the good-natured sparring sessions between Lily and her brother. Gods knew they went at it often enough, but they were always grinning, cracking jokes, clearly not out to do real damage.

Unlike now. The amount of strength and pressure Lily was putting into the choke—she was killing Basil. Her brother.

Shit. As sentinel, his orders were straightforward. Watch Maeve MacKenna—currently living at the Murrays'—and don't interfere unless Maeve's life was in danger. Arawn wanted Maeve alive for him to claim at a time of his choosing, but he couldn't care less if the Murrays slaughtered each other in the meantime.

But Alek cared. Whatever was driving Lily to this kind of violence, it wasn't normal, it wasn't good, and when Lily snapped out of it, the fact she'd killed her brother would haunt her forever. He couldn't let that happen.

Before he could second-guess his decision, he grabbed a

fist-sized stone from the ground and hurled it at the French doors to the kitchen. His missile hit a terracotta flower pot and shattered it. The crashing noise startled Lily, and she apparently snapped out of whatever was riding her. Or at least found enough presence of mind again to realize to some extent what she'd been doing, if her panicked scrambling away from Basil was any indication.

She jerked up her head, looked toward the door leading from the kitchen into the house, and the next second she barged out of the French doors into the backyard. A moment later the Elder witch, Hazel, head of the Murray family, entered the kitchen. Ah, so Lily was running from her mother.

While Hazel rushed to Basil's side, tending to him, Lily kept fleeing through the backyard—straight toward the spot at the end of the property where Alek stood, pressed as closely up against the wards as he could manage without being fried magically. Heart pounding a million miles a minute, he could only stare while Lily raced closer. He should move. Arawn's spell would hide him from her, sure, but he should step aside anyway, let her pass. But his muscles were locked, his brain unable to give the command to shift out of the way.

And then Lily scaled the fence—her movements so graceful, sleek, and elegant like a gymnast's, it transfixed him where he stood—and the next thing he knew she stumbled right into him. He grabbed her reflexively, steadying her with his hands on her upper arms, and the heat of her skin a branding caress. Her scent crashed into him, so much stronger than when he'd been close to her earlier. It was a mix of the heavy fragrance of some exotic flower and the aroma of rain-soaked earth. He inhaled a deep lungful without thinking and got lost in it, his head spinning.

Lily's wiggling yanked him back into the real world. He grunted at the punches and kicks she landed—she sure as hell knew how to fight, and had enough strength to back it up. He had to get to her to calm down, though, before she did some real damage, either to him or herself. And he couldn't let her run, not in her current state of panic, without making sure she'd be okay.

"Stop," he said, and it came out growlier than he intended.

Lily shivered and stilled for a second. Just when he thought she'd come out of her panic, she bit his arm. Hard.

"Fucking hell, woman." He ground his teeth and couldn't help loosening his grip a little.

Enough for Lily to twist out of his hold. *Dammit.* She'd run three steps before his fuse blew. He tackled her, making sure to turn them both sideways so he wouldn't crush her.

"Umpf," Lily wheezed—and went right back to fighting him tooth and nail to get away.

He turned her around so her back was on the ground, straddled her to keep her in place. When her eyes, swirling red and black, met his, startling him with an impossible implication, she stopped struggling. Her lips parted on a soft inhale, her features gentling, an echo of her reaction when he met her head-on in the street after he fed from the *morbus.* And damn if it didn't have the same effect on him. His heartbeat hammered in his ears, his stomach did that annoying flip, and his blood heated and rushed unerringly south.

Get a grip. Neither the right place nor the right time to be thinking along those lines. There was something more pressing than his unrequited attraction, something that corroborated the theory her changing eye color had sparked. Her strapless dress exposed her upper arms, shoulders, and top cleavage, and what was appearing on that smooth-looking skin was straight-up unbelievable. Swirling henna-colored lines and dots, forming graceful symbols, gradually emerged like a tan setting in.

Lily was developing a *tvaglakshana*.

She caught herself while he was still reeling and resumed her struggle. He barely moved fast enough to avoid her punch. Grabbing both her wrists, he pinned her arms next to her head.

"Stop," he ground out. "I don't want to harm you, but if you don't stop fighting me, I may hurt you without meaning to."

The red in her eyes blazed. "And I'm supposed to buy your 'don't mean you harm' bullshit when your whole act is rape-y as hell?"

"What?"

"Seriously? Oh, well, sure, being tackled and then pinned to the ground by a strange male works out so well for most women."

That made him do a mental double-take. He blinked, looked down at their position...and it hit him how that had to come across for her. *Shit.*

"I wasn't going to—" He pressed his lips together, exhaled through his nose, and moved off her while keeping a hold on one of her wrists. "Just to get this straight—I have *never* forced myself on a female, and I'd rather hack off my hand than sexually assault you."

"But you're okay with wrestling me to the ground?" She tugged on her arm, trying to get him to release her.

He rose to his feet and pulled her up to standing as well,

making sure not to loosen his grip on her wrist. "Let's start over. My name is Alek, and I'm trying to help you."

"Uh-huh. You know what would help?" She leaned in and loudly whispered. "Letting me go."

Her words sounded light, almost flippant, and she did a good job of acting as if she was in control. The chaotic maelstrom of energy in her aura spoke a different language. Just underneath the surface of her projected calm roiled a clusterfuck of emotions. Not to mention her aura was decidedly not that of a witch anymore. His mind struggled with accepting the facts in front of him. *This can't be real.*

And yet all his senses told him the same thing, pointed to only one conclusion. However much of an impossibility it was.

"I can't let you run." His voice was raspy, his brain rattled by what he was seeing.

"Right," she shot back, her tone dripping acid. "Because you want to finish what your buddy started, don't you?"

He frowned, stumped. "What?"

"Oh, don't tell me you're not in cahoots with that other life leech. You know, the one who shot me in the ass with a dart gun *like I was fucking game during hunting season.*" She spit the last part out through clenched teeth, her aura erupting into a wave of sparks.

Anger of his own fired through him. "You've been shot?"

"Like you didn't know."

"I didn't," he snarled, infuriated at the mere thought of someone hurting her. Then his brain caught up. "A dart gun?" His mind raced, connecting the dots.

"Well, whatever roofie drug your buddy put in that dart, he needs to check the recipe. It's not working the way you guys intended, is it?"

He was too preoccupied with putting the pieces together to even get mad at her assumption he was involved. "What'd he look like?"

"Red and black eyes, psychotic expression..." She waved her free hand. "Just your run-of-the-mill life leech."

He took a deep breath and battled down his irritation. "I'm not working with whoever attacked you."

"Right. Then how about you let me go? I'm really trying to kick the habit of lurking behind my family's backyard, so if you don't mind, I'll be on my way." She tilted her head and smiled sweetly.

He swallowed. "Can't."

"Because you *are* working with him."

He shook his head. "Because you're turning into one of us, Lilichka."

The shock that hit her was palpable in her aura, rippling out in waves of bone-deep cold. She blinked several times, her face a mask of indifference at complete odds with her energy pattern.

It took her multiple attempts to speak. "The fuck are you talking about?"

"You're turning into a *pranagraha* demon. Like me." He paused, hesitating over whether he should make that connection right now. Well, better to get it out there as well. "Like the one who shot you with that dart."

She shook her head, first slowly, then faster, faster, until he was sure her brain would suffer some kind of damage from all that jerking. She stopped, laughter spilling from her. "Oh dear gods, you're certifiably insane." Holding her stomach with her free hand, she kept giggling.

Alek watched her for a moment. Denial sure wasn't just a river in Egypt. She was trying so, so hard to laugh it off, but underneath the abrasive notes of derision in her voice pulsed a terror so great, so consuming, he felt the chill of it spreading to his own heart.

His thumb stroked over the thin, sensitive skin on the inside of her wrist. "You'll have noticed your senses are heightened," he said, his voice calm and soothing. "How's your eyesight?"

Lily stopped laughing.

"See the world more sharply than before?"

She swallowed, her eyes skittering away from his.

"How 'bout your sense of smell? Notice how scents are much stronger than before?"

A muscle ticked in her jaw.

"You've got *pranagraha* eyes. They change to red and black when you're pissed, hungry, or..." He trailed off.

Lily's gaze focused on him. "Or?"

He couldn't help the half-smile tugging on his lips. "Horny."

She cocked a brow.

"Then there's this." He gestured at the light brown signs spreading over her cleavage, shoulders, and upper arms.

She shifted her stance into a more defensive position, not taking her eyes off him. "My female assets?"

"Your *tvaglakshana*."

"There's really no need to throw insults around."

He bit back a smile. "It's a kind of living tattoo-slash-birthmark. We are born with one symbol over our hearts, and then it grows from there, with more symbols appearing when you have significant life experiences. In a way, they're a key to understanding what made you you. Every *pranagraha* demon has one." He paused, taking a meaningful breath. "And now you have one, too."

"You really are crazypants," she whispered.

"See for yourself." He waved at the *tvaglakshana* again.

She hesitated for a moment, then looked down her cleavage. With a harsh gasp, she tugged on the arm he was still holding, her other hand reflexively touching the skin now adorned with elegantly curving ancient symbols. He didn't let go of her wrist, but stepped closer so she had more leeway to study the markings.

"Holy powers in a can, how far do these go?" Her aura exploded into a kaleidoscope of colors, graying out quickly with a shudder.

"It's different for each *pranagraha*, but at your age, most likely they'll reach down to your stomach and the middle of your back."

She started scratching at the symbols with her free hand, her movements frenetic, her scent laced with acidic fear. Her claws sliced out, tearing thin red gashes in her skin.

"Don't." He caught her other hand as well, held it tight and away from her body to keep her from harming herself further.

At a rustle in the leaves to his right, he froze. Lily stilled as well, scanning the area, eyes swirling with fire-licked obsidian once more.

"My mom," she whispered.

Alek whipped his head around, stared in the same direction as Lily. And sure enough, Hazel Murray was moving toward them through the dark. She was obviously trying to be stealthy, but a *pranagraha* demon would still be able to pick up on the subtle sounds she made.

Lily yanked on her hands, elbowed him in the side and tried to break free. "Let me go." A hushed command,

31

threaded with rising panic. "She can't see me. Please, I need to leave. She can't see me like this."

"Hush." He whirled her around, her back to his front, clasped her to him with one arm around her waist, and covered her mouth with his other hand. "Don't make a sound, and she won't see us."

Lily's heartbeat was so fast and loud it pounded in his ears. Panting through her nose, she grabbed the wrist of his hand covering her mouth, but didn't pull it away. A buzz of electric energy zinged through him at her touch. Her body pressing into his like this, her toned curves nearly rubbing up against him, it sparked a rush of desire down to his groin.

He clamped his teeth together and directed his thoughts to granny panties and other unerotic images. Lily sure wouldn't appreciate his erection poking her lush bottom right now.

Her panting stopped as she held her breath, her face turned toward her mother when Hazel stepped into the small clearing, almost close enough to touch. Alek's breath stalled in his throat, too, his heart skipping a beat.

Magic crackled in the air. The force of the Elder witch's power brushed up against his skin, like a thousand fine needles stinging. He tried to inhale, found it impossible. His chest seemed bound by tight ropes.

Hazel surveyed the clearing, her brows pulling together in a frown. When she looked straight at the spot where he and Lily stood in frozen fear, he thought that would be it. *She'll see us.* And he had no doubt that if the Elder witch found him—a demon—basically holding her daughter in a death grip, he wouldn't live another minute. Witches were notoriously unforgiving toward demons who snatched one of their own...

Hazel shifted her attention to another spot, and she moved past Alek and Lily without any sign she'd registered their presence.

Relief sucked all strength out of him, made his muscles quiver. He loosened his grip on Lily and stepped back a little, though he kept one hand around her wrist. Lily peered in the direction her mother had gone, waiting a few heartbeats.

Then she rounded on him. "What kind of dark demon magic was that?" she hissed, keeping her voice down. "Is that part of a life leech's powers?"

"*Pranagraha,*" he corrected her.

"*Prana-*what?"

"*Pranagraha.* It's the name of my demon species." He nodded at her. "Yours as well."

She scoffed. "Sure. Tell me, when did you stop taking your medication?"

He decided to ignore that jab. "And for your information, that concealment spell isn't one of our powers." He jingled the necklace. "It's a charm."

Lily focused on the necklace, then glanced at his hold on her wrist. "And it concealed me as well, because you're touching me."

"That's how it works."

She pinned him with a piercing look, suspicion evident in her furrowed brow. "How did you get that charm?"

Alek hesitated. How much should he tell her? Instinct and his experience over the past decade warned him to be careful with what information he revealed to her. Nominally, she *was* his enemy. Circumstances had changed, however, and things weren't as clear-cut anymore. If he wanted her to trust him enough to let him help her, he needed to give her something in return.

"The charm is part of my job equipment," he said. "I work for Arawn."

Her aura flared, a wave of dark red lashing out. In her eyes, fire licked at the black.

Holding up his free hand in a gesture of appeasement, he added, "Calm down. I'm not here to hurt your family. My task is to keep an eye on Maeve MacKenna, make sure nothing happens to her."

That apparently baffled her. She blinked, frowned. "You've been watching Maeve?"

"Yes. For a while now." Time to get the conversation on track again. "When I saw you attack your brother tonight, it looked like you were about to kill him."

Lily jerked, her expression shuttering, her energy pattern icing over.

"You were, weren't you? Because you're turning into a *pranagraha* demon, and you're hungry and driven by instincts, and you snapped and lunged at him. If I hadn't thrown that rock at the patio and startled you, you'd have either choked Basil to death or taken his *prana*."

Her throat muscles worked underneath her silken skin as she swallowed hard. "*Prana*? Like, breath?"

Of course, as a witch, she'd know some basic Sanskrit, since the ancient language was used for many spells. "That's one of the meanings. Another one is 'life force.' That's what we *pranagraha* demons feed off of."

He stepped closer, his gaze holding hers. "Let me help you. I don't know what caused this, but I can show you how to deal with being a demon. How to avoid randomly hurting people. I can teach you how to feed. And you'll have to,

34

soon." He raised his free hand, tapped a symbol on her shoulder. "The color of your *tvaglakshana* is an indicator of how much *prana* you have left. It's darkest when you've just fed, and gets lighter the more life force you lose. When it fades until it's nearly the same color as your skin, you die." He stroked her wrist again, in small, soothing circles. "Your *tvaglakshana* is very light. You're burning energy by the second, just by going through the transformation. You'll need to feed tonight."

"No." She shook her head again, her energy trembling with flickers of cold, and tugged on her arm once more. "No. I'm fine. I'll be okay. I can figure this out on my own." Her face twisted into a sneer. "I don't need a *demon* to help me out."

"That's exactly what you need, seeing as you're turning into one yourself."

She flashed her teeth at him, her eyes a storm of red and black. "I. Am. Not."

She didn't signal her move, not a twitch giving away her intention. So when her fist hit his solar plexus with the force of a pissed-off, martial-arts-trained female, there was only one logical result. He wheezed, doubled over, and fell to his knees. If he were human, that blow would have him curled up in a fetal position for long, long minutes. As a demon, it still incapacitated him for about half a minute.

Enough time for Lily to get away.

CHAPTER 4

N ote to self: before you start running away in a brainless
frenzy, make sure you have shoes on.

Lily leaned against the side of a building, her breath
sawing in and out of her lungs, and gingerly lifted one foot
to look at the damage. *Good grief in a fuck-it bucket.* The bare
skin of her sole resembled a plowed field. She set the foot
back down, grimacing at the pain.

For a moment, she let her head rest against the wall
behind her, listening to her pulse roar in her ears.

You're turning into a pranagraha *demon...it looked like you
were about to kill your brother...you're hungry and driven by
instincts...you'll need to feed tonight...*

The demon's words echoed in her mind, a swirling,
confusing, irritating mess of messages she felt no inclination
to make sense of. He—what did he say his name was? A-
something. A...lek—was clearly certifiable. Demons weren't
turned like vampires. They were born, a separate species.
There was no way in hell a witch could just transform into a
demon.

Although *something* was playing havoc with her system, that was for sure. And it obviously had to do with whatever that other life leech shot her with. But turning her into a demon? Laughable. She just needed some time to figure this out by herself. Or maybe...with help.

Taking a deep breath, she pushed away from the wall and studied her surroundings. She hadn't noticed much where she ran, fleeing as if in a trance, but apparently she'd made it right into downtown Portland. On foot. *Barefoot.*

Cringing when her soles touched the concrete, she took a few careful steps while orienting herself. *Ouchouchouch.*

The large illuminated sign of Powell's World of Books loomed just a block ahead. Wow. Within a few minutes, she'd run a distance that would normally take at least a half an hour on foot. Or maybe her sense of time was off. *Like everything else about you, hm?*

She heaved an annoyed sigh and half-sat on a railing, putting one foot up on her other knee to ease the pain. *Okay, let's think this over.* She needed to find a place to recuperate and then start figuring out what the hell happened and how to fix it.

Home was not an option. Just thinking about her mom and Baz—*Baz!*—and facing them after what she'd done gave her hot flashes of shame. And what would she say? *Oh, hi, bro. Really sorry about trying to choke you to death, no hard feelings, right? Just FYI, though, it might happen again, because even now I'm feeling the urge to suck the life out of you.*

And she did. Every time she thought back to that moment, the only thing stronger than her guilt and shame was that unrelenting hunger, that drive to take, take, take.

Kill.

"Shut up," she whispered and buried her face in her

hands, trying to stifle that insidious voice in her head. "Shutupshutupshutup."

Where else could she go? Merle's? If she were to confide in anyone, it would be her best friend, and Lily knew Merle wouldn't judge her, would help her out, no questions asked. If only Merle lived closer, but it was even farther from here to the MacKennas' than it was to home. Lily couldn't walk that distance, not with these shredded feet. She couldn't hail a cab, because she had no money on her. Her cell phone lay happy and useless in her purse...which she'd left at home. And modern times being what they were, with everyone so dependent on having their mobile devices handy at all times, she didn't even know her best friend's phone number by heart, so she couldn't ask to use someone else's phone to call her.

She was well and truly stranded in a big city in the middle of the night, with nothing but the slinky club dress she was wearing, which probably gave people all the wrong ideas about her profession.

The clicking of high heels on concrete made her look up. A college-age girl was walking down the street, keys in one hand, shooting her a furtive glance as she passed.

Lily's heart beat triple time. Her vision narrowed on the human female, on the strong, delicious glow of her life force. Warm, golden, and so, so enticing.

Take.

Eyes on the human, she stood.

The female stepped up to the entrance to the apartment building a few doors down. The keys jingled in the night as she unlocked the door. She threw a look over her shoulder at Lily, and startled. With a soft noise of fear, she opened the door, slipped inside and slammed it shut.

Lily trembled where she stood, realizing she'd stalked the girl several feet. Skin clammy, her stomach a torrent of despair, she raised her hands, stared at her claws, the smears of blood where they had sliced out of her fingertips.

Her breath left her in a rush.

This is not real. Not. Real.

Someone grabbed her from behind, an arm snaking around her waist. With a snarl, she delivered an elbow strike to whoever was attacking her, and when the guy grunted and released her, she whirled around and swung at him.

The stranger blocked and retreated a step, hands raised in a signal of peace. "Sorry, thought you were human."

Her heart skipped a beat, the words *But I am* stuck in her throat. She studied the guy, his demon aura brushing her senses. Human-looking, he belonged to the *hirudo* species, a nasty race of demons who fed off humans' hopes and dreams and other positive feelings. Wouldn't be too much of an issue if that was all they did, but the effect of the feeding was where the nasty came in. A *hirudo* actually drained the human of these feelings, leaving the victim with only negative thoughts and a vicious depression that often led to suicide.

"You know," the *hirudo* said, sidling closer again, "I usually don't go for demon females, but for one fine as you, I'd make an exception." He tilted his head, his gaze raking over her, then focusing on her cleavage. "I'd love to see how far down those markings of yours go."

"Excuse you?"

"Hey, if it's a matter of price, I can pay."

Her claws slid out some more, the sting of it welcome. "I am," she ground out through clenched teeth, "having the worst night of my life. The last thing I need is to be propositioned on the street like I'm a hooker."

"All right, all right, no need to get bitchy." The demon raised his hands again, palms out, and backed away. "If you change your mind, you can find me at *Nine Circles*." He nodded down the street behind him and then walked off in that direction.

What. The. Actual. Fuck.

By all rights, this meeting should have ended in bloodshed, and not because of the way the dick talked to her—though that did make her want to smash his face in. His kind didn't hit on witches. If they did, it was the literal *hit a witch*, as in, beat her to death before she can kill you. A *hirudo* and a witch running into each other? Fight to the death, every time.

But that was the thing, wasn't it? He didn't think she was a witch.

While all the details she couldn't explain away anymore slowly trickled through the wall of denial in her brain, she trudged down the street, only half-aware she was going in the same direction as the *hirudo* demon.

What if that life leech—Alek—was right after all? What if she was indeed turning into one of his kind? Just for argument's sake... She swallowed hard, her throat constricting to the point of pain. Involuntarily, she looked down at her right shoulder and studied the beautiful, weird markings that looked like a cross between Chinese characters and Arabic script.

What'd he call them? *Tvug-luck-shunna* or something like that. The color was that of a faint henna tattoo, only a shade darker than her natural light tan. *When it fades until it's nearly the same color as your skin, you die.* Alek's words whispered through her mind, made her heart stutter.

Then her stomach growled loud enough to wake half of Portland. A clammy sensation clung to her skin, and shivers racked her limbs. She grew lightheaded, as if she hadn't eaten all day. Darkness crept in from the edges of her vision. Blinking to clear her eyes, she stumbled over a crack in the concrete. Where normally a missed step like that wouldn't have done more than make her gait falter for a second, it was now enough to send her flying toward the pavement.

She was barely able to twist so she'd land on her ass instead of kissing the concrete. Pain exploded in her hips, her bottom, and her palms, which she'd used to steady herself. Gods dammit, she'd never been that clumsy. Breathing hard, she got to her feet with a groan. Little lights danced in front of her eyes.

What if it was true? What if she needed to feed, take someone's *prana* just to survive the night?

Oh, gods. She tried to stifle the nausea turning her stomach into a cauldron of puke-a-lot.

A movement farther down the street caught her attention. Someone was walking in her direction. Her senses sharpened, homed in on the potential prey...*yes, human.* Her mouth watered. Her breathing flattened, nostrils flaring as she picked up the scent carrying on the breeze. Intoxicated. *Easy prey.*

"No." Lily spun around, pressed against her temples with her hands balled to fists. "Snap out of it."

Eyes wide, she scanned the street, was about to run in the opposite direction of the approaching human just to get the fuck away from temptation, when her attention snagged on the illuminated sign of a bar—*Nine Circles*. Her breath stuck in her throat. *No way.*

She knew that building. The old two-story housed an appliances repair shop that no one ever seemed to frequent, or at least she'd never seen anyone going in or out when she walked past. She had definitely never seen a bar on the ground floor. She'd gone down this street a few days earlier, and there hadn't been any construction.

There was something in the air around the perimeter of the bar... She squinted and walked closer. *Power.* Magic shimmered along the lines of the building, and it held the distinctive hallmarks of demon magic.

She sucked in a breath. The bar was protected by wards, demon wards. Which would explain why she'd never noticed it before when she was a wit—Realization stung her heart. Shaking her head against the onslaught of emotions barreling through her crumbling wall of denial, she stalked forward on an impulse.

Without giving second thoughts time to catch up, she yanked open the door and stepped gingerly into the bar.

Warm, moist air enveloped her. The door clunked shut behind her, and though it was darker inside than outside, her eyes adjusted immediately. There was a bar stacked with booze to her left, and what looked like several separate seating areas taking up the rest of the space. The different, almost secluded, sections each had a distinctive design in colors and shapes that distinguished it from the others. A sign hung from the ceiling in the middle of each seating area. The one closest to her read *Limbo*, the next one over *Lust*, followed by *Gluttony*.

Pieces clicked together in her head. *Nine Circles...* The

bar's theme was Dante Alighieri's *Inferno*. At least demons appreciated irony.

The patrons scattered across the pub barely looked up when she entered, and went right back to their business as usual. Demon auras brushed up against her senses. She registered a few other energy signatures as well, shifters and nymphs, maybe, but the majority of the guests were demon.

The last pieces of her wall of denial collapsed in on themselves. This...the fact she was standing here unchallenged... was impossible in and of itself. Any other time before tonight, if she'd walked into this bar by herself—as a witch —she'd be buried under a pile of hostile demons by now, exhaling her last breath.

Get a move on. You can throw your pity party later.

Drumming up her courage, she strutted straight to the bar and signaled the demon behind it, who was busy putting together a cocktail. He came over and nodded in greeting, shaking the mixer.

"Hey," Lily said, "I've got a question and was wondering if you could help me out. Do you know if anyone here tonight works for the Demon Lord?"

The bartender—a burly guy with a huge jaw, two of his lower canines extending out of his mouth and almost touching his nose—frowned down on her.

Agh, he was clearly not too happy about her nosiness. She gave him a charming smile and leaned forward a little, not so much as to seem too obvious, but enough to give him a great view of her cleavage. A girl had to use her assets.

The frown melted away, and he raised his brows, an appreciative glint in his eyes. He jerked his head toward a corner booth in the *Lust* section. "Guy in the red shirt."

"Thanks a lot, sweetie." She tapped the bar and walked over to the booth.

The guy in the red shirt was a shifter of some sort, gleaming black hair, light brown skin, up-tilted eyes which were currently focused on his cell phone while he lounged in his seat. Another male—human-looking, blond hair and light skin—sat on the opposite side of the booth, his aura giving him away as demon.

Lily stopped in front of the table and cleared her throat, one hand resting on her hip. "Hey."

"Thanks, luv, but I'm not buying," the shifter said, without deigning to look up from his phone.

"I am," the demon piped up, straightening in his seat.

Anger rushed through her veins like a wave of sparks. Her face heated, and she had to clench her hands to fists to keep her claws from slicing out. "I heard you work for Arawn?"

The shifter still didn't raise his eyes. "He doesn't solicit hookers either."

"I do." The demon leaned forward.

Her feet ached. Every cell in her body was screaming at her to feed, and her internal organs felt like they'd at some point started to digest themselves. She was dying of shame after almost killing her brother, and reeling with the uncertainty of what was happening to her. And here she was, being mistaken for a hooker. *Again.*

She snarled and turned to the demon. "I am *not* a sex worker, and if you don't stop ogling me like one, I'll punch your eyes so far down your head, you'll be shitting them out tomorrow."

The demon gulped and sat back slowly.

She faced the shifter again, who had finally looked up

from his phone and now studied her with mild curiosity. "I need to get in touch with a demon who works for Arawn. He's a li—a *pranagraha*, like me." Phew, good save, there. "His name's Alek. Do you know him?"

"Maybe. Why do you want to talk to him?"

Lily gave him a sweet smile. "*Pranagraha* business."

"What's in it for me?" He put an arm on the backrest of the booth, dark eyes fixed on hers.

Ah, crud. She had no money to bribe him. *Well, time to take a risk.* "Avoiding a broken nose when Alek finds out you refused to put me in touch with him?"

He stared at her for a long moment, then chuckled. Humor glinted in his eyes, revealing a devastatingly handsome side of him. "You've got balls, luv. All right. What's the message?"

A sigh of utter relief slipped out. She glanced around, grabbed a nearby chair, pulled it up to the table and plopped down, easing her aching feet. "Can you call him right now? Tell him I'll take him up on his offer."

The shifter cocked a brow, one side of his mouth tilting up in a suggestive half smile.

She bristled and clenched her teeth. "Not that kind of offer." And without looking at the demon on the other side of the booth—who'd perked up again—she pointed a finger at him and growled, "Don't even."

Grinning, the shifter made the call. "Hey, Alek. Listen, I'm at *Nine Circles* and I've got a *pranagraha* female here who's looking for you. Goes by the name of—" He gave her a prompting nod.

"Lily."

"—Lily," the shifter repeated. "She says—" He stopped, blinked, and held his phone away from him to stare at the screen. "Wouldn't even let me finish. I hate it when people interrupt me. So rude."

She barely kept herself from bouncing in her seat. "What'd he say?"

The shifter pocketed his phone. "He's on his way." He gave Lily a slow once-over, frowning at her legs. "Why are you barefoot?"

৩৯৩

FADING.

Lily stared at her demon tattoo above the neckline of her dress. The signs had become lighter again. The marking was fading more and more. *Shit.*

"Whatever you're hoping to find in there, I could help you look for it."

She looked up from her cleavage at the shifter's buddy in the booth seat and slowly said, "Well, I could suck you…"

The demon straightened, a happy grin spreading on his scraggy face.

"…dry of your life force," she finished, giving him a saccharine smile. "I *am* hungry, you know. Ravenous, really. So, you offering?"

His color turning ashen, the demon cleared his throat and scooted back in the booth seat. The shifter chuckled and sipped his drink.

Smirking, Lily leaned back in her chair. She'd only guessed life leeches were feared among demons as well, but it was good to know for sure. And she'd be damned if she told that jerk she didn't have the slightest idea if she could actually take his *prana,* or even how to feed at all.

Her head spun, and the earth threatened to tilt and toss

her off her chair. She breathed in deeply, exhaled slowly, and grabbed the seat for purchase. Her heart stumbled on its too-fast rhythm. Cold sweat licked her skin. Damn, this was getting serious.

"You okay?" The shifter's dark eyes studied her with disturbing focus.

Don't show weakness. She locked her spine, but retained her hold on the seat cushion to conceal the trembling of her limbs. "Sure. Fine and dandy."

She might be sitting here without being accosted, seemingly accepted by the bar's patrons, but the fact was, they were all predators here, each and every one. And predators pounced on weakness like bargain hunters stormed stores on Black Friday. Vulnerability was an invitation, strength and power a requisite for getting respect.

The door to the bar opened, and even though Lily had her back turned, she knew with instinctual awareness who walked in. That dizzying charge of electricity, the one she felt when she first saw him, and again when she ran into him behind her house, it sizzled over her skin, raised the soft hairs on her arms and neck.

She twisted in the chair, her eyes locking onto Alek as he made his way through the throng of patrons. The crowd parted to let him through, demons and shifters alike skittering out of his way after one glance. She couldn't blame them. He was a contained explosion of violence tempered with authority, everything about him— his expression, his stance, his movements—projecting the kind of *don't fuck with me* attitude of someone used to being in charge—and used to enforcing that status. There was something primal, fierce, and yet inherently noble about the way he carried himself, bringing to mind images of ancient warriors bloodied in battle, yet living by honor.

And he moved with purpose—toward her.

The same thrall that held her spellbound and unmoving when he grabbed her wrist in the street after he killed the *morbus* now stalled the breath in her lungs as she watched him approach. Gods *damn*, he was a fine male specimen. His navy long sleeve shirt stretched over an impressive chest and broad shoulders, ridges and valleys of muscles visible underneath the fabric. Dark gray jeans hugged his narrow hips and strong thighs in a way that made heat curl in her lower belly.

He came to a stop in front of her and she realized with a start how rude it was to keep staring at his groin area. Swallowing, she focused on his face. The ambient lighting tinged his blond hair in a reddish glow, threw gentle shadows on his hard features. Stubbled jaw, long, straight nose, and expressive brows set over eyes which were currently black striated with flickering fire.

"Lily." His voice, low and with just the right amount of scratchy to make her insides tingle, slid over her like rough silk. "Are you all right?"

She started to speak, croaked, and cleared her throat. "Um, sure."

Alek glanced at the shifter and nodded in greeting. "Quentin. Thanks for calling. I owe you one."

"And I plan to collect," Quentin replied, a mild smile on his face.

Alek turned to her again. "Let's find a place to talk."

"Nice meeting you," she said to Quentin as she stood.

Pain stung her soles, and she bit the inside of her lip to keep from wincing. She walked slowly so as not to telegraph the fact she was injured, following Alek to a cocktail table in another corner, secluded enough that their conversation would remain private. She looked at the table and groaned inwardly. No barstools, nowhere to sit. This would hurt. *Suck it up, buttercup.*

"You need to feed," Alek began without preamble, studying the lines of her markings. "Like, right now."

Her knees wobbled. Just a little, just enough to make her grab the table top. "How?"

"There are two main ways to take *prana*. Either you draw in someone's breath, or you drink their blood. Breath is more convenient." He waved a hand. "Gets less messy."

She grimaced. "Breath it is."

"To take it," he said, leaning in over the table and holding her gaze, "you have to get up real close to your prey and inhale their breath with the intent of absorbing their life force." When she wanted to ask again *how* to do just that, he tapped his head and added, "You have to visualize it. It's a mind thing, a switch you have to flip right in here."

"This brings back uncomfortable memories of that one time when a friend dragged me to that New Age guru's workshop."

The corners of his mouth twitched up, and the lines around his eyes crinkled. "You may have to try several times, but I'll help you through it."

Sobering, she grasped the edge of the table tighter to stave off another wave of dizziness. "Why?"

"Well, it's hard to visualize it at first. Most *pranagrahas* need practice to get it right when they transition."

"No, I mean, why are you helping me?"

He was quiet for a moment, his eyes fixed on her with an intensity that made her legs rubbery. Or maybe that was another bout of near-fainting due to whatever was changing her. Drumming his fingers absent-mindedly on the table, his gaze still holding hers, he said, "I can't just let you suffer on you own. Wouldn't be right. You need help, so I'm giving it to you."

"That's mighty noble for a demon. Especially considering I'm your enemy."

"Used to be." His hand stilled on the table. "You're one of us now."

Her heart cracked a tiny bit. She pushed that hurt down, locked her knees to keep standing, but still, the haze in her brain grew, the dizziness taking over. She swayed, and her hands slipped off the table top.

"Whoa." Alek caught her, his strong arms winding around her waist, pulling her to him.

Reflexively, she grabbed his shirt. Male heat and power enveloped her, and his scent stroked along her senses. *Autumn winds and wood fires.* Her lips parted as she drew in his essence.

"You should bottle that," she whispered—and hey, what happened to her verbal filter?

"I don't think we have time to search for prey in the city." His mouth was level with her eyes, and, for the life of her, she couldn't tear them away from his lips. "There's another way."

Those lips, though. Hmmm...

"It's not as good as a full feed from a human source, but it'll tide you over until tomorrow night."

The one on the bottom had just the right amount of full-ness. To nibble on. To lick...

"It's called *pranada*, one *pranagraha* giving a boost of energy to another."

...to suck.

"Lilichka. Are you listening to me?"

"Huh?"

He put one finger under her chin and tipped her head up until her eyes met his. "I can give you breath."

CHAPTER 5

L ily's eyes—glazed over, little flecks of red sparking within the usual indigo depths—finally focused on his.

"I can give you *prana*," he repeated. His thumb stroked over her cheek for a moment, for a heartbeat. "It's an intimate connection. Do you understand?"

She nodded, then shook her head. Her gorgeous dark blue eyes widened when it hit her. "You're gonna kiss me."

"Basically, yeah." He didn't point out that a lip-lock was not usually necessary in order to exchange *prana* by breath. There was only so much gentlemanliness he was capable of all at once.

She focused on his mouth again, and her pink tongue slipped out to lick her lips. He held back a groan. Not making this about sex was already hard enough. That visual prompt did all sorts of wicked things to his mind—and body —inappropriate as it was, considering the situation.

"Well, okay," she said slowly, the sweet scent of her

arousal twining around him, proving she was just as affected by him as he was by her. "But don't get any ideas."

You mean beyond the ones I already have? "You'll feel my *prana* as an energetic push, a kind of warm tingle that goes beyond just breath. When you feel that, make sure you breathe it in. You need to picture pulling that energy inside. The rest will work itself out."

"A'ight," she slurred with all the proper enunciation of a drunk.

Time was running out. Her *tvaglakshana* was so faded, it was barely a tinge darker than her skin tone.

He turned them around so her back was against the wall and his body shielded her from the other patrons. Sliding one hand to the nape of her neck, he angled her head up as he lowered his mouth to hers. Her lips were warm, inviting, and a flash of heat and desire lit up his nerve endings while he finally, *finally* kissed the female he'd been fantasizing about for months now. The one he never thought he'd be able to touch, let alone make out with.

Yet here she was, melting against him, her fingers digging into the fabric of his shirt, curling into his pecs. She opened her mouth to him further. He valiantly fought to keep his need in check, to start gathering his *prana* and transfer it to her, but when she tentatively pushed her tongue into his mouth, licked over his lips, he was done for.

Groaning in the back of his throat, he met her tongue, played with it, the intimate touch sending a thrill through his system, down to his groin. His cock hardened and pushed against the fabric of his jeans. Her arousal flavored the air, intoxicating, delectable.

Somewhere in the back of his mind warning bells

sounded off. *Stop this, now.* As much as he wanted to keep kissing her, it wasn't right, not like this.

He focused and gathered part of his *prana*—a radiant, burning flow of energy suffusing his whole system, its incandescent center in his chest—and pulled it up. Infusing his breath with its power, he exhaled into Lily, bestowing his life force upon her. She jerked when she felt it. Her arms wrapped around his neck and she pushed closer to him, pressing the length of her body against him while she sucked his energy inside her.

Holy fuck.

He'd heard about what it was like to exchange *prana* with an unrelated adult female, but no description came close to the overwhelming reality of it. Her pull on his energy triggered an electric shock of pleasure, zapping through his veins, his muscles, down to his toes. She felt it too, if the explosion of lust in her scent and the stifled moan humming in her throat were any indication. His groin tightened to the point of pain. Part of him flowed into her, fused with her essence, bound her to him. And fuck if he didn't want more of him inside her, to feel her clenching around him while he claimed her as his in the most primal of ways.

Her body undulated in his arms as she breathed him in. Feverishly, with growing urgency, she rubbed herself against him, her belly stroking over his hard cock in moves that made thinking all but impossible. And yet he had to check out of this, for both their sakes.

With more effort than it would take to rein in a horde of four-year-olds on a sugar high, he broke the kiss and drew back. His breath, now only carrying the normal amount of *prana* again, came in short, brutal pants. Lily followed his retreat, her mouth seeking his, but he held her gently at bay.

She whimpered her protest. Her eyes snapped open, meeting his with fire-streaked obsidian.

"Shh. It's enough." Just to make sure it really was, he checked her *tvaglakshana* again. The symbols were now a light brown henna. It would do. He pushed aside the neckline of his shirt to examine his own *tvaglakshana* on his shoulder. As he'd thought. He'd given her about half his life force —good thing he'd just fed, or he'd be dead by now.

He looked back at Lily. "How do you feel?"

Her eyes were still a storm of red on black, her cheeks flushed with color. "Wired. Like I had a huge cup of coffee. And—" She broke off, the blush taking over her whole face and neck.

She didn't have to finish that next sentence. The violent streaks of sexual arousal in her aura, as well as the alluring scent of her feminine desire, spoke loudly enough.

"Yeah, that." He couldn't hold back the grin itching to take over his face. "Happens sometimes after a feed."

"Right." She pulled her arms from his neck and cleared her throat.

He took her hint and stepped back a little to give her space. "You'll probably crash soon." She frowned, so he explained more. "If what you're going through is anything like the normal transition to maturity for our kind—and from what I've seen so far, that's what it looks like—your body's working in overdrive to change your metabolism to demon. It burns a helluva lot of *prana*, and it means you'll tire quickly and need more rest than usual."

"I feel fine."

"Give it a few minutes."

"No, really, I feel like I could totally stay out all night and —" Her knees buckled and her breathing stuttered.

He grabbed her shoulders and held her up. Her eyelids drooped, and her head lolled to the side. *And here we go…*

She jerked up again. "I'm awake. I'm awake." Her hands flailed, then grasped his shirt. She stood still for a few seconds, her breathing flat, staring unfocused past his shoulder. "Okay, maybe I'm not fine."

He exhaled and nodded. "You need to lie low for a while. I'll take you to my place."

"No funny business, Mr. *Prana*-gremlin."

"*Pranagraha*," he corrected her with a smile.

She waved a hand. "Tomay-toes, tomah-toes." Her tone was light, but he felt the tremor in her aura.

She was alone, faced with changes beyond her comprehension, no friends or family to support her right now, and she was about to go home with an unfamiliar male who used to be her enemy. Yeah, he could see how it would frighten her, even if she'd never say so out loud.

"Would it help you trust me," he asked, acutely aware of how his rough hands felt on her silken skin, "if I swear on my mother's ashes not to touch you without your consent?"

🙐🙐

LILY SNAPPED HER HEAD UP, HER HEART MISSING A BEAT AT HIS words—at the solemnity of his tone. His eyes—black speckled with red right after he'd given her *prana*, now gold-rimmed silver again—held hers, unflinching, without blinking, displaying an earnestness that moved her.

"Would you?" she asked softly.

"Yes. If that's what it takes to make you feel safe with me."

He really meant it. He'd swear on his mother's ashes,

56

and every line on his face, the erect way he held himself, the calm yet determined pattern of his energy told her he wouldn't give an oath like that lightly. Many people these days threw vows around as if they were small change, having lost all sense of the binding magic a verbal pledge like that used to hold. The male in front of her, however, seemed to not only remember the inherent power of an earnest vow, he *respected* it.

Something deep inside her shifted.

"I believe you," she said.

"I haven't made the vow yet."

"You don't need to. I can see you mean it."

He stared at her a moment, then nodded once. "Let's go."

When he took her elbow as they walked, she shook her head. "I'm okay, really."

He studied her closely, saw far too much while he assessed her stance, the way she moved. A frown creased his forehead, and he looked down at her feet. "You're hurt."

"It's a scratch." She tried to hold in her wince when she stepped on a crumb on the floor. A fucking *crumb*, and it felt like someone stuck a serrated pincer up her sole.

"Show me your feet."

"It's really not my fetish."

"*Lily.*"

With a hopefully sufficiently annoyed sigh, she lifted one foot for him to see.

"All right, that's it." And before she could so much as squeal her protest, he'd scooped her up, one arm under her knees, one behind her back, and was carrying her out the bar.

Instinctively, she looped her hands around his neck. "That's so not necessary."

"Your soles are shredded."

"A flesh wound."

"You can't walk."

"Can too. The Black Knight *always* trium—"

"Yes, yes, I'm sure you could still bite my leg off. Got it. Doesn't change the fact I'll be carrying you."

A smile blooming in her chest, she stared at him. "You totally got that reference."

He winked at her, his lips curving up. Not a lot of guys she met could pick up on when she quoted Monty Python, let alone run with it and play along. And none of them had a grin that could melt her core.

"You should have told me your feet are injured." The admonishment in his tone. *Pfft.*

"Oh, is that the secret *prana*-grapes code for 'pick me up and haul me around?' I gotta remember that."

He gave a noncommittal grunt and kept carrying her down the empty street, around a corner and into an open parking lot. Stopping in front of a black pickup truck, he murmured, "Hold on."

She tightened her grip around his neck as he let go of her back and fished his keys out of his pocket.

"You can put me down."

"Nope."

"Believe me, my dainty female feet won't disintegrate on contact with the ground for the few seconds it takes you to unlock the car."

"Shush."

He unlocked the truck while still holding her, opened the passenger side door, and set her down on the seat with a gentleness that shook her. She was still perturbed by the level of care he took with her when he got in the driver's seat and started the engine.

Desperate to fill the tense silence while squashing whatever was stirring inside her, she blurted out the first question that popped into her mind. "How long have you worked for Arawn?"

His hands gripped the steering wheel harder. "Almost ten years."

"How did you get into his service?" she asked, because, apparently, her social filter, which should have yelled "sore spot—change subject," had decided to take the rest of the night off.

It took her a moment to realize the crunching sound wasn't the tires crushing gravel but his teeth grinding. "He enlisted me against my will."

"I take it he can be very persuasive."

"Worse than a kid blackmailing you to get a cookie."

Interesting choice of a comparison. She studied him for a moment, giving in to the spark of appreciation for the masculine profile of his strong jaw and nose while he kept his attention on the road. "You don't like working for Arawn, then."

"Can't wait until my tenure with him is over."

"When's that?"

"In a month."

"Why do you hate him?" And yep, her social filter had fled the car.

He glanced at her, flecks of red glowing in the silver of his eyes. "You are inquisitive, aren't you?"

"Pathologically curious. It's a flaw."

Looking back at the road, he said, "Just because I'm

demon doesn't mean I feel any loyalty toward Arawn beyond what is required of me by my contract with him."

"But he's the Demon Lord. Shouldn't that…" She waved her hand. "…mean something to your kind?"

He took a deep breath. "First, he's not lord of all demons. That's a misconception on the witches' part. There are many demons and otherworld creatures who don't belong to him. Second, he's not even a demon. Why anyone would think to dub him lord of a species he's not even part of is beyond me."

"He's not a demon?"

His face shadowed. "No. And don't ask me what he is. No one knows. The only thing that's clear is that he's unlike anything most of us have ever seen or felt."

"And he wants Maeve."

Her thoughts, bleak as they were when talking about a being as obscure and dangerous as Arawn, darkened even more when she remembered the ordeal of her best friend's little sister, the girl who was as much of a sibling to Lily as she was to Merle. They'd all but grown up together, what with the Murrays and the MacKennas so close as to almost count as one family. When Maeve was kidnapped by a demon, Lily had shared Merle's pain, her heart aching for Maeve, who'd long been believed to be without powers.

As it turned out, Maeve did have massive powers, but they were bound inside her. In fact, she possessed a magic so great, that Lily's aunt Isabel had instigated the abduction to use the demon to harvest Maeve's powers for herself. That such devastating betrayal of the sacred witches' code to never harm each other had been perpetrated by someone from her own family had shattered Lily's heart.

Never was a witch to hurt another of her kind. It was anathema, the highest sacrilege.

"I'm only tasked to watch her," Alek said, yanking Lily from the painful past to the present. "I don't know any more than you do about his grand scheme."

"He wants her for her powers, obviously."

"Everything Arawn does is meant to increase his power."

She peered at him. "But you're not privy to his plans."

"If I were, I couldn't tell you." He glanced at her a fleeting moment, a grin flirting with his mouth, before he focused back on the traffic. "But as it is, I'm only one of his enforcers, not his right hand. I'm not involved in governing his dominion. I get my orders, I follow them."

He steered the car onto St. John's Bridge, passing underneath the lofty pillars of the bridge's gates. To their right, the lights of Portland twinkled in the night, reflected on the black waters of the Willamette River. Late as the hour was, there were still people awake, buildings lit, the city big enough to join the club of those that never sleep.

"Where do you live?" she asked without taking her eyes off the haunting beauty of a heart of concrete and stone, a city pulsing with life, even in the dead of night.

"St. John's. We're almost there."

A few minutes later, he pulled up into the driveway of a cottage-style home in a quaint neighborhood.

"This is...nice," she said as he turned off the engine.

"You sound surprised."

"I am."

He faced her, one corner of his mouth tilting up, a glint in his eyes. "What did you expect? A ramshackle shed in a rat-infested dump?"

She cleared her throat, her cheeks heating. "Not that bad."

He stared at her, unblinking.

"Just a little bad," she murmured.

Shaking his head, he opened his door. "You seem to have a lot of misconceptions about demons."

"I'm beginning to see that." She tried not to ogle his butt while he got out of the car. Really did. And failed. But damn, those jeans fit him like nobody's business.

With a sigh, she pushed open the passenger side door and swung her legs out, wanting to slide down from the high truck seat, when he appeared in front of her and grabbed her waist.

"Nice try," he said and hefted her over his shoulder. Like some bad-mannered firefighter. That scoundrel.

"Oy." She tapped his back with her palm. "You're over-doing it, Mr. *Prana*-grunge. Put me down."

"*Pranagraha.*" He continued to haul her up the stairs to the front door.

"Did you know," she said, bouncing with his steps while he unlocked the door and walked inside, "that Wife-Carrying is a sport? Originated in Finland, but they've got championships here in the US, too. You should apply."

He set her down on a couch in the living area, and lingered after placing her on the sofa, his arms on the cushion on either side of her, his face close enough that she could feel the heat radiating off him. He had a strange expression, features tight and gaze searing, as if her blithe words had affected him somehow, had hit on something he hadn't expected.

Longing pulsed between them, so strong, and yet so fleet-ing, Lily wasn't sure she'd interpreted it correctly. She blinked, sucked in air, and the next second he shifted away, leaving her shaken and wondering if she'd imagined whatever had passed between them just now. Well, going by how fucked-up her system and senses were, it very well could have been her mind playing tricks on her.

"Sit tight." Alek walked over to a door toward the back of the house. "I'll be right back."

She took advantage of the moment to study the room. Always one to catalog every new place, she was inherently curious about how other people lived, about the details that made up their personal space. She took her time perusing the puzzle of things that made up Alek's.

A large flat screen TV—naturally—dominated the opposite wall next to the front door. Shelves framed the media center, filled with books and DVDs. Behind the couch she was sitting on stood more shelves on the wall, holding more books, and what looked like picture frames and knickknacks that seemed more suited for a person older than Alek, and with a definite feminine touch. He'd mentioned his mother was dead. Wasn't hard to guess he'd kept some of her belongings in his home—which had probably been his parents' before him.

To her right was the kitchen area, the cupboards painted a bright green, with a small dining table set to one side. One door led to the back of the house, where Alek reappeared, holding two bowls, a washcloth and a towel slung over his forearms.

After setting the equipment on the table, he knelt in front of her and tapped her right shin. "Lift your foot."

"You really have a fetish, don't you?"

He shot her a look that was all kinds of dark and hotly bothering at the same time. "Your wounds need cleaning."

"Well, if you insist." She raised her right foot. "Makes me glad I get regular pedicures and painted my toenails."

He set one of the bowls on the floor. "You'll need to soak your sole in here for a minute so the worst of the dirt can come off."

She gingerly lowered her foot into the bowl. The water was pleasantly warm, not searing, but still the contact stung her to the point she locked her jaw to keep from uttering a sound of pain.

Alek's eyes flicked from her foot to her face, narrowing on whatever tiny clues she hadn't managed to hide. Damn perceptive predators. He didn't comment, however, just calmly studied her expression in a way that had her almost squirming with the impulse to finger comb her hair or fix her makeup. Which probably resembled the Joker by now.

"You've got…" He wet the washcloth, and reached out to her, wiped at her forehead before she could jerk back. He lingered close for a moment, his focus intense, consuming. "Blood," he said, leaning back again. "You had some blood there."

"Yeah," she croaked, her breathing flat. "Thanks."

He gave a nod, then gestured for her to raise both feet so he could switch the bowls. While her left foot was now soaking, he dabbed at the underside of her right, his face serious, entirely focused on his task. His movements were careful, gentle, his hand holding her foot up by her ankle branding her with his heat. Every now and then he glanced at her face.

"Does it hurt?"

She shook her head, biting the inside of her lower lip as a counterpoint to the pain in her sole.

"Liar," he said, his tone as gentle as a caress, a smile in his eyes. He switched to the other foot. "I'll be more careful."

"Really, you don't need to..." She trailed off, unsure how to talk to this male who treated her with a kind of tenderness that rattled her, toppled all sorts of firmly entrenched opinions she'd held for so long. Her heart thumped madly.

He raised his eyes, the gold a luminous ring around the silver. "You're not used to having someone take care of you, hm?"

"I'm not a kid anymore, so no. I can take care of myself quite well."

The nurturing warmth of her mom had been curbed by Aunt Isabel's drive to make sure Lily would grow into a witch strong enough to one day inherit the family's power, even though she'd never been first in line as heir. Isabel's own daughters were slated to carry that responsibility. Until they were murdered, one by one, by vengeful demons. With the irony of fate, her aunt's foresight in training Lily as a future Elder witch had almost become just that—foresight, or an especially cruel self-fulfilling prophecy.

"I know you can," Alek said. His thumb stroked over her ankle, sending a pleasant shiver up her leg. "Sometimes you want to take care of someone else, not because you think the person can't do it themselves..." he dabbed at the arch of her foot, gentle, so fucking gentle "...but because it soothes a need inside you." The look he sent her shot straight through her defenses. "And it's your way of showing you care."

An inexplicable lump formed in her throat, and suddenly the only thing she could think about was swallowing past it without choking.

The slow clicking of claws against wood startled her. She tore her gaze away from Alek's sincere expression and twisted to look behind her. An old dog trudged through the open door leading to the other rooms and made his way to the couch. He stopped next to Alek, who set down the wash-cloth and ruffled the mutt's fur.

"Hey there, buddy." Alek's voice lowered to a soothing pitch, his words infused with warmth and affection. "You want to take a look at our guest, hm?"

The dog—probably at least partly a German Shepherd-Labrador mix, his dark brown fur graying around his muzzle—sat down and licked over Alek's hand.

"This is Grant," Alek said, still scratching the dog's flappy ears. "Grant, this is Lily." He took Grant's head in both hands and gave him a hard stare. "She's off-limits. You hear?"

"I'm not sure I want to know why you need to tell him that, or what exactly that means."

Alek shrugged one shoulder, rubbing his neck, his face coloring. "He likes to hump people's legs."

"Charming."

He sighed. "Yeah, well, he's fixed, but he still *thinks* he's got the right equipment. Although he never seems to remember how to go through with it. He starts humping and then just stops with a confused look on his face…"

Lily snort-laughed, then clapped a hand over her mouth. "Sorry."

Alek's grin made her chest flutter with tingles. "'Sokay. It *is* kind of funny."

"How old is he?"

"Fifteen."

"Wow."

"Yeah." He rubbed Grant's neck and scratched under his muzzle, a tender gleam in his eyes as he looked at his dog. "I've had him since he was a pup."

Another misconception toppled. Learning a demon

would have a pet, and display this kind of affection and attachment to it corrected her perspective by several notches. "You're really not what I thought you should be," she said quietly.

A side glance from this unconventional demon. "We'll have to work on your flattery skills."

She wanted to smile and shoot back a quip, but a wave of nausea made her gasp, the room spinning too fast around her.

"Lily?"

His face, his form, were a blur, while darkness crept in from the edges, and somehow the couch threw her off.

"I've got you," was the last thing she heard before heat and autumn winds engulfed her, her mind slipping into the black silk of oblivion.

CHAPTER 6

L ily jerked awake, coated with sweat, her heart pounding madly in her chest. She blinked, her breath coming in pants, her mind entangled in the lingering images, sounds, and sensations of the dream. Nightmare, more like. Gasping, she clutched the sheets as the full extent of the horrid memories flooded her consciousness.

Her hands around Baz's neck, claws breaking his skin. His eyes, bloodshot and wide with terror. He paws at her to let him go. A dark whisper deep inside her enjoying his struggle. A drumming force within, lusting after the inevitable end to his struggle.

Kill.

A whimper tore from her throat. What had she done? What had she become? More than anything, she wanted to see Baz, tell him how sorry she was, make sure he was okay. And yet, trumping that urge to make amends was a shame so devastating it shriveled every good intention she had.

She couldn't face him. What if he looked at her with disgust, or hate, or...worst of all...fear? She couldn't bear the thought. Not when they'd always been so close they finished each other's sentences, could hold entire conversations just by exchanging looks.

Fighting down the corrosive hurt spreading from her heart, she took stock of her surroundings. A darkened room, its one window heavily shielded, with only a minuscule glow around the edges giving away that it was daytime outside. She was sitting on a sofa bed in the corner, the rest of the room dominated by workout equipment—a weight-lifting bench in the middle, a punching bag hanging from the ceiling in the other corner, a treadmill on one wall.

She swung her legs over the side of the bed and paused. Ugh, she still had on her once-sexy, now-filthy dress, plus the grime and dirt accumulated during one hell of a night. And not the good kind of hell. Grimacing, she glanced at the markings covering her cleavage and shoulders, then looked away quickly. *It's still real.* It had really happened.

Swallowing hard, pain lancing her chest, she stood and walked out of the room. She followed the narrow hall to the front of the house. The scent of coffee, bacon, and something fried tantalized her senses. Her mouth watered and her stomach growled on cue.

When she entered the main living area, Alek was at the stove, turning something in a pan. The kitchen light lent his hair a glow like dark, burnished gold. She paused with her full focus locked on his form, her breath stalling in her lungs.

His dark red T-shirt seemed to hug his shoulders and back just so, as if caressing the taut muscles that bunched and rippled with his every move. From underneath the short sleeves flowed the symbols of his demon tattoo, down to his elbows. The sight of those elegant lines curving over his biceps, running over his tan skin in strokes of light-brown henna, it stirred a primal appreciation in her. Credit where credit was due, and those symbols, the way they adorned his arms, they were *beautiful*.

As was he.

He was cooking with the same concentration he'd applied to washing her wounds, and she guessed he'd bring that kind of attention to every task he did. It lent him an air of focused control and security, and damn if that wasn't sexy as fuck. Her stomach fluttered, and heat pooled between her thighs.

"Hungry?" he asked without taking his eyes off the stove.

"More than you know." And for far more than just food.

"Dinner will take a few more minutes. You can jump into the shower in the meantime." He pointed at the door to the other rooms with the spatula, muscles flexing in his forearm. "Bathroom's the first door on the left. I laid out towels for you."

"Um. Thanks." She pressed her lips together, remembering she had nothing else to wear after taking the shower. Just the thought of having to slip back into this dress…

"Oh," he said, "and I figured you might want to change into something else, so I ran over to my brother Dima's and borrowed a few things from his mate. She's about your size, give or take an inch, so maybe it'll fit you."

"You—you ran out?" Her eyes flicked to the heavily covered windows blocking out the day. "Isn't sunlight lethal to *prana*-graffitis?"

His lips twitched. *"Pranagrahas,"* he said, not looking up from the frying pan. "And it's not immediately fatal. It just drains us of *prana* more quickly. We can stand a few minutes of full exposure, and when we're covered from head to toe, we can stay out a bit longer, though it's a risk we rarely take."

But he had. For her. Just to get her some damn clothes. "Thank you," she said, her voice husky.

"My pleasure." He met her gaze for a searing moment then nodded toward the couch. "I put the clothes over there." He scratched the back of his neck, eyes trained studiously on the pan again. "Uh, Tori said the panties are brand new, she just bought them recently and washed them, but they haven't been worn yet."

She pressed her lips together, a grin wanting to steal across her face. "That's, um, good to know."

She was about to flee for the emotional safety of the bathroom when he asked, "How are your feet?"

Taken aback, she stopped mid-stride. That's right, her feet. She hadn't felt any pain or discomfort padding across the hardwood floors after waking up. Lifting one foot, she inspected the sole. Smooth skin, unscarred.

"Healed?"

"Yeah," she muttered, baffled. "Not a scratch left."

"Perks of being a *pranagraha*."

"That *is* neat."

Alek opened the oven, peeked inside, then closed it again. "More severe injuries can still cripple us or leave scars, but stuff like that?" He shrugged, muscles rolling in his shoulders. "Heals in no time."

"Great perks." She gave him a tight smile and hurried to the bathroom, where she chucked her dress and underwear, stepped into the tub, and turned on the shower.

The splash of cold water was a welcome shock.

Yes, the healing was a great perk. An advantage many would covet. And a few people probably wouldn't even mind the darkness that came with that perk, the urge to kill, the necessity of taking someone else's life force to survive.

She shivered despite the now-hot water pelting down on her. Even if being demon came with immortality and super powers like flying, or waking up with perfect makeup and no morning breath, she'd trade it in for being a witch immediately. Deep inside her, where her familiar magic should be, where it had pulsed and glowed since she came into her powers, was a hollow ache. A ravine of empty darkness. If she focused on it too long, she'd fall into that black chasm.

Who was she, if that which had defined her for more than twenty years was stripped away? If her identity as a witch was removed, what was left?

Maybe she didn't even want to know, was afraid to find out.

Reeling from the force of having the rug yanked out from under her, it took her several minutes to realize she was rubbing so hard over the demon markings she'd chafed her skin raw. She took a deep breath, held on to what little peace of mind she had left, and finished showering. After toweling herself dry, she dressed in the clothes Alek had risked himself to get for her.

The black panties—no frills or fancy stuff, just cotton with a little lace on the sides, the way she liked it—fit her well enough, as did the skinny jeans. The red sports bra did an acceptable job of keeping her girls in place, and she pulled the dark blue tank top over it. A dark red cardigan and a pair of black boots completed the ensemble. She wiggled her toes against the front of the boots, where she needed just half an inch more for a perfect fit. They would do, though.

First chance she got, she'd have to thank Alek's sister-in-law—or would that be sister-by-mating?—for her generosity.

When she joined Alek again in the kitchen, he'd already set the table. Bacon, sautéed vegetables, bread rolls, and basically what looked like the entire contents of his fridge covered the table.

"Sit," he said while emptying the contents of the skillet into a bowl, then set a glass of juice in front of her. "You like mango, right?"

"Uh, yeah. How do you—" She broke off, understanding dawning. It was a habit of hers to eat out on the back deck during summer when the weather was fine, whether that be breakfast or dinner. "You saw me. When you watched Maeve."

One side of his mouth curved up in a charming half-smile. "I promise it's not as stalkerish as it sounds. I was doing my task as sentinel, keeping an eye on the mansion. You happened to be there, too, so I...noticed. Coffee?"

And he'd picked up on the sort of juice she always drank —even though she was not even his target. Her heart started a mad gallop. "Sure," she muttered, accepting the mug of coffee he handed her. And remembering the fact that Arawn was staking out her family's home, his covetous eyes on Maeve, she made a mental note to warn her mom and Merle the first chance she got. As soon as she was able to talk to them again without shame heating her face, that was.

"What would you like on the bread?" he asked as he turned back to the frying pan. "I've got salami, cream cheese, peanut butter, jam..." He nodded toward the table and the abundance of food on it.

She was so stunned by the care and attention he'd put into making dinner for her, all she could do was take a sip of coffee in the hopes of maybe jump-starting more of her usual mental capacities. She spotted sesame bread among the assortment of food on the table—her favorite.

Slowly, she set the coffee mug down. "Why am I getting the feeling you've more than *noticed* me in the past?"

Instead of answering, he turned and set the bowl with what he'd fried in the skillet on the table. Steaming hot fried potatoes, made the way her mom always prepared them, German-style and roasted to perfection. Her favorite dish.

Inside her chest, her heart thumped around like a trapped rabbit. Breath leaving her in a dizzying rush, she stood and took a step back from the table, from him. "What is this about? There's more to your helping me than just an altruistic drive, isn't there?"

Alek met her look, his expression serious. "If there is?"

"What are you playing at?" Suspicion crawled over her skin like a thousand tiny spider legs.

He hesitated, took a deep breath as if gathering courage, and said, "I like you."

She blinked, her chest and stomach still tight with wariness. "Right. Okay."

"No, I mean...I like you as in, I want you in my life."

Her throat had gone dry at the intensity of the look he was giving her. Like she was the one bright spot in his life, the one thing he craved more than his next breath, the treasure he'd do anything to obtain.

She cleared her throat. "What do you mea—?"

"I want you to mate with me."

۞

"Mate?" Lily's eyes were locked onto Alek's, depths of

indigo that drew him in like nothing else. "As in bond-for-a-lifetime-squeeze-out-a-bunch-of-demon-spawn-and-live-happily-ever-after? That kind of mate? Or do you mean the have-hot-and-mindless-animal-sex-and-part-ways-without-strings-attached kind of mate?" She sounded so hopeful when she babbled out the second alternative.

He prowled toward her. "The first one. Lifetime, bunch of demon spawn, and happily-ever-after. Though I do plan to include the hot-and-mindless sex, too." He caught her gaze, made sure she saw the intention in his own. "But I want the strings. I've wanted you since the first time I saw you at the beginning of summer, but you were a witch, and I couldn't have you. Now you're a *pranagraha*, we're compatible to mate. And that," he said, dropping his voice to a sensual caress, "is what I'm playing at."

A part of him worried this was a little too straightforward. Too much, too soon. He'd thought about taking more time to court her, to win her heart bit by bit before proposing. If she were any other *pranagraha* female, that would have been his route of choice. But Lily's case was different in one essential point: He might very well not have enough time to woo her as was proper. If whatever happened to turn her into a demon was reversible somehow, it was logical she'd want to find out how and become a witch again. Unless...

Unless he gave her a reason to stay demon.

So he'd decided to lay his cards on the table, to let her know he was serious about her. And didn't human females usually appreciate honesty, and a male who was in it for the long haul?

She blinked, shook her head, disbelief written all over her face.

"I'm perfect mate material," he said, going on to list his assets, ticking them off on his fingers. "I'm smart, healthy, strong, I can provide for you, protect you, I can cook, I clean up after myself, I'll always take care of your pleasure, and I make cute babies."

Her mouth fell open. "You have children?"

"No, but I have a twin brother, and he has three kids. They're the cutest buggers you'll ever see, and since we share the same genes, my kids will be just as cute. At least." He waved his hand at her. "With you as their mother, they'll be gorgeous."

For the second time in as many minutes, her mouth fell open. She closed it. Opened it. Then closed it again, making the most adorable imitation of a fish out of water he'd ever seen. "You," she said slowly, moving her head back warily while keeping her eyes on him, "are the most crazypants person I've met in my life."

"Not crazy. Determined. I'm well aware of what I want, and I'm going for it."

He stalked toward her, stopped just short of invading her personal space, though close enough to see the flutter of her pulse on her throat. It had sped up while he prowled over to her, and as he raised his hand, ran his finger over the sensitive skin where her neck met her shoulder, she uttered a soft, feminine sound of pleasure. It made him wonder what she would sound like in wild abandon, hot and sweaty underneath him, open and trusting. Would she cry out when he made her shatter with ecstasy?

"I want to make you mine," he said, and damn, his voice was as rough as the crude urges raging inside him, this potent, devastating mix of hunger, desire, and possessiveness.

As he rubbed her collarbone—with more gentleness than he'd thought he was capable of in his current emotional state —she leaned into his touch for a moment, then seemed to catch herself. She stepped back, the scent of her growing excitement a tantalizing fragrance that belied her retreat. "Tell me, is this normal *prana*-gravy behavior, or are you just a special kind of insane?"

He chuckled at her creative misuse of their species' name. "Male *pranagrahas* do have a strong mating urge, and the older we get, the stronger the urge. There are fewer females than males around, so females are coveted. But I don't want you because you're the next best *pranagraha* female. Not because of what you are." He followed her retreat, just a small step, careful not to threaten her, but enough to keep her body aware of his. "I want you because of *who* you are."

She narrowed her eyes. "And you think watching me prance around our backyard for a few months has given you extensive knowledge about who I am. Well, congratulations on knowing my favorite food and juice, that's a real nice touch, but frankly, my dear—" she leaned forward, jutting out her chin, the movement a dare and a warning at once "— you have no fucking idea about who I am."

Ignoring the warning, he took her up on the dare, leaned in, and paused a few inches from her face. The air between them heated. "I know enough to know I want you. You're funny, clever, a fighter, loyal to a fault, passionate, and beautiful. Not to mention hot enough to make a demon forget his name. I want you in my life, by my side." He lowered his voice to a murmur. "In my bed."

She inhaled softly, her pupils dilating. Her eyes skittered down to his lips, and his whole body tightened, remembering their kiss. Judging by the fresh tendrils of arousal in her scent, she remembered it too.

"I'm not even attracted to you."

He cocked one eyebrow and sauntered around her, looking pointedly at her jeans.

She half turned around, following his movements with narrowed eyes. "What are you doing?"

"Checking for fire." He hooked one finger through a loop in her pants, tugging gently. "These must be burning like hell right about now."

"I'm not lying."

"*Tsvetochek*, you do know our sense of smell still surpasses that of humans, even when it's dulled during the day?"

It took her a moment. Then her eyes widened, and her cheeks blazed an adorable tomato red. Clearly trying for furtive, she clenched her thighs together. Which he of course noticed, glancing down. Amusement and desire vied for supremacy. He ignored both and went with calm observance, dragging his gaze up her body again before focusing on her eyes.

She cleared her throat, took another step back. "What does *tsvetochek* mean?"

"It's Russian for *little flower*."

A small crease appeared between her brows.

"Your name," he said, his lips curving up without his conscious doing. "You're named after a flower. Thought it was fitting."

The frown on her forehead smoothed away, like rain-clouds clearing from the sky—and the smile that graced her face then was like a ray of sunshine, warm, open, radiating joy. "I like that," she whispered.

That smile of hers, it shot straight through to his heart, filled the cold and aching places. How often had he dreamed of her giving him a radiant smile like this one?

With his finger still hooked through the loop of her jeans, he pulled her closer again, until her front all but brushed against his own. His every sense alert, he studied her body language, ready to let her go at once if she gave the smallest sign of rejection or fear. She didn't. Though her hands flexed, fingers fidgeting, and her brows drew together just the tiniest bit, her attention darted between his eyes and his mouth, the overtone of excitement in her scent deepened, and her lips parted on a slow exhale as her body swayed oh-so-slightly toward him.

Yes.

Anticipation humming through his muscles, he leaned even closer, ready to remind her how explosive they could be together. Her breath whispered over his lips. Her finger-tips grazed his shirt.

Claws clicked on the floor, and then a muzzle pushed its way between both of their legs. Lily startled and pulled away. Fidgeting, she tugged at her clothes—which hadn't even been disturbed, much to his chagrin—and looked at Grant. The old traitor of a dog wagged his tail, sporting a happy canine grin.

Alek rubbed a hand over his face, inwardly cursing Grant's new cockblocking tendencies. Well, to be fair, Alek had never brought a female home before, so Grant had never learned to leave him alone when he got physically close to a date.

"Um, I think he's peeing," Lily said, yanking him back to the present situation.

A situation that was just getting worse.

With a barely-held-back groan, he turned to Grant, who was indeed emptying his bladder on the kitchen floor, all the while happily wagging his tail. "He does that when he's excited. It's gotten worse with age." He grabbed the roll of paper towels from the counter and started wiping up the mess. "It's okay, buddy," he muttered to Grant, his voice soothing. "You're okay. I'm not mad at you."

He scratched Grant's ears, and then applied cleaner to the peed-on area as well. He'd still have to use some urine neutralizer, too, but that could wait until later. Right now, he had to get back to convincing one searingly hot witch-turned-demon that staying on the dark side had more perks than cookies.

He washed his hands and faced Lily. "Sorry about that."

"No problem." She didn't sound disgusted or embarrassed as he'd feared. In fact, a small smile tugged at her lips, her eyes warm as she glanced at Grant. "We used to have a cat that started having bladder issues when she got older. She couldn't hold it in anymore, and we could tell it was embarrassing for her. We set up so many litter boxes all over the house for her that people thought we had three dozen cats. But it helped. And she was so grateful."

She met his eyes, and for a moment, he basked in the affection and warmth in them, the softness of her features. Then as if a switch had been turned, her expression shuttered and she glanced away, clearing her throat. "Um, I think it's best we stop this."

His stomach made a dive for the ground. "Stop what?"

"I know you offered to help me, and I agreed, but I don't feel it's right, considering."

"Considering what?" Man, he felt like a parrot. A frazzled, confused, feeling-like-a-moron parrot.

"Your intentions." She gestured at him. "The whole wanting-to-mate thing. It...makes me uncomfortable. If I'd known you were into me like that, I would have never accepted your help. I'm not looking for a serious relationship —not usually, and especially not now. So." She paused, bit her lip. "I think it's best I leave. Thank you for what you've done for me. I wish I could pay you for the clothes, and your help. If I had my wallet on me..."

"Whoa." He held up his hands, heart racing, his blood running cold, not just with the imminent threat of her departure, but with the implication in her words. "Let me make one thing clear. You don't owe me. I don't expect you to pay me." He let his arms fall to his sides, hands clenching. "*In any way,*" he added, making sure his voice carried his indignation at even the hint that he was looking for a reward of the physical kind. "I'm not that kind of guy."

She shook her head. "I didn't mean to imply that. But even if you don't expect me to repay you that way, you're not just helping me out of kindness. You do have an agenda, a goal you hope to achieve. It doesn't feel right to accept your help when I know you want something from me that I can never give you."

Her words struck him like a blow to the gut. Scratch that, the strike was worse than the solar plexus hit she'd delivered last night. He was losing her. Losing the one chance he'd had at winning her favor. He pushed that hurt down, gritted his teeth and breathed through his nose, exhaled through his mouth to center himself. His mind raced to analyze the situation, to see if there was something salvageable.

Lily crossed her arms in front of her chest, shuffling her feet. "If you could tell me where the next bus station is..."

"I'll take you home." Fuck that, he wasn't going to let her

roam on the public transportation system. He'd drive her, even if it broke his fucking heart to facilitate her leaving.

She shook her head, a haunted expression on her face. "I can't go home."

Right, she'd attacked her brother and was probably still too racked by shame and guilt to deal with it. "You can stay with me," he tried again. "I won't pressure you into anything, or expect you to mate with me." Of course he'd *hope* for it. And use whatever skills he had to smoothly court her and change her mind without scaring her away.

"No." She briefly closed her eyes. "I can't do this. It's not fair." One of her hands came up to rub the markings peeking out from under her neckline. "I'll go to my friend's house."

"Merle MacKenna?"

Her eyes darted up, widening slightly. "Yes."

"I'll drive you there."

CHAPTER 7

Lily sat silently while Alek steered his truck through the early evening Portland traffic. Outside the car's window, the last light of sunset painted the sky in hues of fiery red merging to indigo.

Her chest and stomach were in tight knots of complicated feelings after the scene at his house. A part of her wanted to nudge him to say something, to break the heavy quiet that had come over him after she blew him off. Gone were the half-smiles and grins he'd directed her way before, gone was the easy way he'd been around her, to be replaced with a tense atmosphere of disappointment and hurt.

And it hurt her.

Surprising, that. And she really shouldn't feel this way. She should be relieved he was complying with her wishes, relieved to get away from a male with intentions that had her legs itching with the urge to run. Well, a part of her *was* glad. Once she got to Merle's, she could confer with her best friend about this whole ridiculous turn-into-a-demon thing, and then get on with solving this mess. After, of course, she confessed to Merle what she'd done to Baz, a prospect that made her tremble with anxiety.

And then there was the small part of her that didn't, in fact, want to leave Alek. Crazy. That's what it was. She hadn't even known him for twenty-four hours. She'd barely scratched the surface of who he was. But still, the way she felt when she was around him...as if something that had been missing—something she hadn't even been aware of—clicked into place. He made her feel safe. At a moment, in a situation when her entire world had come crashing down around her, when she wasn't sure anymore who she was, he'd managed to somehow steady her.

But he wanted more than she was willing to give, and she wouldn't take advantage of his offer of help if it meant stringing him along. She was going to turn back into a witch, and he wouldn't be able to mate with her then. And even if she were to remain a demon—which she was *not*, dammit—she'd never agree to mate with him. Or anyone else. Knowing that, she couldn't stay around him and lead him on by accepting his help.

Alek pulled the truck up into a parking lot sandwiched between three-story buildings.

She turned to him with a frown. "Why are we stopping here?"

Shutting off the engine, he said, "You need to feed." Before she could interrupt, he went on. "Think about it. You're running low on *prana* again, and you'll need to take someone's life force before the night is over. What do you think will happen when I drop you off at Merle's house, and you're hungry, your instincts taking over?"

Well, hell. She hadn't thought that far. He was right. The last thing she wanted was a repeat of her attack on Baz. If her guilt was eating her alive about that incident already, she didn't want to imagine her emotional state if she also lunged at her best friend. She'd never be able to look at herself in the mirror again.

But just the thought of having to take someone's life—she shuddered. "Do I really need to *kill*? Can't I just, like, nibble a little on someone's *prana*? Like I did with yours?"

He shook his head. "That's only to tide you over in an emergency. It's not enough to recharge you fully. You need to take someone's whole life force if you want to survive."

She locked her jaw. "No one innocent."

"Don't worry. I'll find someone who deserves it."

Her eyes met his for an instant. "How?"

"Auras. *Pranagrahas* are exceptionally good at reading them. Once you learn how, you'll find it very easy to pick out humans with especially strong *prana* and souls stained beyond redemption."

She studied him silently for a few seconds. "You mean to tell me you only kill bad guys?"

He shrugged. "I can't change the fact I need to kill to survive. But I have a choice about who to kill. I can be selective with my prey. Why should I take the life of an innocent mother of two if I can instead kill a murderer? Or an abuser? It makes no sense not to make that distinction."

"Do all *prana*-grinches make that choice?"

"No." The corners of his lips twitched, and despite the bleakness of her situation, the fact she could make him smile with her continued malapropisms of his species' name let her heart sigh. "Many don't care."

"But you do." She eyed him with new-found respect, this male who fit in none of her neat little compartments.

"I live to shatter your misconceptions, Lilichka," he said

with a smile. "And I'll teach you how to take someone's *prana*."

The look he gave her... *I'll be there for you*, it said. *I won't let you deal with this alone.* And damn if it didn't make her feel better about facing this part of her new demon nature.

Throat tight, she whispered, "I appreciate it."

He gave a curt nod and got out of the truck. She followed him onto the street, round a corner and toward a small park.

"Where are we going?"

He threw a glance at her over his shoulder. "A place where I've found suitable prey in the past. Chances are I'll find more."

They walked into the park, following the path that led them to a pergola. A man was leaning against the pavilion's railing, smoking a cigarette. The air around him pulsed with darkness, his aura dulled by a nasty tinge. While Alek and Lily approached, a harried-looking woman hurried up to the man and said something to him. They exchanged something, and the woman left as quickly as she'd come, her energy pattern trembling and crackling.

"A dealer?" Lily asked, unable to keep the growl from her voice.

"Yep."

"You knew you'd find him here?"

"Not him in particular. Someone like him. I took out another one here a few weeks ago. Seems like whoever he's working for likes to keep this corner in business."

As they drew closer, the guy's aura became more pronounced, easier to read. The darkness in it clung to the air like sludge to boots. Underneath it pulsed his life force, beckoning like the finest treat. The man stood straight when he saw Alek, his eyes assessing him, probably trying to figure out if Alek posed a threat or was a potential customer.

"Let's not talk," Alek said when he reached the dealer.

The guy's eyes glazed over and he nodded.

Lily blinked. "You're using mind control?"

"Yep. So can you, once you learn it." He caught her gaze. "I'll take this one. I think it's better if I feed first. You can watch and see how I do it, and then I'll find someone for you."

Her chest drew tight. "All right."

He shot her a glance, noted her discomfort. "This guy here," he said, his voice a rumble in the dark, "doesn't just deal with drugs. The taint of his aura hinted at something darker, and I checked his mind to make sure. So, if it makes you feel better, know that he has a penchant for cruelty that will make you nauseous."

She narrowed her eyes. "Like?"

"He likes to set animals on fire."

She sucked in air through her nose, her lips pressed together tightly.

"He used to have a dog," Alek went on, while the dealer leaned against the pergola's railing, his eyes unfocused. "Taped his muzzle shut, and watched him try to eat, laughing at the dog's despair. He watched him starve." Alek's aura flashed like lightning in a storm, and she could have sworn she heard thunder.

"Enough," Lily rasped, her breathing fast, her blood a rapid of rage. "Do it."

Alek nodded once. "When you feed, it will be a bit different from when I gave you *prana*. I pushed my life force into you, which made it easy for you to grab it. Taking *prana* by making a kill will be trickier. You'll have to keep control over your prey's mind so they don't fight you, while at the same time burrowing into their soul and pulling their *prana* out. Which is why we'll be feeding from humans tonight, since their minds are easier to manipulate."

She raised both brows. "So I could always take *prana* from demons?" That first night she'd seen Alek...yes, he'd fed from the *morbus* demon, hadn't he?

"Yes. It's just harder. Riskier."

That's a risk I'm willing to take. Well, if she were to stay demon, that was. Which she wasn't. Nope. So that was a problem she didn't even have to deal with. *There.*

He grasped the guy's collar and pulled him close. "Watch."

Alek's aura sizzled with power while he leaned in, clasping the guy's jaw with one hand and opening his mouth. The man didn't struggle, his mind apparently still firmly in Alek's grasp. Alek didn't press his lips to the dealer's, instead stopping a mere centimeter from his mouth. The human's aura lit up like an overfired light bulb. He uttered an agonized moan even as his limbs remained limp under Alek's control.

And then Lily saw it. Glowing warm and golden, the *prana* left the man's body, flowing out of his mouth and into Alek's, whose energy pattern blazed brighter the more life force he took from the human.

The glow of life around the dealer dimmed, then went out like a snuffed candle. The light in his eyes disappeared. Alek let go of the guy's collar, and the man slumped to the ground. Aura pulsing with new power, eyes a swirl of red and black, Alek turned to her.

He was magnificent.

Every inch of him projected strength and primal potency,

that same air of command and prowess he'd worn when he walked into *Nine Circles*, only now it was jacked up by a thousand percent. Muscles bulged underneath his T-shirt, beckoning her to touch. His scent wrapped around her like a siren's call, wood fires and crisp fall nights, enticing her senses. He looked at her with an intent focus, the promise of indulgent sin in his eyes.

Hoo, boy.

Heat flooded her system, her skin sensitizing as if in preparation for touch. Mouth suddenly dry, she parted her lips on a gasp as he stepped toward her.

An explosion of light flashed past her and hit Alek straight in the chest. He stumbled back, features slackening in shock, and barely caught himself on one of the pergola's pillars.

Breath stuck in her throat, Lily whirled around. Alek's attacker was running toward them, hand stretched out in front of her, residual magic glowing around her.

Selene. Through the haze of red fury spreading in her mind, Lily recognized her as the granddaughter of Elder witch Juneau Laroche.

"Stop!" Lily yelled at her, but her cry drowned in the roar of magic as Selene threw another spell at Alek.

He convulsed, bellowed in pain, and fell to his knees.

The red haze in Lily's brain whipped into a storm.

Magic pulsed in the air, flowing from Selene to Alek. She held him tightly in her grip, knocking up the power some more with a twist of her hand and muttered word. Alek screamed and collapsed completely.

She was going to kill him.

All rationality, reason, and sense was erased in a violent surge of primal instincts, and Lily was no more. In her stead emerged a female predator with a single focus, all her fury concentrated on one target—the witch torturing Alek, her male. With a snarl, Lily lunged at her. She intercepted the witch as she was running to the pergola, her tackle slamming Selene to the grass. The witch let out an ooomph, gasping for air from the impact.

Lily straddled her, her vision drenched in blood and wrath, and punched the female straight in the face. And again. And again. How dare she attack her male?

The witch cried out and flailed against the onslaught of blows, obviously too overwhelmed by the barrage to even form a spell. The urge to maim and kill to protect her own driving her every move, Lily struck and hit and punched.

Hunger roared to life again inside her. She had a human pinned to the ground. A human with a glowing life force.

She grabbed the witch's arms, held them in a death grip above her head, and then leaned in. A dark, dark need deep within barreled its way to the forefront.

Take.

Her lips almost touched the female's. She exhaled, preparing to drill into the witch's soul to extract her *prana*.

Someone grabbed her around the waist from behind and yanked her off the human. Strong hands handled her with take-no-bullshit efficiency and slung her over an impressive male shoulder. She struggled, growling her anger at being denied her meal, and caught a glimpse of the witch sniffling on the ground, propping herself up in obvious pain while the demon who carried Lily ran away, and she lost sight of her prey.

CHAPTER 8

A lek flung open the passenger side door to his truck and placed Lily on the seat with as much care as the urgency of the situation allowed.

"Buckle up," he barked and slammed the door.

He jumped in on the driver's side, started the truck, and tore out of the parking lot. Heart racing a million miles a minute, he forced himself to slow down enough to avoid cop attention. He focused on his breathing—in, out, in, out—centering himself in the sensations of the air leaving his nose, his chest heaving.

His pulse decelerated. His thoughts cleared.

That was a close call.

He shot a glance at Lily. "You okay?"

She had her fingers buried in her hair on both sides of her face, her palms pressing against her temples. "I attacked a witch."

"Yes." He didn't know what else to say. He couldn't even start to process the fact she'd done so to help him.

"I almost killed her." She was staring out the window, her eyes troubled, her face ashen.

"But you didn't."

"Not for lack of trying. If you hadn't pulled me off her…"

He moved before he could second-guess himself, reaching out to clasp one of her hands. Gently he squeezed, anchoring her. The scattered, oscillating colors in her aura calmed, smoothed out. She exhaled—and squeezed his hand back.

"You were overwhelmed," he said, warmth spreading in his chest, "acting on instinct. This is all still new to you. You shouldn't blame yourself."

"Doesn't matter." Her voice was but a rasp. "They will."

"Who?"

"The other witches."

He frowned. "She attacked you. You defended yourself. In my book, it's justified to fight back."

She shook her head, still holding onto his hand, firming her grip. "You don't understand. I attacked a witch." She faced him then, shadows in her eyes. "It's anathema. The highest form of treason among our kind. And it wasn't even in self-defense. I defended *you*. A demon." Her lower lip trembled. "I just committed the worst crime possible in my community. Well, second worst. You kept me from doing the worst."

He struggled for words. Hell, he'd never been good at talking. Dima, his twin brother, was the one to look to for verbal reassurance. He'd never had to console a female before, and certainly not one as desolate as the witch-turned-demon sitting next to him. And yet he wanted nothing more than to ease her pain, lift her sorrow, and make her believe everything would work out fine.

He cleared his throat. "Your situation is unusual, Lilichka. Far as I know, there's never been a witch before who was transformed into a demon. If you'd still been a witch, you wouldn't have reacted that way. Your entire system is in uproar. Your mind is too rattled yet to leash your instincts. I'm sure the other witches will acknowledge that and make concessions."

She turned away, staring out the window with an air so forlorn he wanted to pull her close and hold her until she felt better. Withdrawing her hand from his, she muttered something that sounded like, "Not bloody likely."

Silence wove between them, filling the truck's cabin with sad tension.

Taking a deep breath, he said, "You still need to feed." He hated that he had to bring it up, now of all times, but the parts of her *tvaglakshana* peeking out from the neckline of her T-shirt had faded to a light henna again.

She jerked, her hands clenching. "Right." A cascade of darkness rippled through her energy.

He parked the truck on the street a few blocks from his target. They got out of the car, the mild night wrapping around them, and he led Lily toward the theater's entrance. He gestured for her to wait with him pretending to peruse the announcements of upcoming plays.

A few minutes later, the doors opened and the audience streamed out onto the sidewalk. He scanned the crowd, the multitude of auras coloring the air in a rainbow of energy. A couple of college-age girls chatting excitedly about the production. A mixed group of men and women, laughing and talking about where to go for drinks. And then there was a smudge within the quilt of colorful auras.

He homed in on the man exuding that energy. Nudging

Lily, he nodded furtively toward the older guy. "There," he murmured, his voice pitched low so only Lily would hear him with her enhanced demon senses. "See that man with the graying hair and red scarf?"

She nodded. "What about him?"

"Focus on his aura. What's it like?"

Her forehead scrunched up in lines of concentration. "It's darker. And it feels...wrong. It's like an oil spill, almost as if it's polluting the air around him. But he's not sick."

"No. At least his body isn't. We'll follow him."

After the man waved goodbye to his friends, he sauntered down the street. Alek and Lily trailed after him, taking care to appear casual, a couple out for a stroll around the neighborhood.

When the old man approached his car, which was parked in an open lot, Alek sped up to catch up to him. He tapped the guy on the shoulder.

The human turned, his expression friendly but wary. "May I help you?"

"Yes," Alek said. "Yes, you may indeed. Let's drive somewhere, shall we?"

He slipped into the man's mind like a breeze through a crack in a window. Easy, so easy. No mental shields at all. Plenty of darkness, though, and he fought bile rising up in his throat at the images he found in the guy's memories. He wrenched control over his higher faculties from him and proceeded to supply the human's mind with instructions for what to do.

"Get in the car," Alek told Lily while mentally ordering the man to open the driver's side door and sit down.

Lily took the front passenger seat, and Alek slid onto the back seat. Under his mental control, the human steered through the nightly traffic, toward a place where Alek could teach Lily without the risk of being interrupted.

"His energy makes my skin crawl," Lily whispered.

"Yeah," Alek said darkly. "Mine, too." He took a deep breath, trying to shake the nausea boiling in his stomach at the details of the man's sick proclivities. Rage a hot simmer underneath his skin, he leaned forward, catching Lily's eyes. "Go into his mind. It's time you learn how."

She glanced at the human, who drove obediently in silence, thanks to the grasp Alek still had on his mind. "I know a little about reading thoughts. Witches can do it, too, you know." There was a slight edge to her voice.

"Not as well as we do. Slip into his mind. Follow the darker threads, the ones that feel like lines of tar. Look for the source."

Her pupils dilated, power sparking off her as she used her demon gifts to dive into the man's mind.

"Do you see his memories? That cluster of thoughts, images, feelings, the one that tastes like three-day-old trash smells?"

She gasped, and shook her head once, hard. Fire and night bled into her eyes, her aura a violent red, exploding outward in a crushing wave. "No. Oh gods, no. Those kids... all those children. I— You fucking bastard." With a roar, she lunged at the human.

The car swerved precariously. Tires screeched. Alek jumped forward, grabbed Lily's hands and pulled her away from the man. Blood dripped from her claws. Her eyes were an inferno of swirling red and black. Snarling, she writhed in Alek's grip, panting, straining to get to the human, who— under Alek's command—had gotten the car under control again.

Lily hissed, baring her teeth. "You godsdamned son of a bitch!"

"Lily, enough!"

"Let me rip out his fucking throat!"

"Stop it." Alek grabbed her chin and forced her to look at him. "Calm down. You get to kill him, okay? Just not now. We're on the road, and he's driving. Do you want us to end up smashed into a tree? Or flagged down by a cop car? Calm. Down."

Her breath came in heavy pants, her eyes still a vivid display of demon rage.

"Breathe, *tsvetochek.*" He caressed her cheek, stroked over the pulse point on her wrist with the fingers of his other hand.

Her gaze roved over his face, locked onto his eyes, and slowly the red and black receded, the natural indigo returning bit by bit. "He's a fucking monster," she whispered, her voice broken.

"Yes." He continued to stroke her, petting her down from her wrath. "That's why I picked him for you."

"How did you know he was going to be there at the theater?"

"I didn't. I just figured chances would be good we'd find someone with a despicable skeleton in their closet. If not him, then someone else. If not there, then at some other joint in the city. You'd be surprised how many there are like him walking around undetected, unchecked."

She blinked, sucking in air through her nose, her lips pressed tightly together. "I always knew the dark figure of these...cases...is a lot higher than the reported one." When she glanced at the human piece of trash again, her eyes reignited with demon red, but this time she restrained herself.

Still, Alek kept one hand on her shoulder, gently massaging her, grounding her with touch. He steered the man's mind to drive the car into the deserted parking lot next to a trailhead, and ordered the guy to sit with idle hands in his lap, staring unseeing out through the windshield.

On the outside, the man was the epitome of calm, a perfect picture of a Zen monk immersed in meditation. Inside, though, his mind was in upheaval underneath the cold control of Alek's grip, his emotions churning, fear eating at him with the knowledge of being in the presence of two predators, both of whom clearly wanted to end his life. Alek didn't do a damn thing to calm the guy's emotions or alleviate his fears. Bastard deserved every fucking second of terror before he drew his last breath.

"Now," he said to Lily, leaning forward again, "our mind-control abilities are stronger than a witch's. Means that, in addition to reading minds, we can insert commands and basically use humans or weak-minded otherworld creatures like puppets whose strings we pull. Think of something for him to do, and then try to push that thought into his brain, like an imperative."

She didn't hesitate for one second. Her eyes blazed with fire, and the next instant, the human punched himself in the face. He grunted with pain. Blood spurted from his nose.

"All right, let's not take this too far." Alek laid a hand on her shoulder, squeezed. "Just FYI, when you make your prey hurt themselves, keep it to non-fatal injuries, and—ideally— ones that will prove to be self-inflicted. One reason I like to use mind control when taking *prana* is to subdue the prey, but another is that the fewer wounds the body has, the less likely the police will rule it a homicide. Too many violent deaths in the city, and the human authorities get nervous. Make it look like a heart attack, suicide, or accident, and you're good."

Her aura pulsed with rage. "I want to hurt him some more."

He regarded her for a moment, studied the darkness in her energy, the bloodlust pouring off her. "How about you take his *prana* instead, hm?"

☼

ALEK'S GENTLE WORDS BARELY PIERCED THE RED MIST CLOUDING Lily's mind. Her body hummed with need, with hunger. The desire to hurt, maim, *kill* crackled over her nerve endings, sparked a low-level buzz of electricity in her system.

She ordered the human to punch himself again. The crunch of his nose giving way under the blow was grimly satisfying.

"Lilichka." Alek put a finger under her chin, turned her to face him.

Reluctantly, she tore her attention away from the glowing temptation of the human's life force and met Alek's silver-gold eyes.

"Stop." He spoke the word softly, and yet it held a punch of authority.

"Why?" Defiance made her clench her jaw tight.

He rubbed his thumb over her chin, brushed her lower lip. "Because, as much as you want to hurt him right now, you might see things differently later. Hunger and the frenzy of feeding have a way of distorting our perceptions. Once you're sated and more in control of yourself again, you'll hate yourself for giving in to that kind of darkness."

"You don't know that. You don't know me."

"Maybe not as well as your friends and family, but I do know a few things. And one of them is that you're kind at heart. You may put on a tough and irreverent front sometimes, acting like you don't take much seriously. But deep down, you *care*. Maybe too much about a lot of things, and that's why you play it off with jokes."

She trembled. Not her hands, though, but rather inside. It was a whole-soul shiver that started deep and spread to the surface. How could he read her so well? The way he casually described her emotional makeup was unnerving.

"If you hurt him," Alek said, his voice a low, rough caress, "it'll hurt you. And I don't want to see you in pain. That's why I'm asking you to stop." His eyes, the gold luminous in the night, held her spellbound.

He was asking her. Not ordering, not demanding. *Asking.*

Something clicked into place inside.

She nodded. "How do I take his *prana*?"

A smile ghosted over his lips, gone again in a second. "You've already been in his mind. Now you'll need to go deeper. I know, I know, it'll be disgusting." He held up a hand to stave off her protest. "But you need to tap into the most primal, subconscious part of him, into his soul. That's where you'll find the center of his *prana*. You'll feel it. Once you got it, grab it and pull it out. Be sure to let go of his mind before you take the last of his life force. If you hold on too long, he'll drag you down with him."

Puffing up her cheeks, she exhaled. "Okay. I can do this."

He squeezed her shoulder. "I'm here."

She sent him a quick look of appreciation and then

focused on the human. Diving into his mind, she resisted the images that barreled toward her. Revulsion crawled over her skin. If she never had to see those memories again, it would be too soon. Suppressing the shiver that threatened at the sick darkness of the human's mind, she burrowed deeper. Layers upon layers of thoughts, emotions, urges, motives, memories. The entirety of a human life, compressed into a what seemed such a small space, and was yet vaster than expected.

Finally, she locked onto the dead center of it all. It held the core—or in his particular case, the nadir, the lowest, basest part—of his soul, his life force. His *prana* glowed here, blindingly bright, even though it was still tainted and smudged in a way that Baz's energy, for example, wasn't.

She mentally grabbed the shining ball of power—and pulled. Back she went through the memories and the sludge and the nauseating sickness of the human's mind, until she resurfaced, reconnected with the here and now, and inhaled the glowing life force she drew from his mouth.

Remembering how Alek had fed, she'd positioned herself so close to the man's face that less than an inch separated their lips. She took care not to breathe through her nose, having no inclination whatsoever to inhale the guy's scent.

Her one hand was braced on the backrest of the driver's seat, and with her other hand she grasped the steering wheel, balancing herself. When the human's *prana* fused with her own, every single cell in her body sighed in relief. The ache in her limbs—which had been a constant low-level annoyance—vanished. Her heart pumped faster, blood rushed through her veins, newly invigorated. Power zapped through her, an energetic current that nourished her. The feeling of becoming hollow from the inside out lessened, dissolved in the joy of being once more complete, healthy, strong.

Somewhere in the back of her bliss-soaked brain, swirled the thought that she'd just killed. Not a demon, but a *human*. Not in defense, or to protect, but to sate her hunger, to slake a need she'd never had before. One she shouldn't even have. One that was *wrong*. The thought latched onto to her, clawed its way to the forefront of her mind, pierced and tainted the joy of the new power coursing through her veins.

Her chest rose and fell with her fast breaths, and she jerked back, her hand groping for the handle of the car door. She caught it, threw the door open and stumbled out.

"Lily." Alek's voice followed her retreat, and then he was jumping out of the car, too.

Heart thumping against her rib cage, she speed-walked away, toward the trail entrance. Alek's footsteps sounded behind her on the asphalt of the parking lot, then muffled on the rain-soaked dirt of the hiking path.

Her breath caught in her throat. *Don't think, don't think, don't think.* She sped up, ran down the trail, deeper into the welcoming darkness of the forest.

"Lily, stop." Alek's voice behind her.

No. She had to keep running. If she stopped, she'd start thinking about what she'd just done. Not only that—she'd *feel* it.

Nope, nope, nope. She could do this, run until—

A hand grabbed her elbow, made her stumble, and spun her around. She gasped and landed in Alek's arms. Her fingers dug into his T-shirt. He steadied her, his hands on her waist.

"Tell me what's going on."

CHAPTER 9

"**H**azel." Merle slammed the door of her car shut and hurried up the driveway to the stately turn-of-the-century villa.

The other Elder witch paused and turned, the tense lines on her face softening as she beheld Merle. "Oh, good. You could make it."

"Do you know what this is about?" They continued up to the front door.

Hazel shook her head, her energy tinged with gray. As it had been since Lily's inexplicable outburst, her unthinkable attack on Basil, and her subsequent disappearance. Merle and Hazel both had spent the past night and following day searching for Lily, in vain. Hazel's locator spell had failed... and there was only one possible explanation for that, one that neither Merle nor Hazel wanted to even consider, much less accept.

Lily had to be alive. She *had* to be.

They rang the doorbell, and after a few seconds, Estelle, Juneau Laroche's eldest daughter, opened the door.

The middle-aged witch blinked, her smile coming a second too late to be genuine. "Hi! Please, come in."

Merle exchanged a glance with Hazel, and they both followed Estelle into the foyer.

"The meeting's in here," Estelle said as she led them to a room in the back. "I'll leave you to it."

"Thank you." Hazel nodded at the younger witch, then opened the door.

The conversation inside fell silent when Merle and Hazel stepped into the wood-paneled room. Seated in a circle on ornate antique chairs, the other Elders, heads of the witch families of the region, looked up at their entrance.

"Hazel, Merle, what a nice surprise." Juneau, unofficial leader of the group by the strength of her powers, gave them a smile that didn't reach her deep green eyes. "I apologize for starting the meeting without you. I couldn't reach you, and wasn't sure if you were coming."

"Oh," Merle chirped, "not a problem. Technology is such a fickle thing, isn't it? Sometimes neither text messages nor phone calls go through, and you only find out about an unscheduled meeting of the Elders by chance."

A shadow prowled through Juneau's aura, there and gone so quickly, Merle could have thought it might have been a trick of the light. If not for that prickling in the nape of her neck, that sinking feeling in her stomach...

"Please take a seat," Juneau said, while a rumble went through the rest of the group, some of the Elders frowning.

Merle glanced at the circle, which had been set for the exact number of witches present before she and Hazel arrived, which meant they had to drag up two chairs from the adjoining room.

As soon as they sat, Juneau cleared her throat.

"As I was saying just before Merle and Hazel joined us," the head of the Laroche family said, the light of the chandelier glinting off her silver-white hair, "I propose we deal with the latest threat to our community swiftly and without false mercy. We cannot allow ourselves to grow mellow and weak. Our kind has not survived this long by trivializing danger."

Merle leaned forward, suspicion a chilly whisper in her bones. "What threat?"

Juneau's eyes met hers. "My granddaughter Selene was attacked tonight." The Elder witch shifted her focus to Hazel. "By Lily Murray."

A collective gasp echoed in the room, the notion of one witch assaulting another so unthinkable, so abhorrent, it was difficult to grasp. Even though a similar violation of the sacred witches' code had been committed only a few months ago, and Merle's heart still bore the scars of it.

Hazel sucked in air, her power quivering and crackling in the air. "What are you talking about?"

"So you don't know." Juneau tilted her head. "It seems your daughter has truly gone rogue, then."

"What," Hazel ground out, "are you talking about, Juneau?"

"Less than an hour ago, Selene happened upon a life leech demon while she was on patrol. He was feeding, and she went to take him down. She was intercepted by Lily, who attacked her and would have killed her if Selene hadn't managed to get away at the last minute by the grace of the Powers That Be."

Hazel's chest rose and fell with her fast breaths. She opened her mouth to speak, but another Elder witch beat her to it.

"This is insane." Elaine, head of the Donovan family

looked at Juneau, then at Hazel. "Why would Lily attack a fellow witch? She's never been anything but an upstanding member of our community."

"Has she?" Juneau raised her brows. "I remember she quite recently undermined our laws by helping Merle avoid justice after she unbound that demon without our consent."

"That demon," Merle snarled, her power brimming around her, "is my husband by law, and he's the reason my sister is still alive. So take care how you speak of him."

Juneau's chilling look slammed into hers, but Merle didn't flinch, didn't blink, just held the other Elder's stare with a backbone of steel and the fire of her line. The air crackled.

"It seems," Juneau said softly after a moment, breaking eye contact first, "that the reason Lily attacked my grand-daughter is that she's not, in fact, a witch anymore."

Silence pulsed in the room.

Merle swallowed, the suspicion that had whispered through her marrow growing into a crescendo of trepidation.

"What do you mean?" Elaine's brow furrowed.

"When Lily assaulted Selene," Juneau went on, her eyes on Hazel, who had become so silent, Merle wondered if she was still breathing, "her eyes flared red and black, and her energy bore the unmistakable traits of demon power."

A murmur rolled through the ranks of the Elders.

"Lily," Juneau said, raising her voice, "has turned into a life leech demon."

The room exploded into shouts and gasps, witches shooting to their feet, arguing over each other. Merle closed her eyes for a moment, the sinking feeling in her gut now turning to a ball of lead, her shoulders slumping forward. And with every bit of the foreboding truth sense that was worked into her powers, she knew Juneau to be right.

"Silence!"

Magic snapped taut like a rope, its vibration rocking Merle down to her core. Every witch in the room heeded that powerful command, all eyes flicking to Juneau, who had risen from her seat.

"No matter the nature of Lily Murray," Juneau said, her voice thunderous, "a violent attack like this cannot go unpunished. I hereby make a motion to indict Lily Murray with treason for assault of a fellow witch. She is to be brought to justice, with whatever force necessary, as the law demands."

Both Merle and Hazel jumped up so fast their chairs almost toppled over.

"No!" Hazel shouted.

"Wait," Merle yelled.

More voices joined them, until the room was once more brimming with the heated discussion of all of the Elders. A cutting hand gesture from Juneau silenced the commotion again.

"Please," Hazel said into the tense quiet, stepping forward, "let's slow down and go about this with consideration and reason. We haven't heard Lily's side of the story yet, and I think we should delay any and all condemnations until she has a chance to explain. She deserves that much, at least."

"I agree." Merle came to stand beside Hazel, meeting each of the Elders' eyes. "And I think we should give Lily the chance to turn herself in or contact us before we hunt her down like a criminal. Besides," she added—despite the visceral knowledge that the accusation was true, but she *had* to give her best friend a fighting chance—"we only have Selene's word about the attack and Lily's supposed transformation."

"Are you implying," Juneau said with lethal quiet, "that my granddaughter is a liar?"

"I'm saying," Merle shot back through gritted teeth, "that we don't have all the information, from both parties, and therefore can't know how much of the alleged threat is real."

Juneau's eye twitched, her power sizzled.

Someone cleared her throat. Merle tore her gaze off the older witch, and focused on the Elder who had made the sound.

"I hadn't thought to mention it," Carissa, head of the Hart family said, a frown marring her forehead, "because I figured it was an internal affair of the Murrays, but..." Her light blue eyes cut to Hazel, and she grimaced apologetically.

"Go on," Juneau said, her attention like that of a cobra.

"My daughter Nina told me that Basil Murray was viciously attacked last night—by Lily."

Hazel closed her eyes, her aura drooping around her like a settling cloak of resignation. Merle sucked in a pained breath. Nina was Basil's new girlfriend, their relationship only a few weeks old, but apparently he'd confided in her about what had happened last night. And instead of honoring Basil's trust, Nina had told her mom.

Who had now told the Elders, pouring fuel on Juneau's fire.

"Is this true?" Catarina, head of the Gutierrez family, spoke up, facing Hazel.

"Yes," Hazel ground out. "But—"

"So," Juneau cut in, "twice now Lily Murray has

viciously attacked members of our community. She is a walking threat, to us and to anyone else, and we need to neutralize her quickly to avoid further casualties."

"Neutralize?" Merle hissed. "She's not a dog to be put down!"

"No? If she truly has turned into a demon, then she is little better than that."

The Elders murmured, some with the distinct sound of disagreement.

Juneau's eyes narrowed, and she tilted her head as she regarded her fellow Elders. "Must I remind you of the many witches murdered, tortured, butchered by demons? Of the blood spilled by these creatures, over centuries, and how they revel in the death they deal? Our laws have been formed for a reason, and they *must* be upheld. Our survival depends upon it." Her voice was sharp like a whip's crack in the air. "Lily Murray has violated these laws, and twofold. As a witch, she has broken our most sacred code, and as a demon she has spilled witch blood, which must be avenged."

Her face a mask of hardness, Juneau stood up straight. "I call for a vote on the motion that Lily Murray be convicted of treason, declared an outlaw, and be brought in to face justice, as required by the laws we live by. All those in favor, raise your hand."

One by one, half of the Elders followed Juneau's call, lifting their hands.

"All those opposed?"

A third of the Elders raised their hands, including Merle, Hazel, and Elaine, with the few remaining ones abstaining. Merle's heart sank, her breath hitched. No.

With a twinkle in her eye, Juneau faced her and Hazel. "I

hereby condemn Lily Murray as an outlaw, to be hunted and brought in with any force necessary, so she can be punished in accordance with witch law. Anyone who harbors her or withholds information regarding where to find her will be complicit in her crimes...and shall face the consequences."

Hazel raised her chin, her nostrils flaring, her eyes shimmering. "Understood."

Merle took Hazel's hand, tugged at her to leave while not looking away from Juneau. "Since we want to honor your decree," she said with venomous sweetness, "we'll get right on searching for the outlaw."

And under the simmering heat of Juneau's stare, they backed out of the room.

CHAPTER 10

"Tell me what's going on."

Alek's voice slid over Lily's heightened senses, soothing and thrilling at the same time. Her breath still fast from her sprint, from the panic and adrenaline pumping through her, she swayed as he pulled her to a stop.

"Talk to me, *tsvetochek*."

"I—I killed him." Her throat felt so raw, it hurt to speak.

He laid both hands on her shoulders. "So you can live. It's not like you—"

She shook her head hard. "I don't want to talk about it."

Avoiding his eyes, she studied the strong column of his neck, the cords of muscles and sinew that were so quintessentially male. So lickable. Without thinking—*can't start thinking, that's dangerous*—she slid one hand up and stroked over the spot where his neck met his shoulder. His demon aura flared, and his muscles went rigid at her touch. She tunneled her fingers into his hair, relishing the silken feel of it.

She needed this. Right now. Right here. To lose herself in

him. To find a counterpoint to the death she just dealt, a light to the darkness within. She caressed his neck, reveled in the heat and male strength underneath her fingers.

He closed his eyes and uttered a strangled sound. "Lilichka." He tightened his grip on her waist. "Stop this, or…"

Her focus was glued to his mouth. "Or?"

He pulled her closer and leaned in, nipping at her earlobe. "There's only so much gentleman in me. Keep this up, and all bets are off."

His deep voice sent a pleasant shiver down her spine, curled her toes. She turned her face toward his. Power sparked in the space between them. His breath—hot, branding—brushed against her lips, but he held back, his muscles taught, his aura vibrating with tension.

"Alek," she whispered against the temptation of his mouth. Closing the inch between them, she licked over his lower lip.

His eyes went demon, an explosion of fire on midnight sky. With a groan that was half growl, he responded. And, oh, he began by unleashing a streak of dominance that had her melting inside.

One of his hands shot into her hair, tangled in the strands, and pulled hard enough to hurt deliciously good while his mouth crashed down on hers. His tongue demanded entrance, and she melted with eagerness to grant it. He licked at her, a hint of teeth grazing her tongue. The sensations—his grip on her hair, the heat of his kiss, his body pressing against hers—sparked a chain reaction of pleasure inside her, all the way down to the aching, needy spot between her thighs.

Yes.

She wanted to drown in him. Acting on an impulse, she

moved one hand down his front, cupped him over his jeans. He groaned and pushed into her touch, deepening the kiss. The urge to stroke that delicious hardness without the barrier of clothing made her tremble. She was fumbling with his belt buckle when he *tsked* and whirled her around so her back was to his front.

"Not fair," she muttered.

All further protest from her ended in a moan as he slid his hand under her shirt, under the sports bra, and up to her breast to tweak her erect nipple. His lips feathered over the curve of her neck, and she tilted her head and rested it against his shoulder to give him better access. He lightly bit the sensitive skin, then licked over it, setting her aflame.

Desire pulsed through her, and she rubbed against him, the feel of his erection against her lower back ratcheting up her need. He kneaded her breast with just the right amount of roughness and demand to make what was left of her thoughts dissolve in a storm of sensation.

"Please." The hoarse word fell from her lips, carrying all the sexual urgency that wrecked her. "I need—"

"This?" He flicked open her jeans and then his hand glided into her panties, his fingers finding and parting her swollen flesh.

"Oh gods, yes..." Her eyelids fluttered shut, and she surrendered to the rush of sweetest pleasure at his intimate caress.

He pushed two fingers inside her, and she gasped at the erotic intrusion. So welcome, so wickedly good. Pumping once, twice, he coated his fingers in her wetness and then used that to circle and tease her clit. Soon her breath came in ragged pants and she reached behind her to hold on to him, because no way could she have remained standing on her own, seeing as he'd turned her legs to rubber with his skillful touch.

"I love how wet you are for me," he murmured in her ear. "How responsive."

As if to demonstrate his point, he pushed his fingers into her again, curled them up to stroke over an area that made her moan and shiver.

He kissed her neck, grazed his teeth over her hypersensitive skin there. "I want to see you shatter. I want to feel you clench around my fingers." He pressed the heel of his hand against her clit, rubbed it hard while thrusting three fingers inside her. "Let go, Lilichka."

She sucked in air, sexual tension and need curling tighter and tighter—and then her climax razed her like a firestorm. All air left her on a moan, while wave after wave of purest bliss coursed through her.

Trembling inside and out with the best kind of comedown, she slackened. He slung one arm around her waist, caught her before she slid to the ground.

"I've got you." The timbre of his voice was the sort of husky that inspired feminine sighs and sinful fantasies.

Her pulse slowed to a normal level. The sensual haze in her brain lifted, and she found herself on a hiking path in a deserted forest at night, held up by a male demon who was as wickedly appealing as he was trouble.

She cleared her throat and disentangled herself from his embrace. Turning away from him, she busied herself with fastening her jeans and adjusting her bra and top.

"Lily." His voice was pitched low, almost gentle.

"Hm?" That top was really stubborn. Just didn't want to be righted.

"Look at me."

She paused in her fidgeting, sighed, and—skin tight with nerves—faced him. There was a harshness about his expression, tension whispering through his aura. Flecks of red flared in his silver-gold eyes.

"Don't run," he said.

She blinked. "I'm not running." Waving at herself, she added, "Still as a statue."

"You know what I mean."

He came closer, gaze fixed on hers with the kind of attention the tiger paid the deer.

"You don't need to retreat from this." He gestured between them. "From us."

Taking one more step, he closed the remaining distance separating them. His heat brushed her skin. His scent curled around her, a most insidious caress.

"Whatever is going on right now in here—" he tapped a finger against her temple, then used that same finger to circle her ear, causing traitorous shivers down to her toes "—stop it. Don't overthink this. Let's take things as they come and see where we end up."

She bit her lip. "I shouldn't have let you—we shouldn't have—" Turning away from him, she rubbed both hands over her face, guilt a sour taste in her mouth. "This was a mistake, and I'm sorry I got your hopes up. I didn't mean to lead you on."

"Hey." He took her hand, tugged until she faced him again. "Back up a second, there. You're not leading me on. I know what I'm getting into. You don't want to mate with me—fine. That doesn't mean we can't enjoy each other for however long this'll last. I'm attracted to you. You're attracted to me. Let's just go with that and have fun."

She shot him a dubious glance from underneath her

lashes. "So you changed your mind? You don't want me to mate with you anymore?"

"Didn't say that." The sly smile he sent her stirred a low hum in her nether regions. "I'm simply opportunist enough to take what I can get."

"I don't think it's a good idea to start a casual thing when you want more than that."

"Are you worried about breaking my fragile heart, Lilichka?" His tone was soft, so soft, but his expression held thunder, his question a dangerous warning.

"I don't want to hurt you."

He prowled closer to her, backing her up against a tree. "I'll take my chances."

"This is unfair to you." A whisper in the dark, her eyes once more riveted to his mouth. Her lips tingled with the sensual memory of what that mouth felt like while it ravished hers.

"Why don't you let me be the judge of that?"

Their breaths mingled in the night air. Desire rekindled in her lower belly. He placed a hand on each side of her head, caging her in. Fire-streaked obsidian invaded the silver-gold of his eyes. She parted her lips—

Alek gasped and stumbled back, clutching his throat. Witch magic sparked in the night. *Again?* What the hell? Lily spun toward their attacker—and jerked to a halt.

Merle MacKenna, her best friend since kindergarten, the one person she trusted most beside her twin, emerged from the shadows, hand stretched out in front of her, keeping Alek in a magical chokehold.

THE MAGIC BURNED ALEK'S SKIN, AND HE CLAWED AT HIS throat, trying in vain to dislodge the invisible vise choking him. He stared at Lily's stricken face as she recognized who had attacked him. The MacKenna witch, older sister to Maeve, whom he'd seen many times over the past few months while watching Arawn's future asset.

"Merle," Lily ground out, her voice shaking, "stop. Please."

The witch's eyes darted from Lily to Alek and back again. "Are you okay? Did he hurt you? What did he do to you?"

Lily exhaled, her aura wavering with relief. "I'm fine. Let him go, please. He's with me."

Merle cast a skeptical look at Alek, not releasing the magical hold she had on him. He uttered a strangled sound at the invisible fire still licking over his skin.

"Merle," a deep voice said from the dark behind the witch, and the next second a male *bluotezzer* demon walked into view. Rhun leaned close to his mate and muttered in her ear—though still loud enough that both Alek and Lily could hear— "Going by their scent, they're on very *friendly* terms, if you catch my drift." He accentuated the word *friendly* with air quotes and a wink.

"Oh." Merle lowered her hand a little. She glanced back and forth between Alek and Lily again, and then her eyes widened. "*Oh.*" The light skin of her face flushed a blazing red. With a flick of her hand a muttered word, she released Alek from her spell.

Sucking in huge lungfuls of air, Alek massaged his neck. The magical burn receded.

Rhun smirked, glancing back and forth between Alek and Lily. "Hope we didn't interrupt anything?"

Lily sported an adorable blush of her own as she cleared her throat. "This is Alek. He's helping me...deal with...with being..." She broke off, her voice cracking.

"Oh, honey." Merle was at her side in a second, enfolding Lily in a hug. They remained locked for a long moment, exchanging whispered words between what sounded suspiciously like sobs.

Alek shifted uncomfortably and caught Rhun fidgeting as well. Their eyes met over the huddling females. Alek gave a slow nod. Rhun repeated the gesture. One demon acknowledging another.

"So," Alek said. "How did you find us?"

"I tracked you."

Ah, yes. Bluotezzer demons had the uncanny ability to trace the energy of other demons. But— "From where?"

"The place where Lily attacked the witch."

Shit. If news of it had already spread...

Merle and Lily broke apart, and Lily exhaled on a shudder. "The others know?"

Merle wouldn't meet her best friend's eyes. "Maybe we should sit down for this. Isn't there a picnic area up ahead?"

"What is it?" Lily's aura vibrated with trepidation.

"Well," Rhun said conversationally, "usually it's a designated area with tables and benches where hikers can sit down and eat."

Merle shot him a glare that would have shriveled many a fine male, and walked farther down the trail. Rhun followed, and Lily glanced at Alek, nodding for him to come along. At the picnic area, Merle sat on the bench while Lily perched on the table, her feet on the seat below. Rhun stood behind Merle and crossed his arms, and Alek decided to take up a position close to Lily, leaning against the table with his hip.

His arm brushed against Lily's shoulder, and she pressed ever-so-lightly against him. That reaction, however small and probably unconscious, infused his blood with delight.

"How is Selene?" Lily asked.

"Her nose was broken, but Juneau healed her. No permanent damage."

Lily closed her eyes and took a deep breath. What looked like shame and self-recrimination blanketed her aura like a shroud. "Okay," she muttered, "on a scale of one to John McClane, how fucked am I?"

Merle blew out a breath. "You're outlawed."

All color left Lily's face. "The fuck?"

What Merle told them next raised Alek's hackles, partly in a visceral reaction to Lily's shock and devastation that no amount of energy control could hide, and which chafed at his heart, but mostly in outrage on Lily's behalf at how she was being treated by her own.

"How is this possible?" he asked, his voice raw from the anger biting at him. "Aren't these your own people we're talking about? How come the witch community is ready to pile on Lily like this? Aren't you supposed to stick together?"

Merle shook her head, sky-blue eyes filled with shadows. "Juneau has been fuming ever since I sneaked Rhun in under her nose. It never did sit right with her that I didn't bind him in the Shadows again, and she's been looking for a way to pay me back for finding that legal loophole to keep him around as my husband."

"It's not just that, though," Lily spoke up, and cleared her throat, trying so obviously to keep herself together. "Merle fighting for—and winning—Rhun's freedom kicked off a shift in thinking for some of the witch families in the community. My mom told me about the change in attitude among some of the Elders. There's now the notion that, maybe, just maybe, we should differentiate more between types of demons and not assume they're all evil." She looked at him with a self-conscious glint in her eyes, probably aware of how she'd held quite a few misconceptions about demons herself when she met him.

Understanding dawned on Alek. "And Juneau doesn't agree with that notion."

"That's a mild way of putting it." Merle grimaced. "She's grown more and more radical in her stance. She keeps rallying support for her views, and never fails to remind every witch she talks to that accepting even one demon among them is a slippery slope, and sure to be the beginning of the end."

Alek met Merle's eyes. "So this is a political issue."

Merle nodded. "It's not really about Lily. Juneau wants to make a point. And she has no problem with collateral damage." She looked at her best friend. "There are others who oppose Juneau and her charges against you, but not enough to sway the vote or start an open conflict with Juneau."

Lily clenched her jaw and nodded. "You haven't asked me yet if I really did attack Selene." She glanced at Merle for a second, then away again.

"Because it's secondary," Merle said softly. "Whatever happened, I've got your back. Like you had mine when Maeve was kidnapped and I went against the Elders."

Lily stared down at her knees. "It's true. I jumped on her. She was going to kill Alek."

Both Merle and Rhun looked at him then, an assessing curiosity in their eyes.

"So," Rhun said, tilting his head at Alek, "we know your name, and that the two of you are chummy, but I seem to have missed the tale of how you met."

Lily filled them in, explaining what they knew so far about how Lily had been turned—which wasn't much—and the ways Alek had helped her, making him sound like a fucking hero. Which let him inwardly preen like a foolish peacock, while he kept up the facade of unfazed, cool male, nodding slowly here and there. Lily smoothly left out the details of becoming intimate, not that Merle and Rhun hadn't already read between the lines and filled in those blanks.

But at the mention of Alek's association with Arawn, an almost visible wave of animosity rolled out from both Merle and her demon husband. Merle sat up straighter, eying him with wariness, while Rhun shifted closer to his mate.

Alek held up his hands, palms out. "Chill. I don't mean harm to either of you, and right now I don't represent anyone but myself."

"But that can change," Merle said, her tone cooler than before. "Your allegiance is to Arawn. Forgive me if I am a bit bristly about the fact you're working for the guy who plans to enslave my baby sister."

"Not to mention," Rhun added with a softness at odds with the threatening darkness in his eyes, "that this same guy is currently using up Merle's power for trivial shit, all the while laughing at her, as if she's his own personal jester."

Alek clenched his jaw, fighting down the surge of annoyance at being associated with Arawn's jerktastic behavior. "Fair enough. Just so you know, I have no love to spare for Arawn either, and I'll be more than happy to leave his service in a month's time."

That bit of information seemed to calm some of the anger flowing his way from Merle and Rhun. Still giving him a little side-eye, Merle dug in her purse and handed something to Lily.

"Your cell phone," she said. "I thought you might want to have this."

"Thanks." Lily cradled the device in her hands, her face shadowing. "So you've seen Baz? How...is he?"

"Worried about you." She grasped one of Lily's hands. "Your mom, too. They've been going crazy, not knowing what's going on with you. After you ran away last night, Hazel cast a locator spell to find you, but it failed..."

Lily gasped. When Alek frowned at her reaction, she explained softly, "Usually, the only time a spell like that doesn't work is if the person you're looking for is dead." She closed her eyes for a moment, her face carved with anguish. "My family thought I had died."

"Not just your family." Merle's voice was low, humming with the sorrow she must have felt. "Until the Elder meeting and Juneau's account of your attack on Selene, none of us knew you were still alive. And then the only thing we knew was that you'd gone rogue and had been snatched away by some demon." At the last word, she glanced at Alek. "That's why I attacked you earlier. I thought you'd kidnapped Lily."

And in light of her experience with demons abducting her loved ones, her reaction was more than understandable. "No hard feelings," he told her.

Merle nodded once, then faced Lily again. "I know you feel guilty for what you did to Baz, but I really think you should talk to him. And your mom."

"Well," Lily said, "considering I've got a huge fucking

target painted to my back, I don't think it's a good idea to go anywhere close to home right now."

"Yeah, I wouldn't put it past Juneau to have staked out your house. Mine, too, probably." Merle shifted on the bench. "Which brings up the question where you're staying until we sort this out. I talked to Rhun, and he can ask Bahram if maybe—"

"She can stay with me." Alek stepped closer to the table, every primal instinct in him roaring at the thought of Lily staying with another male—an incubus, to boot.

Merle narrowed her eyes and opened her mouth to speak, but he added, "I can hide her. I'm a demon, the witches don't know me, I've got no connection to you that they know of, and there's little chance she'll be found at my place." He caught Lily's gaze. "My offer still stands. I'll help you, no strings attached."

She seemed to consider this, her indigo eyes thoughtful. "I'll need to find the demon who shot me with that dart, so we can get to the bottom of this and reverse whatever he did to me."

The sting in his chest was instinctual, the idea of her turning back into a witch cutting him deep. He pushed that hurt down as best he could, and masked the pain he knew would show in his energy pattern. He needed more time to win her heart, to make her fall for him to the point where she'd want to stay demon...for him.

"Even more reason to stick with me," he told her, his voice projecting a calm he didn't feel. "The jerk who shot you is a *pranagraha*. Who better than one of his own to help you hunt him down? I know the places our kind likes to hang out, I've got resources you guys don't have access to. Stay with me, and I'll help you look for him." Not that he *actually* wanted to find the guy, but if it meant he got more time with Lily, he'd do it.

She slowly nodded. "No strings attached, right?"

"Right." He ignored the yearning in his heart. Couldn't let her know how much he wanted those strings.

"All right." Lily jumped off the table. "Merle, can you look in your books for any precedent for this happening? What are the chances of reversing whatever it is?"

The ginger-haired witch regarded her for a moment, a crease building between her brows. "If this is magic-born, I've never seen anything like it. From what I can feel, there's nothing left of you that is witch. You seem to have completely turned into a demon."

Rhun nodded. "Your energy pattern is uniquely demon. I could trace you."

"And you've got all the qualities and attributes of a *pranagraha*," Alek added. "You feel like one to me."

A tremor went through Lily's aura, but she nonchalantly waved her hand. "All right, I think we've established I'm eligible to enter demon pageants and all." She looked at Merle. "Can you fix this?"

You don't need to be fixed. Alek bit back that response. Lily would skewer him for it, however true it was for him. If she'd been beautiful before, she was glorious as a demon female. An undercurrent of lethal prowess hummed in her aura, her creamy skin practically glowed in the moonlight, and the dark blue of her eyes seemed to have ripened and deepened after her transition, to resemble a particular shade he'd never seen in human eyes.

He wanted her more now than ever before, and he'd love for her to see herself the way he did.

"Well, if it is magic," Merle broke in Alek's thoughts,

"then—in theory—there should be a counter-spell. There's always a way to reverse a charm, the trick is finding out how. If it's some kind of established magic, we should be able to find it in the books, and possibly a cure, too. I can't make any promises, Lil, but I'll search everywhere…and you know me. No stone unturned and all."

"Thanks."

"Is there anything more you remember about the attack or the attacker? Any detail could help."

Lily thought for a second, then startled. "Oh! Of course, why didn't I remember that? The dart. It got lost when I fought the demon off, and I didn't have the time to retrieve it, but maybe it's still at the place where he attacked me. You could analyze the potion inside if you find it, right?"

"Yes." Merle perked up. "Yes, we could. That's great. Where exactly is that spot?"

Lily explained it to Merle, who promised to comb the area.

"If we find it, I'll get right to analyzing it and let you know."

Lily hugged her. "Thank you."

"No need," Merle whispered back. "We'll make this right, Lil. We'll keep trying until we get you back."

Her only reply was an even stronger hug from Lily, before they moved apart.

Rhun snapped his fingers. "I almost forgot." He walked over to Lily, pulled a small bag from his jacket pocket and handed it to her. "Welcome to the Dark Side. Here are the cookies."

Merle gasped and smacked his shoulder. "Rhun!"

He turned to his mate, shrugging and holding his palms

up in a touching display of wounded innocence. "What? The least we can do is give her the damn cookies."

"Where'd you even get these?" Merle's eyes widened. "Wait—*that's* what you had to get when you stopped at the gas station?"

Rhun just smirked.

"I swear I can't take you anywhere," Merle muttered then turned to Lily. "One more thing before we leave."

Lily raised her brows.

"Call Basil. And your mom." Her voice gentled. "They're desperate to hear from you. And I know all three of you need to talk this over."

From the look on Lily's face and the flavor of her aura, one could have thought Merle had ordered her to organize her own execution.

CHAPTER 11

Lily watched Merle and Rhun drive away in Merle's car. They'd given Alek and Lily a ride to Alek's truck, which was still parked close to the theater where they picked up the human Lily fed from.

She quickly directed her thoughts away from the man, still not willing or able to deal with what she'd done. Why sink down a spiral of despair when denial was such a convenient option? Yep, denial it was.

Unfortunately, blocking out the topic of her feeding—on top of the already tabooed subject of her attack on her twin brother—meant her mind greedily latched on to the next big issue in her life right now, the sizzling attraction she felt to one fine demon male, currently getting into the driver's seat next to her. She'd readily block that subject, too, but there were only so many things she could successfully suppress at once.

Alek slammed the door and started the engine, and his enticing scent filled the confines of the truck's cabin within seconds. Crisp autumn nights, burning wood, and an essence of *male* that made her want to purr. Oh, she was in trouble.

Because his intimate touch felt way too good, and the fire he'd sparked in her with just a few adept moves of his fingers was too addicting to be anything but dangerous. If he could make her shiver and melt like that without even taking her clothes off, she didn't want to imagine what he was capable of between the sheets, skin-on-skin, sweat-slick and hot, bodies tangled in passion...

"Lily," he ground out.

She startled. "What?"

"You can't do this."

"Do what?"

"Get aroused while I'm driving." His fingers clenched hard around the steering wheel. "Your scent is making me crazy. If you don't simmer down, I'll pull over, drag you into the backseat, and lap up every last bit of you."

Her eyes widened. Heat flooded her lower belly, his words evoking not only more memories of how he'd pleasured her before, but a number of new fantasies.

"Hell, Lilichka." Alek cursed and rolled down his window.

She couldn't help it. She laughed. He looked so tortured, so adorably struggling to remain in control of himself.

He shot her look as dark as it was sizzling. "I'll get you back for this." Focusing on the traffic again, he sobered. "I know you want to get right on searching for the *pranagraha* who shot you, and I'd love to help you out tonight, but I need to go to work. I already switched shifts with another sentinel last night so I could take care of you, but I can't find anyone who will swap shifts tonight."

Right, he did have a job. Watching her home. Just

thinking about that brought a sting to her heart. *Push it down.*

"So," he said on a deep exhale, "I'd suggest you could come with me, but that would mean you have to hold my hand the entire time in order for the invisibility charm to work on you as well. Not sure you'd like to be shackled to me like that the whole night. Plus, I don't think it's a good idea to bring you anywhere close to your house right now, what with Juneau's witches probably patrolling the whole area."

Lily decided not to further explore the numerous ideas her unruly mind came up with at the mention of being shackled to him. She cleared her throat. "Yeah, we should avoid that."

"You can stay at my place until I get back." He held up a hand to stop her as she took a breath, ready to speak. "I know you'd like to look for the demon, but I'd rather not have you roaming the streets alone."

Her hackles rose at his domineering words.

"Stop growling." He sent her a quick look. "Think about it. You'll be more successful searching for him with me there to show you around the demon underbelly of the city. The risk that you'll be spotted by other witches is high when you're on your own. I can take you on paths unknown by witches. And," he added, glancing at her again, "you're still adjusting to being demon. Not that I think you'll be the Hulk on the loose, but…"

She narrowed her eyes at him. "Say it. You think I can't control myself."

They stopped at a red light, and he faced her fully, his eyes without mercy. "Can you?"

Grinding her teeth, she breathed through her nose, anger

a rising pulse in her blood. The light turned green, and he broke eye contact to drive on.

She looked out the other window, clenched her hands to fists and quietly said, "I don't know."

It took a lot for her to admit that, and the truth tasted bitter on her tongue.

"I know this isn't easy for you," Alek murmured. "And I'm not pointing it out to be mean or to rub it in. I just need to be sure you won't get hurt."

She was itching to give him some form of *I can take care of myself* spiel, but the fact was, he did have a point. And damn if it didn't grate on her to acknowledge that. "All right," she said. "I'll stay at your place while you're gone."

His shoulders lost some of their tension, and he shifted into a more relaxed position behind the wheel. "We'll go looking for the *pranagraha* first thing tomorrow."

Back at his house, he came inside with her and pointed to the kitchen. "You can eat anything you find. If you want to lie down, the spare bedroom you slept in last night is all yours."

Grant came trotting over, having noticed his master was home. He wagged his tail with all the vigor of a geriatric dog, which in effect was little more than a tired wave.

"Hey, buddy." Alek bent down to scratch the mutt's ears. Looking up at Lily, he said, "I'll walk Grant around the block real quick before I head out. If you do decide to sleep later, best keep your door closed, or he'll end up in your bed. He doesn't do well with boundaries."

"Got it."

Alek grabbed a leash from a hook next to the door, snapped it on Grant's collar and went outside, the dog trudging after him.

Ten minutes later—Lily had helped herself to a bowl of Alek's cereal and was munching that sitting at the kitchen table—Alek and Grant returned. The dog trotted over to her and lay down on top of her feet, resting his head on his front paws.

"If he bothers you, I can order him to lie down on his blanket." Alek pointed to a cozy lounging area in the corner of the living room.

"No need. I don't mind him." She leaned down to pet Grant's head. "As long as he doesn't get too excited," she added, eying the furry old guy.

"I hope he won't pee on you." Alek grimaced and muttered, "And I've always wanted to say *that* to a female."

Lily grinned and winked at him. Returning her smile, Alek turned to the door.

"Oh," he said and faced her again. "Almost forgot. Let's exchange numbers." He grabbed a pen and notepad from the counter, scribbled on it and handed her the note. "Call me if you need me. I'll be there as soon as I can."

"Okay."

He got out his cell, and she rattled off her number while he typed it in before he left.

And then she was alone. Well, not quite. There *was* a snoring dog on her feet.

❧

TEN MISSED CALLS AND FIFTEEN TEXT MESSAGES.

When Alek mentioned her cell phone, it reminded Lily that she hadn't checked it since Merle gave it to her. Since it was running low on battery, she plugged it in using a cable she'd spotted in Alek's living room tech area. Most of the calls and messages were from Baz, her mom, and Merle, along with some other witch friends like Lenora and Keira. The calls from her family and her best friend had stopped shortly after she attacked Baz, so she assumed they had found her phone by then. The other witches called right after the Elders meeting, when her phone had still been on mute.

And she had no inclination whatsoever to call back any of them. Having Merle in the know and on her side was enough right now, and she'd explain everything to the others once this unfortunate episode was over.

She turned the ringer on her cell up loud enough that she wouldn't miss it if Merle or Alek called her, and then proceeded to snoop around the house. Nothing unethical like peeking into drawers, but whatever was openly on display was fair game.

Turned out Alek was a Star Wars fan, and either he had some brownies living here with a creative streak, or Alek actually enjoyed folding origami of Star Wars characters and props. One whole board in the living room shelf was lined with little Yodas, the Millennium Falcon, a bantha, R2D2, and many more items and figures from the movies.

Her cell phone rang, and she jumped about two feet. Pulse racing, she looked at the caller ID. *Baz.* A flush of adrenaline tingled along her nerves. Thumb hovering over the "accept call" button, she faltered. *No, I can't do this.* Not yet. She swiped the call away so it would go to voice mail.

And her heart broke just a little at the silence that followed, shame heating her face. Throat suddenly thick and raw, she took a hitching breath, chucked the phone on the couch, and turned away.

With her heartbeat still thundering in her ears, she continued her exploration of the living room. She paused in front of a couple of framed photos of grinning kids. Two boys, about ten and five, and a little girl who couldn't be more than a year old. Alek had mentioned he had a brother with kids, so these had to be his niece and nephews. She could definitely see some of Alek in the boys, which made sense if their dad was Alek's identical twin.

A strange feeling twisted her chest. Almost like…longing. Which was ridiculous. She'd never been keen on having children. She accepted the fact she'd one day have to have at least one little critter, seeing as she'd become head of the Murray family and responsible for carrying on the line. But that could be done without a husband. Single mothers were much more common these days, and for that, she was truly grateful. No way was she going to get stuck in a marriage.

Or a mating.

An image of her mom rose from a dark corner of her mind. Her nowadays radiant face shadowed, her brown eyes tinged with sadness that latched onto Lily, sank into her bones while she watched her mom cringe at the venom in her dad's words. Words that should have made any self-respecting witch bristle and fight, and yet…Hazel said nothing, did nothing, just…endured.

A ding from her phone jerked Lily back into the present. And there went her heart again, stumbling in her chest. Dammit. She grabbed her cell and checked it. The message was from Merle. Phew.

So, what's the deal with that demon you're hanging with?

She typed back, *Did you find the dart??*

She only had to wait a few seconds for Merle's reply.

Oh, yeah, that. Found it. Working my mojo on it. So, while that is bubbling, tell me all about that pranagraha *who couldn't take his eyes off you. He looked positively smitten.*

Lily couldn't help grinning, and not only because of Merle's understated way of revealing they were one step closer to solving whatever happened to Lily.

Alek, she texted. *His name's Alek.* She sobered, the grin slipping off her face. *And he's not just smitten, he wants the real deal. As in, mating for life.* A prospect that kicked her whole system into flight mode.

Merle's response was a single, most eloquent, *Thewhawhaaaa?*

My reaction exactly, Lily typed back. *I told him no, but...*

She was pondering how best to describe the quagmire she was in with Alek when her cell rang again. Barely escaping another heart attack, she clutched her chest and calmed her breathing. It was Baz. She should really talk to him. But— Stomach sinking, she mentally hopped on her nope-octopus and noped away from that scenario. She let the call go to voice mail, again. And her heart broke, again. *I'm sorry, Baz.*

Her phone dinged with a message from Merle.

DID HE HURT YOU?? I SWEAR TO THE GODS I WILL SEND HIS ASS INTO THE SHADOWS.

Even though it was ridiculous, and she knew it, Lily actually held the phone away from her to mute the screaming-via-text. She'd apparently taken too long to finish her text and Merle had gotten the wrong impression.

Whoa, hakuna your tatas, girl, Lily replied. *He didn't. He's an okay guy. You know, for a demon.*

Then what's the but for?

Lily sighed. *I told him I don't wanna mate, but he's still interested in "having fun."*

And you're not?

Yes, I am. I mean, have you seen him?

As a prim and properly mated/married female, I feel obliged to withhold any comment on that.

Lily snickered. *Right. Anyway, I'd love to jump his bones, and he said he's okay with no-strings sex, but knowing he does want those strings makes me feel like I'm leading him on if I have sex with him.*

Have you talked to him about that?

Yes. He still wants to boink.

Lil. We had a discussion about using that word.

It's totally legit. Merriam-Webster has it.

Moving on. So, are you his mom?

What? Ew. No. Why the fuck would you ask that?

Because you're not responsible for his happiness, and it's not your job to protect his feelings. He's a big boy. He can watch out for himself. If you want to have fun with him and he wants to have fun with you, and he's okay with your boundaries, then go for it.

Huh. If you put it that way…

Just want to make sure my BFF gets some.

Saucy wench.

Merle sent her a grinning emoticon. *All right, gotta go examine that dart some more. You take care, okay?*

Always.

No sooner than she'd sent off the text did her phone ding again. She checked it, expecting another message from Merle, and stopped short. She didn't recognize the number.

Has Grant peed on you yet? the text read.

Realizing it was Alek, she grinned and typed back, *Shouldn't you be watching my house?*

I am. I've successfully trained myself to multitask, you know.

She chuckled. *Impressive. So, I'm guessing nothing much is going on right now?*

Nope. Your mom is in the library, and Maeve is upstairs in her room. All quiet except...

???

Well, your brother is pacing the kitchen staring and cursing at his phone.

Her stomach dropped through the floor. She hesitated a moment then texted, *He's been calling me.*

Ah. Not ready to talk to him yet?

The sigh that escaped her chest felt like the weight of the world. *I can't. What am I supposed to tell him?*

How about sorry?

Like that's so easy.

It is. You're the one who's making it complicated.

She stared at her phone, fizzing with annoyance. Before she could send off any of the sharp retorts tingling at her fingertips, Alek texted another message.

Merle mentioned he's worried about you. She didn't say anything about him being mad or holding a grudge.

Alek was typing some more, so Lily stopped her own texting and waited.

He's been trying to talk to you, and going by what I've seen and heard so far, it's not to yell at you. Lily, you're stalling not because he's hasn't forgiven you. It's because you haven't.

That gave her pause. Could Alek be right?

You need to talk to him. Not just for his sake, but for your own, too. It'll help you make peace with yourself.

She sat there on the couch, staring unseeing across the room. Damn, that demon had her pegged. Maybe she did need to forgive herself. Still easier said than done, but she could at least try.

Her phone dinged with another message from Alek. *You still with me?*

She shook herself and typed back. *How come you're so good at this shit? Do you have a psych degree?*

Nope, just some experience with messing up and owning it.

She bit her lip. *Thank you.*

You're welcome. Now please call that poor guy. His pacing is stressing me out.

Grinning, she texted, *You're such a delicate flower.*

Watch it, tsvetochek.

So that was how that word was spelled.

Taking a deep breath, she opened her list of recent calls, and tapped Baz's name before she could think twice. It dialed and rang once. Then he picked up.

"Lil?" His voice sounded strained.

A lump lodged in her throat, closing off her air supply and all ability to speak. She swallowed, trying to get something—anything—past that lump. Her heart raced so fast that little spots of light danced in her vision.

"If you start making Darth Vader sounds," Baz said, his voice shaking despite his nonchalant tone, "I'll still know it's you. Beauty of having caller ID."

A laugh bubbled up, slipped past the lump in her throat and broke through the grip of fear around her heart. She sucked in a huge lungful of air and leaned back against the couch. Her hand trembled while she held the phone to her ear.

"If I were to prank-call you," she said, eyes filling with tears, "I'd scratch two knives together right next to the phone." Baz hated the sound of metal on metal so much, he had a physical reaction every time he heard it.

"Now that's more like it." He paused, his voice quieting. "You scared me there, Lil."

Annnnd the lump was back. "I'm sorry, Baz." She rushed the words out before she lost the ability to speak again.

He made an impatient sound. "I don't mean you attacking me."

"But—"

"If you're hung up on that, you need to let that crap go. I don't hold it against you, so don't even."

She swallowed hard, the knot in her chest easing a bit.

"I was scared for *you*."

How was Baz always better at admitting his feelings than she was? Shouldn't it be the other way around, him being a guy and all? But truth was, Basil had been more open with emotional stuff since they were kids.

She took a deep breath, released it with closed eyes. "I'm scared, too." There, she'd said it.

"Are you okay now? Like, how does it feel to be…"

"A demon?" She grimaced. "I miss my magic. It's always been there, but now it's just—gone. And…there's this darkness." Looking down, she fumbled with a thread of fabric on the couch. "Like, every violent impulse I've ever had, magnified and more powerful. In the literal sense, there's *power* behind it. I've only just scratched the surface of what I can do, and I know I could tap even more of it." She tugged at the thread then let it go. "But I'm afraid to."

"Merle said there's a life leech helping you?"

"*Pranagraha*," she corrected, and went on to tell him about Alek, finishing with, "He's kind of the reason you're still alive. If he hadn't thrown that stone at our back porch…"

"So I should hold off on the brotherly intimidation I have planned?"

The pressure on her chest eased at Baz's casual way of

distracting her. "I'm not sure he'd be intimidated, but I appreciate the thought." She pursed her lips. "How are things with Nina?"

She could swear she heard a growl. Her brother *never* growled. "If I could break up with her twice, I would." After a pause, he added, "I'm sorry the Elders found out."

"Not your fault she blabbed to her mom."

"I shouldn't have told her."

"You really need to let that crap go," she said with a grin, giving back his own excellent advice.

Baz laughed, and she hadn't known how much she'd needed to hear that sound until now. "Keep in touch, sis."

"I will." And she meant it.

CHAPTER 12

The sky was already brightening with the advent of dawn when Alek came back. And if she hadn't already known she was in trouble with him, the way her every female instinct sat up at attention at the sight of him, the prickling of delight running through her veins when he smiled at her sure did the job. Something restless inside her settled as soon as his energy brushed hers.

He walked Grant around the block in record time to avoid the first light of day, then whipped up a delicious omelet, and sat down at the table with Lily.

"Have you slept at all?" he asked while she cleaned her plate.

"Nope. Was too wired." Although now the lurking exhaustion caught up with her, and she stifled a yawn.

He nodded, his silver-gold eyes trained on her. "I think it's best if we catch some sleep during the day and then start the search for the *pranagraha* as soon as the sun sets. I couldn't get out of working tomorrow night, but that's not until midnight. We'll have a couple of hours to look for him, and I'll be off watch duty the following two nights. That should give us plenty of time to find the fucker."

She was too tired to argue about going out to track down the demon sooner, so she just shrugged. "All right."

He put the dishes away. "Before we call it a night, there's something I'd like to try. Remember how I told you your *tvaglakshana* chronicles major life events? It might hold a clue about how you were turned into a demon, maybe even tell us exactly what happened. I could check it for you."

She pursed her lips. "You just want to ogle my goodies, don't you? You wily *prana*-gecko."

He choked on a laugh. "Well," he replied, molten heat in his eyes, "I'd never pass up a chance to check you out naked, but—whether you believe it or not—that's not why I asked. I really do think your *tvaglakshana* may hold some clues. And, since the marking grows from your heart outward, with the newer signs on the fringes, it's likely that the symbols about your turning will be on your arms, stomach, or lower back." The wicked grin he shot her caused a happy tingle in her belly. "Very likely not on your breasts." His gaze lingered on said area and his voice dropped to a level that would be dangerous to the self-control of females everywhere. "Beautiful and tempting though they may be."

She cleared her throat, trying not to show her disappointment that he wouldn't have to look at her girls. "Um, these signs. When you read them, they tell you things about me. Important things. Like a psychological profile, right?"

His eyes shot up to meet hers, embers of red glimmering in the silver-gold. "Yeah."

"So getting naked is a big deal for *prana*-gizmos. You'll

know all that stuff about each other." A flicker of anxiety whispered through her. "If you know how to read the signs, that is."

And she couldn't. Even if they got to the point where she saw him without his clothes on, she wouldn't be able to tell what his signs meant. He could read her symbols, her life chronicled before him, the code to who she was, but she wouldn't be able to claim the same insight into his character and life.

He studied her with too-perceptive eyes, the gold ring seeming to glow around the silver. "Tell you what, we'll do a trade. I show you mine, and you'll show me yours." And before she could reply, he reached up, grabbed the collar of his shirt, and yanked it over his head and off.

The synapses in her brain short-circuited. Her thoughts ground to a halt.

All...those...muscles. Good *gawds*. Her eyes couldn't decide which delicious part of him to drink in first, there was just so much yumminess going on in front of her. His demon tattoo sprawled over ridges and bunches of muscles, from his well-defined pecs—strong enough for her fingers to get a good grip while digging in—over his broad shoulders, with trapezius muscles worthy of fawning over, to his bulging deltoids and biceps. And his abs... Scratch six-pack. He boasted an impossible eight-pack. And damn, did she want to lick, trace those demon markings adorning his skin, all the way down to the waistband of his jeans...lower.

Bursts of heat sparked all over her skin, flamed out and to the center, settling with a throbbing need between her thighs. Her fingers tingled, claws slicing out, wanting to mark him.

He stilled and inhaled deeply, closing his eyes when he breathed out again. A tremor went through his aura, and when he opened his eyes, hints of red and black were just vanishing, leaving the normal, controlled silver-gold. Still, a note of lust remained, mirrored in his aura, and it almost did her in.

"This symbol here," he said, his voice on the good side of rough, his finger tapping a sign on those magnificent abs of his, "depicts the first time I killed to take *prana*."

Something in his voice made her look up. "How old were you?"

"Seventeen."

"Damn." A pained whisper.

"I hated it. I threw up right after, losing all the energy I'd just taken, but that wasn't the worst part. My father was there. He'd taken me to make my first kill, and he laughed at me when I lost it."

The sharp bite of hurt spiking through her chest mingled with white-hot anger. She bit off a curse, wanted to say something else, but Alek was already moving on to the next sign.

"This is the sign for my twin, Dimitri. Or Dima, as we call him." He tapped a symbol close to his heart. "And these here are for my other brothers, Kolya and Yuri." He indicated two other signs, distributed across his chest.

"You've got *three* brothers?"

"Yeah. Nikolai—Kolya for short—is the middle kid, and Yuri is the youngest. He moved out a couple of months ago." Before she could ask more questions, he pointed at another symbol. "This states that family is the most important thing in my life."

The fingers of his left hand found an elaborate sign on his

right arm, circled it with care. "The symbol for my parents' death."

She held her breath, released it on a sound of sympathy. "I'm sorry."

He nodded, still looking at the sign. "These symbols tell how they died when I was eighteen."

Shock vibrated through her. *So young.* "How..." She shook her head. "Sorry. I shouldn't pry."

"Arawn killed them." He kept looking at the symbols, a muscle flexing in his jaw. "Well, he killed my father, and since *pranagraha* mates are tied to each other in life and death, my mom died as well."

She stepped back and gasped, rendered speechless by the implication of what he was saying.

"If you're wondering how I ended up in his service after that," he said quietly, his aura a violent storm, "this part of my *tvaglakshana* tells you." He tapped the elegant, flowing lines, their beauty in such stark contrast to what they stood for. "Arawn came to me after my parents died and offered to provide for me and my brothers. Apparently, he hadn't intended to kill my mom as well. Said he was unaware that her life was bound to my father's. Hell knows whether he felt the need to make amends or whatever, but he offered to pay for our livelihood until we came of age." His nostrils flared as he clenched his jaw and breathed out through his nose. "I threw his fucking charity offer back in his face and spit on it."

Lily swallowed, her heart aching for him... To have lost his parents so young and then to have their murderer insult him with an offer like that. "What happened then?" Based on what she knew of the Demon Lord, he wouldn't have reacted kindly to anyone spitting anywhere close to him.

"Arawn gets what Arawn wants," he said, the bitterness in his voice cutting her like a knife. "He threatened me until I agreed to enter his service for the duration of ten years. Incidentally, he timed it to end when Yuri would come of age, and my salary was the exact amount he'd offered to pay for our living expenses."

What must it have been like to be forced to work for his parents' killer? No wonder he hated Arawn. "You'll soon be free of him, right?"

He simply nodded, a grim smile twisting his mouth.

The urge to reach out to him was so strong it made her hands shake. So she just gave in, laid her hand on the symbol that stood for a kind of heartache she couldn't imagine. A shudder went through him at her touch, the streaks of hurt in his aura quieting, dissolving like mist clearing from a field in the morning.

He laid his hand on hers, squeezed, and then moved it down his arm, onto another sign. "This one stands for the birth of my oldest nephew, Luka. He's almost ten now. He kills me with his charm, you know."

The warmth in his eyes almost killed *her*.

"And this sign..." He led her hand up to his shoulder. "This is when I bested Dima in kickboxing. He was always better, had won the local tournament several years in a row. But not that night. It gave me the confidence to know I could accomplish anything if I put my mind to it." A small grin tugged on his lips, lips she wanted to explore so much it hurt. "To this day, Dima claims I put something in his food to make him lose that time."

"Did you?"

"No." He tapped the symbol, his eyes dancing. "The sign proves it. Not that he'll admit it."

She bit her lip, fighting a smile. "Of course not."

He went on to point out signs and explain their meaning, twisting to show the ones on his sides, his shoulders, his back. He kept guiding her to the symbols, and—for the life of her—she couldn't withdraw her hand. Not because he held onto it. She was sure he would have let her go if she tugged it away.

But she simply couldn't. It was as if he were a magnet and she the metal that was drawn to him, as if her next breath depended on her being able to feel the satiny heat of his skin beneath her palm. She followed his lead, reveling in the sensation of his muscles bunching at her touch, relishing the way his aura trembled when she moved her hand.

When he finally turned to face her again, after what felt like an eternity and only a minute all wrapped into one, she could have written a comprehensive essay on his life with the information he'd given her. But it felt so much more personal. It seemed as if he'd let her share the experiences through her touch, a connection forged by tactile sensation and more, as if she'd soaked up a part of him.

Her hand came to rest on his chest when he turned back to her, over his heartbeat. A steady, reassuring drum against her palm, reverberating all the way through her body, into those places already grown hot and hungry. For more touch. More heat. More *him*.

"Well," he said, his voice a rumble she felt through her hand, "I showed you mine."

Mine. The word echoed through her pleasure-hazed brain as she surveyed the rippling expanse of male gorgeousness she'd just explored. *Mine*.

She blinked, shook her head to clear it. *Careful*.

Wrestling her thoughts halfway in order, she slowly stepped back, grasped the hem of her tank top…

…and pulled it off over her head.

༺ºༀº༻

ALEK SUCKED IN A BREATH. HIS BODY TIGHTENED, HIS VISION sharpened, going demon at the sight in front of him. Lily in nothing but jeans and bra, the fabric thin enough to showcase her hardened nipples.

Which of course made *him* harden.

Slow. He needed to go slow with her if he wanted to do this right. She hadn't quite agreed to his proposition to have a casual fling, so he needed to tread carefully.

Clearing his throat, he indicated the signs visible on her shoulders, arms, and beneath her collarbone, down to the sweet upper curve of her breast, a curve he ached to follow with his lips. "I'll check those symbols first."

As if in a daze, she nodded. "Check. Symbols. Right."

His fingers itched to trace those signs, the elegant, delicate swirls, the curved lines and dots. He shoved his hands into his pockets instead, resisting all that temptation. He let his eyes rove over the smooth cream of her skin, studied the symbols on the exposed areas, looking for a clue. In vain.

"There's nothing on here about your transformation." Damn, his voice had dropped gravelly low. "I'll check your stomach."

A tremor ran through her, body and aura alike. The black of her pupils widened, the red around it blazing up. "Okay."

When he sank to his knees in front of her, she uttered a barely audible gasp, the muscles in her abdomen flexing as if expecting—*craving*—his touch. He'd gotten down on a level with her stomach just to see the signs better, he told himself. Not to bring his face that much closer to the one part of her body he wanted to lick above all others. Nope. Not at all.

The faint outline of abs underneath her skin tempted him to run his fingers over the muscles, make them flex under his caress. She was athletic, beautifully so, the strength she'd gained through rigorous martial arts training drawing him to her all the more. Some males didn't like their females kick-ass capable, wanted them soft and sweet and vulnerable. Alek had bedded some women like that, and every damn second of being with them, he'd been afraid he'd break something. He much preferred a female who could hold her own, with the strength to keep up with him and take all he had to give, from rough play to passionate power.

And damn, now his cock was rock-hard, and at such an uncomfortable angle in his jeans that he shifted, trying to relieve the strain. The fact that the musky scent of her arousal wrapped around him, so much stronger, more enticing from where he crouched only inches from its source, didn't exactly help his predicament.

"So?" Lily's husky voice startled him.

"Huh?"

"The sign? Is it there?"

"Oh." He harrumphed, shot a glance up at her. "Right. The sign."

She pressed her lips together, obviously trying to stifle a grin, but the glint of amusement in her eyes was unmistakable. Humor, though, wasn't the only emotion gleaming there. The fiery red in her demon gaze flared up, glowing embers of lust.

Damn, he could bask in that stare forever, would upend the world to keep her looking at him like that. With an effort, he dragged his focus away from her stunning eyes, and examined the markings on her abdomen. Nothing about her turning into a demon here, either. Shaking his head, he stood, catching her eye again. "Your back. Sometimes the newest signs emerge down the line of the spine and spread from there." She hesitated only a second, then nodded and turned.

A quick glance and—*there*. To the left of her spine, a symbol combination that spoke of change, one so massive it would disrupt fabric, biology, instincts, mind, body, heart, and soul. He swallowed hard. This had to be it. He leaned in closer, studied the intricacies of the combination, the way the signs flowed into each other, creating new meaning.

Without thinking, he reached out to graze his fingers over the signs. Lily gasped and looked at him over her shoulder.

"You found it?"

He nodded, his focus not on her words or the sign, but on the silken heat of her skin.

"What does it say?"

He ran his fingertips along the lines of the symbol combination, enjoying the way her aura spiked with pleasure at his touch. "If I'm reading this right," he said, his eyes flicking up to meet hers, "it says that what turned you was more than just demon magic."

Her brow furrowed.

"I honestly have no idea how it could have been demon magic at all," he muttered, "because neither *pranagrahas* nor any other species I know of possesses the kind of power necessary to trigger this transformation."

She nibbled on her lower lip, her mind almost visibly working in overdrive. "There's always power we don't know of," she murmured, as if stating a side note. "You said 'more than just demon magic.' Does it say what that 'more' is?"

He inhaled deeply and nodded. "Yeah. But it doesn't make sense."

"Spill it."

"Lilichka...the signs speak of witch magic."

CHAPTER 13

Hints of daylight glowed around the heavy-duty sunblock panel over the window, casting the bedroom in a dim twilight. Not that the gloom had done Alek any good. He'd tossed and turned for what felt like hours already, his mind and body too restless to drift off.

He flopped onto his back and stared at the ceiling, silently cursing his honesty.

Why did he tell Lily about the signs he'd read on her back? He should have just kept that info to himself, for several reasons, not least of which was that the less she learned about the details of her turning, the longer it would take to eventually change her back—if that was even possible. He had his doubts, but in any case, he shouldn't share clues with her which could point her to the one thing that would destroy any future he could have with her.

Plus, him telling her that little tidbit was one hell of a mood killer. All that lust saturating the air while he read her *tvaglakshana*, all that pent-up sexual tension, the hunger in her eyes? Vanished like a burst bubble as soon as he told her about the witch magic.

He could still taste the shock in her aura, like a splash of cold water. Her eyes had widened, she'd turned, and asked him a million times if he was sure. When he said yes, she grabbed her top, muttered something about having to think, and disappeared into the spare bedroom, the door closing behind her with a click that resounded loudly in his heart.

Way to go there, Sasha. Lily was already skittish, and he'd gone and ruined what could have turned into a *very* pleasurable morning.

He scrubbed a hand over his face, stifling a groan of frustration.

The doorknob turned. He whipped his head up, eyes fixed on the door, which slowly swung open. In the shadows of the darkened room, a female shape slipped inside, closing the door behind her.

Lily.

Even though his demon senses were reduced since it was daytime, he picked up her unique scent, and it sent a hum of excitement through him. He didn't move, didn't make a sound, simply waited to see what she would do.

Her soft footsteps padded on the hardwood floor, her shadowed shape coming closer. The mattress dented as she perched on the edge.

"Are you asleep?" Her voice was but a whisper.

"Somehow nobody ever believes me when I say yes."

Her grin was a flash of white in the dark, a fleeting thing, gone again the next second. "Does your offer still stand?"

"'Course. I'll help you, no matter what."

"Not that one. The other offer."

He frowned, then it clicked. And his body responded

immediately, his cock hardening in an instant, tenting the sheet. "It does."

"Casual fun, right?"

He nodded and scooted to the side, making room for her on the bed. "Casual fun."

She crawled onto the mattress, over to him, and straddled his waist. The oversized T-shirt she wore—one she'd apparently found in the closet in the spare bedroom—rode up to her hips, revealing her sleek, muscled thighs. His hands landed on those thighs before he could think better. Dammit, but he'd been dreaming of stroking her legs ever since he first saw her in shorts.

Lily inhaled softly, and the scent of her arousal caressed him like the finest aphrodisiac, potent enough to make him lose his mind. "I can't make any promises," she whispered.

"Don't expect you to." He'd take what she was willing to give right now, and he'd work hard until she wanted to give more.

He stroked his thumbs over the insides of her thighs, smiling at her small sound of pleasure. Placing her hands on his chest, she leaned forward and kissed him. A chaste meeting of lips at first, until she licked over his lower lip and then nipped at it. He felt the pull of that move all the way down to his groin, and his dick twitched in response.

"Hmm, that feels promising," she murmured, and pushed her pelvis against his erection, the heat of her core burning him through the sheet.

He slid his hands from her thighs up, clasped her hips, and pressed her even closer, bucking up to meet her at the same time. She gasped at the increased friction. Her nails dug into his chest.

"Take off your shirt." His voice scraped somewhere on the dark side of rough.

Without missing a beat, she did as he asked, grasped the hem of her T-shirt and pulled it off. He had his mouth on her breasts before she'd thrown the shirt to the side. Crying out at his speed, she clung to his shoulders while he licked a circle around her left areola, coming closer and closer to her nipple. Once he reached the puckered nub, he took it between his teeth and pulled gently.

She threw her head back and moaned.

He used his tongue to toy with her nipple while he kneaded her other breast, rubbing his thumb over the hardened bud of that one as well. Lily rocked against him rhythmically, sliding her hips and core along his cock. Even through her panties and the sheet, he felt her arousal dampening the fabric. It drove a tremor of need through him.

He released her nipple to murmur against her flushed skin. "How wet are you, *tsvetochek*?"

Leaning closer, her midnight hair cascading around them like a black waterfall of silk, she gave him a smile that made his heart stutter and desire tighten his balls at the same time. "Why don't you check?"

He tightened his fingers around her waist, and had it been nighttime, his claws would have sliced out to nick her skin. Just a little. Just enough to mark her, to let her know she was playing with a male who'd push her.

With a move that made her squeal in surprise, he flipped her onto her back, with him snug between her legs. Her long black curls spilled onto the mattress, her eyes wide, the indigo luminous in the dimness of the room. The sheet was still wedged between their bodies. He removed the nuisance with a growl and went for her panties next. They hit the floor somewhere. He didn't care.

All he could focus on, in that instant, was the alluring perfection of the sight in front of him. Between those supple legs, which he planned to lick inch by inch, was the one spot he was aching to get his mouth on. A small triangle of dark curls topped her intimate flesh, pink and glistening with moisture. The scent of her excitement—heavy, sensual, quintessentially feminine—filled his nose, so strong, so heady, he groaned in anticipation.

"I've been wanting to taste you for so long," he said, settling in between her legs, running his hands from her knees up to the sensitive inner curve of her hips, "it may take a while until I'm done here."

Lily gasped, rolling her pelvis underneath his touch. "By all means, taste away."

That was an invitation she didn't have to issue twice. He dove in, taking care to work his way around her clit, driving up her excitement with licks and kisses and clever use of his fingers until she writhed against him. Her fingers tangled in his hair, tugged and pulled in response to his moves, a small, delicious hurt that zinged down his spine and gathered more heat to center in his groin.

And, holy hell, the taste of her. A sweetness he hadn't guessed from her scent mingled with the musky flavor he expected, and it drove him wild. He wanted—needed—to see her shatter again, to feel her inner muscles spasm around him in ecstasy.

He pushed two fingers inside her, let his tongue dance around her swollen clit. "So tight," he muttered, pumping in and out. "Can you take more?"

She moaned and tugged on his hair, pulling him closer to her. "Yes, please."

Her open enjoyment—unabashed, rapturous, confident in her own body—was a drug to his mind, heightened his own pleasure. He could play with her like this for hours, lost in the sensual tangle with a female who knew exactly what she wanted, and was comfortable asking for it.

But this wasn't just any female, and that was what made his heart soar, his soul hum with bliss. This was Lily, his Lily, whom he'd pined for all summer. He finally had her in his bed, and the reality of her blew every fantasy he'd had over the past months to smithereens.

"You're abso-fucking-lutely gorgeous," he spoke against her heated flesh—and she came with a husky moan.

He pushed a third finger inside her while her orgasm was still ebbing, closed his lips around her clit and sucked. Her hips bucked off the mattress and she climaxed again, her hands clenching in his hair so hard she might have pulled some of it out.

Not that he'd mind if she did.

He pushed her, relentlessly, working his tongue along her plump lips, teasing and coaxing, while he kept fucking her with his fingers. Every once in a while he checked her expression, made sure she was along for the ride and enjoying what he did to her. Just going by her moans and garbled encouragements alone, she was having the time of her life. At some point he had to hold her hips down with his other hand because she was wiggling and thrashing so much, even though she kept pulling him closer with her hands tangled in his hair.

He grinned against her intimate flesh.

When he finally decided he'd had his fill of his own

personal Lily feast—at least for tonight—she was all but liquid. He wiped his mouth on her inner thigh, nipping it in the process, and his tiny bite didn't even make her wince. Under heavy lids, indigo eyes aglow with languorous contentment met his gaze, and a lazy smile flirted along her lips.

"I think you broke me." Her voice was sex wrapped in velvet.

"Good thing we heal fast."

He crawled up her body, leaving kisses in his wake, though not with the intent to excite her any more. He was petting her down, his touch soothing, relaxing. From the looks of it, she really was done for the day.

Her sleepy look traveled down from his face to his chest, to his rock-hard cock pushing against his boxer briefs. She half-heartedly reached out, but he grabbed her hand, kissed it, and tucked it next to her head as he lay down beside her.

Lily looked at him and raised an eyebrow, even that small movement filled with exhaustion. "What about you?"

"Not this time." She was half asleep already.

"You're a strange male," she murmured.

He pushed a lock of her hair behind her ear, feeling a small smile start in his heart and take over his face. "Because I'd rather enjoy sex with fully conscious females?"

"Hm." She closed her eyes and settled deeper into the pillow, her voice drowsy. "But I didn't even get to play with your dick."

He chuckled. "You'll get your chance."

"I better," she whispered, and then she was out like a light.

CHAPTER 14

"I really don't know nothing about it!"

Lily watched the alp struggle against Alek's hold. He held the tiny nightmare-inducing demon pressed to the wall of the tunnel, one of many that apparently ran underneath Portland, used to travel hidden from witch eyes. To say she'd been surprised when Alek led her down into the vast system of underground passageways was an understatement. All this time, she and her family and friends had patrolled the city for demons, and they'd been right under their feet.

As a requirement for taking her along, Alek had made her vow to keep the passageways a secret from the other witches—a binding oath of power. As much as it grated on her to be unable to tell her mom or Merle about these tunnels, she understood why Alek insisted on her silence. Many of his friends or family were demon, and, given the current climate among witches, if knowledge like this leaked to Juneau and her followers, it could be used to devastating effect against all demons—whether they were evil or not.

"Let's try this again," Alek said, and brought the lemon he was holding in his other hand closer to the alp's face. "I've got a few more of these in that bag over there, and unless you want me to shove them all into your mouth, you're going to talk."

The alp's black eyes widened in panic, and it whimpered. "Please, no, not the lemons! Anything but the lemons!"

Lily couldn't help snorting a laugh. She'd known alps didn't like the citrus fruit, but she had no idea they were actually terrified. Apparently, as Alek had explained, when you shoved a lemon in their mouths, they went limp and paralyzed. And spraying a little bit of lemon juice on their skin prevented the little demon creatures from changing shape. If Alek hadn't squirted some of the lemon juice on the alp, it would have already shifted from its standard form of a dwarf-like humanoid being—an ugly-ass one, if she were honest—to a moth or a snake.

Alek wiggled the citrus fruit suggestively. "Talk."

"All right, all right," the alp sputtered. "I seen him, okay?"

"Where?"

"Over in the harbor quarter. Where the ships dock. He supposed to live there, in one of them empty containers."

Alek glanced at her, then back at the alp. He let the little demon go, but raised the lemon in warning. "Good. Now, if I find out you told me shit, I'll be back with a whole tub full of lemon juice and dunk you in it."

The alp shuddered and scurried away.

"Well," she said, fighting a grin at Alek's unique interrogation method, "let's hit the harbor."

It had taken some careful asking around among Alek's contacts—he'd been careful to be specific enough to get good answers but not enough to arouse suspicion—until they found someone who knew someone who might have more information about a certain *pranagraha* they were looking for. Even after Lily remembered more details about the guy, like he had short, dark hair and a scar over his left eye, it was like finding a needle in a haystack.

The *pranagraha* community apparently wasn't all that big, but it lacked any kind of organization, so individual *pranagrahas* didn't necessarily know every other member of their species who lived in the area. Alek didn't recognize the guy from her description, and he was careful not to ask around other *pranagrahas* too directly, in case the demon he probed for information was friends with the one they were looking for and would warn him.

So, after spending the better part of the available hours until midnight cautiously tapping non-*pranagraha* sources of information, they'd finally been pointed to the alp. According to their source, someone saw him hanging out with a *pranagraha* who fit their description. Unfortunately, even the alp didn't know the demon's name.

Using the tunnels as much as possible to avoid being spotted by witches, Alek and Lily went to the harbor quarter of Portland. They spent the next hour checking every container for signs of habitation. Other than a few rat nests, a family of raccoons, a very pissed pixie colony, and a demon couple—not *pranagraha*—busy having a fuck-fest, they found nothing, not even a scrap that hinted at the possibility the *pranagraha* had recently lived here.

With a groan of frustration, Lily leaned against the wall of the last container they'd just opened. "That was a bust."

Alek pressed his lips in a grim line. "I'll have to pay that alp a lemon visit after all."

"That tiny bastard." She straightened. "So, we're back to square one. Any other ideas where to look?"

He checked his phone. "Not right now. I'll have to be at work soon." Pocketing the cell again, he looked at her. "Tell you what, while I'm at my post, I'll text some of my contacts in Arawn's network. Someone has to know something."

She crossed her arms over her chest, frustration and anxiety tensing her muscles. "I don't like the idea of sitting around idly for the rest of the night. I need to *find* this jerkface."

Merle had called her earlier with the news that she and Lily's mom had analyzed the serum in the dart as thoroughly as possible, and their findings corroborated what Alek had read in her demon tattoo—whatever the exact spell, the magic was a mix of demon and witch. How that was possible, they didn't know, and it was one reason Lily still needed to catch the *pranagraha* who shot her. The information her mom and Merle had gleaned from the serum was enough for them to start looking for a reversal spell, but the more info they had on the exact nature of the power used, the better.

Magic was such a finicky, ambiguous force. One detail could radically alter the makeup of a spell, and thus the counter-magic necessary to reverse it. If they didn't learn what exactly had been done to create the serum, they might find a spell to turn Lily back, but it could very well have undesirable side effects.

Yeah, she was so not keen on that.

Alek stepped up to her, cupped her face with his hand, the silver in his eyes swirling. "I know you're antsy to get him, but you can't go out on your own. It's too risky."

She narrowed her eyes, raised her chin. "I could use the tunnels."

"Nope. For two reasons." He held up one finger. "You don't know the tunnel system, which means you could easily get lost." He raised a second finger. "There's actual, real demon traffic going on down there."

She couldn't help it—she snickered.

He groaned and rolled his eyes. "Oh, come on."

"What?" she asked, the snicker turning into full laughter that had her belly aching. "Demon traffic? *Down there*?" She gestured. "Have you met my mind? How can it *not* go there?"

He pressed his lips together, a muscle feathering in his cheek. He was so obviously trying to appear stern, but the sparkle in his eyes and the flicker in his aura gave him away. And it only took a couple of seconds for the amusement to take over. A gorgeous grin broke across his face, lighting up his eyes, bringing out his crinkling laugh lines—and a small dimple in one cheek.

How had she not noticed that dimple before? Good gods, that alone could have stolen her heart.

Sizzling heat replaced the laughter in his eyes, and his aura pulsed with sexual intent. The next second, he had her shoved against the container wall, his thigh between her legs, his mouth on hers. His powerful body pressed against hers, all hard planes and virile strength.

"When you look at me like that," he muttered when he broke his bruising kiss, "all I can think about is how fast I can get you naked with your legs wrapped around me."

Desire blooming in her core, she slid her hands down and under his shirt, stroked over the taut muscles of his abdomen. "I wouldn't mind some of that demon traffic about now." To emphasize her point, she hooked her fingers in the waistband of his jeans and tugged.

His aura blazed into a storm that scorched her own energy. Red and black bled into his eyes, glowing in the dark as he gave her a look that was making her sweat in the best of ways.

A loud clang startled them both. Somewhere over in the next row of containers, the trip-trip of small feet on wet concrete sounded, moving away. She caught sight of a rat-sized creature scurrying from one shadow to the next.

Alek stepped back, regret set in the lines of his face. "Not here, Lilichka. And not right now."

She puffed out a breath. "You're right. Let's go."

৩৯৫৩

THEY'RE LOOKING FOR ME.

Drake watched the hellrat he'd stirred up from its slumber scuttle past the container he'd climbed—past Lily and the *pranagraha* male she was with.

Damn him. He balled his hand into a fist, his claws slicing out and into the flesh of his palm until blood dripped down onto the container roof. That male...the son of a bitch had dared lay a hand on Lily. *His* Lily.

As far as he could tell, she wasn't mated yet, but it was only a matter of time. The way she reacted to that fucking bastard... He gritted his teeth hard enough to pop a muscle in his jaw. He had to get her back before the other male claimed her as his mate. Drake hadn't risked his hide stealing that vial of serum and shooting Lily with it, only to have her snatched away from right under his nose by another *pranagraha*.

The thought of her with another male made his blood boil. Ever since he saw her while she was out on patrol one night a couple weeks back, he hadn't been able to shake the desire for her. She made him yearn like no other female had ever done before, and he'd come to understand it was because she was meant for him. She had to be. Why else would she incite this kind of need in him, when she hadn't even been born a *pranagraha*? Well, he'd taken care of that little obstacle.

She was his, and he'd make sure to stake his claim. Once he mated with her, no one would be able to take her away from him, the mating bond tying her to him beyond the reach of anyone else, demon or witch. And he'd make Lily see that no other male could compare. One night with him, and she wouldn't even look at another *pranagraha*.

He carefully climbed back down the container once Lily and his rival were out of earshot, and followed them from a safe distance, taking care to stay downwind. If Lily were alone, he'd have jumped her already, but he couldn't fight both her and the male. He'd have to tail them and wait for his chance, maybe see where they stayed. It wasn't her family's home, that was for sure. He'd staked out that one for the past two nights, but had caught no sign of Lily returning home. Checking on her friend's house—that ginger-haired witch with the *bluotezzer* mate—had been a waste of time, too.

He'd begun to fear he'd lost her to the maze of the city, had come here to grab the last of his stuff from the boat where he'd been living for the past weeks—it was time to move again—when she showed up, just like that. His own personal miracle.

And didn't she look heavenly tonight? A vision of bliss

wrapped in sin. This was the first time he'd seen her after her transformation, and her new demon aura sent a thrill down to his balls. He couldn't wait to get her alone, to see her eyes flare with red and black when she looked at him. She might fight him at first, but that was fine. It was part of the mating dance, and, if he was honest, the idea excited him. It would make it so much sweeter when she finally submitted.

Lily and the *pranagraha* approached the hidden entrance to the underground tunnel system, and his heart rate spiked. It would be tricky to follow them in there without being noticed.

The male scanned the area, then opened the secret door to the derelict, boarded-up shed. After sniffing the air inside, he nodded at Lily and waved her in.

Anxiety vibrated down Drake's spine. He tensed, ready to run out of his hiding spot behind the fence, and around the container compound, to follow them underground. His cell phone rang, and his heart stuttered. He flattened his back to the fence and pushed the button to mute the call. *Shit.* He should have remembered to turn it off. A glance at the caller ID had his stomach roiling with trepidation.

Seth.

He knew what the other *pranagraha* wanted. Drake had ignored several calls from him already, as well as a text demanding he pay Seth a visit ASAP. Sweat beaded on his brow. He couldn't face Seth yet, not before he'd mated with Lily.

Pocketing the muted phone again, he peered around the fence. The door to the shed was closed…no sign of Lily or the male. He made his way over to the entrance and followed them inside. The trap door flickered into view under his hand, the concealment spell recognizing his demon nature and releasing its hold.

Making sure the coast was clear, he lowered himself into the tunnel. Sniffing the air, he tracked the route Lily and the male had taken, until he came to a T-junction in the tunnel. The faint trace he'd been following dissipated in the breeze of another creature's scent. Someone else had come through the tunnel here after Lily and the *pranagraha,* and the astringent smell overpowered any other note in the air.

Fuck, fuck, fuck.

He'd lost them.

CHAPTER 15

Alek made it back home just as the blue-gray of predawn gave way to the rose blush of impending morning. He quickly walked Grant around the block, eying the daylight crawling closer and closer.

Once back inside, he pulled the shutters down and locked them. He expelled a breath of relief. That had been close. Not that the daylight would have burned him to a crisp in seconds, but he'd rather not lose any more *prana*.

Speaking of which…

"Lilichka," he said, catching her attention as she put away her cereal bowl. "I'd like to show you something."

A saucy grin quirked up one corner of her mouth, and she wiggled her brows while she sauntered over. "Is it biiiiii-iiiig? Will it shock my delicate female sensibilities and make me gasp and clutch my pearls?"

She slid her arms around his waist, her hands stroking over his ass and up to the front, where she started unbuckling his belt. His pulse kicked up and a bolt of desire shot to his groin, blood rushing unerringly south. *Down, boy.*

"As much as I appreciate your straightforward willingness to get me naked," he muttered, plucking her deft hands off his belt, "this is not what I meant."

Her lips pulled into a pout, and it was the cutest damn thing he'd ever seen. "You promised I could play with your cock."

Hot damn. That mouth of hers... A new wave of lust flooded his body, her dirty talk making the part she'd mentioned stand at expectant attention.

"Later." As much as he wanted to get her in his bed again —or on any other available surface, really—and as much as he could tell she needed the outlet, evident in the humming tension in her body and the hints of frustration in her aura, showing her how to preserve her *prana* would also help balance her mind and body and calm her down like nothing else.

She sighed. "You keep dangling that carrot in front of me, but I never get to taste it."

He choked on a laugh. "You'll get the carrot, *tsvetochek.* After I show you how to extend your life force so you won't have to take *prana* quite so soon again."

That sobered her a bit. Her eyes lost the glint of humor, and she stepped back from him. "Oh? Do tell."

"In a nutshell, it's a method of controlling the flow of your breath with the aim of keeping more of your *prana* inside your body. It's called *pranayama.*"

She frowned. "That's a yoga technique."

"Yeah, that's where it originated. We adapted it to our needs."

He sat cross-legged on the rug in front of the couch and gestured for her to join him. Still looking rather skeptical, Lily lowered herself to sit across from him.

"Okay," he began, "so you already know we need to absorb someone else's life force regularly to replenish our own. Here's why—breath carries *prana*, so every time we exhale, we lose a bit of it. And this is where breathing techniques come in. By controlling the flow of the breath in and out of the body, you can control the flow of *prana* as well. With practice, you can get to the point where regular sessions of breath retention and deep, slow breathing will reduce the amount of *prana* that gets lost with an exhale."

"But only during a *pranayama* session, right?"

"Nope. That's the beauty of it. Do this regularly, and you'll lower the loss of *prana* in general. Without this, you'd have to make a kill every other night or so, depending on your activity level. With *pranayama*, you'll be able to gradually increase the time between feedings to several days, if not weeks. You're recalibrating your body, in a way." He tilted his head. "As long as you still keep up regular *pranayama* practice, that is."

She nodded. "Got it."

"Good. To start, center yourself and focus on your breathing. It helps if you close your eyes."

"I've done a little yoga and meditation before."

"Perfect. Then you know the basics. Direct your awareness to your breath, feel how it leaves your body, focus on the sensations of it. How it flows through your throat, how it tickles your nose."

He let her breathe quietly for a few minutes, giving her time to calm down and reach the optimal mindset. Her aura settled a little, some of the tension leaving her body. Her shoulders relaxed. The lines in her face eased.

"Now," he said, keeping his voice low and soothing so as

not to disturb her focus too much, "visualize your life force, see how it glows, carried on your breath."

She opened one eye to peer at him. "Are you sure you don't want to start a side business as a New Age guru? You've got the lingo down pat."

"Lily." He suppressed a grin and put on his best stern face. "Focus."

"All right, all right." She closed her eye again.

"Do you have a visual hold on your *prana*?"

"Well, it *is* a slippery little bastard. Kinda hard to pin down, really."

"*Lily.*"

"Fine. Yes, I see it."

"Good. I'm going to teach you about *bandhas*, which are—"

"Bonds, or bands, I know." There went that one eye again, candescent indigo glittering at him with just a hint of amusement. "I did learn a little Sanskrit."

"Right. In *pranayama* practice, *bandhas* are four main parts of the body used to block the air flow. That's useful for when you try to prolong the pauses in breathing, which is part of training your body to retain more *prana*."

He went on to teach her how to activate each of these blocks, showing her three different techniques for slowing down and arresting the breath. Having practiced Fire Breath with her—a series of quick breathing followed by a deliberate, long pause after an inhale before exhaling with control—he did a couple more training sessions of deep breathing with her.

The sun had long since risen, his demon senses dulled with the advent of day, and with them his ability to read auras. Still, he could tell from Lily's body language and facial expression that she was now deeply relaxed, had shaken off the acrid tension, no doubt caused by their failure to locate the other *pranagraha,* and made worse by the time she'd been forced to sit idly at home while he was on watch duty.

Good. He hoped her mind had found some peace as well. He hated seeing her so frustrated—hated that he was partly to blame. Sure, they'd had little to go on in terms of information about their target, but he'd contributed to that by deliberately sabotaging the search.

As it was, he'd led Lily around the city on an interesting, albeit fake, hunt for information, only asking contacts whom he knew wouldn't be able to offer anything of value. Deep inside, his conscience burned with shame over breaking her trust like this. She was the one person he wanted to be honest with at all times, and yet being honest with her would drive her away.

From what he'd gleaned when he checked her *tvaglak-shana*—although not as closely as he'd have liked, lacking the time to read it thoroughly—Lily was deathly afraid of getting stuck in a committed relationship, and somehow that fear was rooted in her parents' marriage. What exactly had caused that emotional hindrance, he didn't know, since the signs he found hadn't spoken of the deeper reasons. According to his intel on the Murray family, Lily's father died a couple of years ago, and Alek didn't have more information on the nature of the marriage between Hazel Murray and her late husband.

Whatever the background there, it was clear he needed to tread extra-carefully with Lily if he wanted to win her consent to mate with him. His current strategy was to spend as much time as possible with her, stealthily win her heart, and make her fall for him. That she'd agreed to have a casual physical relationship with him should make it easier. And he wasn't above using the full arsenal of his sensual skills to draw her in further, make her crave the pleasure of his touch until her heart came along for the ride, too.

How did that human saying go? *All's fair in love and war.*

He studied her serene expression, the peaceful way she sat in lotus pose with her hands resting on her knees. Her chest slowly rose and fell with her deep, calm breaths. She was a natural at meditation and *pranayama*.

"So," she said without opening her eyes, her quiet voice reminiscent of the low, soothing tone used by Zen masters, "do I get to play with your cock now?"

⚶

LILY HEARD THE DISTINCT SOUND OF ALEK SUPPRESSING A SNORT of laughter, and opened one eye to peek at him, joy bubbling in her chest. Teasing him was so much fun.

"And here I thought you were the epitome of relaxation," he said, the silver in his eyes glittering.

"Oh, I am." She unknotted her legs from their wedged position and crawled closer to him. "Doesn't mean I forgot you still owe me a carrot."

He glowered at her, the brute. "I don't think I'm comfortable with that particular vegetable comparison."

"Well, I'm sure I can come up with a better one...once I get a good look at it." She let her finger trail down the front of his shirt, over those taut muscles she still planned on giving a thorough sensual exploration, to the waistband of his jeans.

Leaning back, he placed his hands on the floor behind

him, balancing his weight on them, and stretched his legs out on either side of her. "You have my attention."

She shot him a quick smile and refocused on the growing bulge visible underneath his jeans. The simmer of desire she always felt around him expanded into a slow, delicious burn, heat centering in all the quintessentially feminine parts of her body. She unbuckled his belt, and flicked open the button of his jeans.

His erection strained against his boxer briefs, the head of his cock almost inching out past the elastic of his underwear. Oh, the plans she had for this... Inhaling the hints of his musky, masculine scent, she sighed and brushed her fingertip over the blunt top of his shaft.

It jumped in response to her touch, and she smiled, enjoying his reaction to her.

She pulled down the zipper, freeing more of his arousal, and dove in without warning. Her mouth closed around the rock-hard evidence of his need for her, her teeth gently grazing the thin fabric of his boxers that still covered his cock.

"Jesus Christ, Lily!" Alek jerked, his muscles locking.

When she glanced up at him as she pulled down the elastic of his underwear with her teeth, his face was harsh with hunger and passion, tempered with just the right amount of amazement. She loved how she could surprise him, topple his notions of what she'd be like in bed.

Using both hands, she finished pulling his boxer briefs far down enough for his erection to spring free. Thick and long, pumped with blood and crowned with a velvety-looking head, it was a thing of beauty. And it made her mouth water, not to mention dampened her panties even more.

"Lilichka..." His voice held the kind of roughness that made her shiver in delight.

"Yeah?"

"The way you look at me right now, you either go ahead and follow through, or I'll have you on your back and my cock inside you in two seconds flat."

His coarse, erotic warning triggered a throb of desire between her legs. "All righty, then."

She leaned down and licked a long line from the base of his shaft to the flared-out head, followed the brim of it around until she reached the front again, and let her tongue dance over the sensitive vein there. Alek exhaled on the brink of a moan, his eyes heavy-lidded as he watched her. Her skin grew tight and hot at his rapt attention, at the smoldering promise of sensual retribution in his gaze.

The taste of him...hmm. Musky, male, and all Alek. Addictive, so she went back for more, licking and nipping and caressing the length of him with her tongue, her teeth, her lips. His cock twitched under her ministrations, the muscles in his abdomen flexing, his fingers digging into the carpet where he steadied himself.

Arriving at the top again, she opened her mouth and swallowed him whole in one smooth move. He uttered a strangled groan, the sound so erotic it sent even more heat pooling between her thighs.

Gods, she loved seeing him react like this to her touch, knowing she made him crazy with pleasure. It was a heady feeling, turning her on in exquisitely wicked ways, and she moaned against him while she teased him with her tongue.

But it wasn't just the effect she had on him that made her own body hum with excitement—she enjoyed sucking him for her own benefit, something she'd never experienced with her previous lovers. With them, she'd done it because they'd asked her, never of her own volition, and while it had been okay, she hadn't particularly gotten off on it.

Now licking Alek, however... Hmm, it was like treating herself to a yummy piece of erotic candy. She relished the taste of him, the feel of velvet stretched taut over steel, the sensation as she slid him in and out of her mouth.

Using one hand to steady him, she let her tongue circle around the head when she came down, and sucked when she moved up again, with a hint of teeth grazing his skin. Judging by the way Alek's grip on the carpet tightened and his breathing quickened, he enjoyed her teasing.

She'd just started playfully licking the sensitive underside of the tip, when he yanked her off.

She glared at him in outrage. "I'm not finished!"

"I need to be inside you," he growled back, and before she could so much as squeal, he'd hoisted her up on his shoulder, carrying her toward his bedroom.

Her back met the mattress, the soft impact still abrupt enough to rush air out of her lungs for a moment. Alek used that instant of immobility on her part to divest her of her pants and was in the process of pulling off her top when she caught up with the change of place and pace. No less eager than he to get naked, she helped him get rid of the rest of her clothes.

"You too," she said, tugging on his shirt.

He complied without hesitation. With a swift move, he took off his shirt, then stripped out of his jeans and underwear and crawled back on the bed. Looming over her like a darkly beautiful vision of sex, he gave her a look that made her quiver in anticipation.

"I'd love to taste you again," he murmured, his voice on

the edge of feral, "but I'm afraid I'm all out of patience for now."

"So am I." She wriggled farther underneath him, hooking one leg around his hips, opening herself to him.

Balancing his weight on one arm next to her shoulder, he leaned down and caught her mouth in a searing kiss, while he slid his other hand down to the juncture of her thighs, to the aching spot so ready for him. His fingers found her entrance, played with her folds, teased the throbbing center of her need.

Yes.

A thought at the back of her mind, pushing forward. "Can *prana*-grendels have STDs?" she asked, her hands on his shoulders.

He paused, his lips twitching. "*Pranagrahas*. And no." His fingers moved against her intimate flesh again, sending shivers of pleasure through her that all but erased her thought process. "And I can't get you pregnant, not until we're mated."

Content with his explanation—and ignoring the undertone of longing in his words—she arched against his touch, craving more. "I need to feel you, Alek."

A tremor went through him when she called him by name. Locking his gaze with hers, the intensity in his eyes threatening to reach parts of her heart she wanted to keep hidden behind a wall, he positioned his cock and entered her.

She gasped at the pleasure-pain of him stretching her in a way that was at once too much and not enough.

He stilled, silver-gold eyes alight with attention. "You okay?"

"Give me a moment," she whispered, her nails digging into his shoulders.

Eyes still locked with hers, he kissed her with a gentleness that contrasted beautifully with the almost-but-not-quite hurt of his erotic intrusion. His free hand tangled in her hair, cradled the back of her head and caressed her neck, slid down farther to her breast. He circled her nipple, brushed his fingertips oh-so-lightly over the puckered tip, inciting small fireworks in her skin and all the way down to where she began to adjust to his size.

She squeezed him with her inner muscles and rolled her hips against him. Smiling against her lips, he took her cue and began to move. Slowly at first, he rocked into her, picking up speed after a few thrusts as her body welcomed him more and more fully, and she matched his rhythm. The slap of flesh on flesh and heated, quickened breaths filled the room, a primal mix of sounds that turned her on as much as the twining scents of their lust, the feel of Alek possessing her in a way that spoke to the most primitive part of her nature.

His fingers tunneling into her hair again, he grasped the strands, pulled until she bared her throat to him. Her heartbeat a drum in her ears, she gasped as he bent to lick the sensitive skin, his teeth nipping at her in a mere shadow of a demand, and yet the primordial part of her brain exploded with warning.

With a series of swift moves ingrained in her through years of martial arts training, she flipped them both over. Straddling him, she lowered herself, driving his cock deep and gyrating her hips at the same time. Alek groaned, throwing his head back against the pillow, his hands gripping her waist.

The niggling feeling at the back of her mind faded now that she was in control, and she let herself go, gave in to the passion burning inside her, and rode him hard. Her climax hit her like a storm front. Setting all her nerve endings alight, the orgasm blew through her with unadulterated force. Thoughts and feelings a scattered mess, she was still in the grip of the last waves of bliss...when Alek drove his hips up and squeezed her nipples—hard.

Crying out, she surrendered to a peak of pleasure unlike anything she'd ever felt. This climax was pure sensual devastation, merciless in its erotic destruction. Light flooded her vision before darkness swallowed her mind.

છ૪ઝ

DARK NEED DRIVING HER, SHE KEPT ON BEATING THE WITCH pinned underneath her knees. Her fists rained down, knuckles bloody, the scent of iron thick in the air. It only incited her bloodlust further.

The witch struggled, a feeble attempt at stopping the wrath unleashed upon her. "Lily, stop!"

The familiar voice sent a tendril of recognition through her, a spike of fear. This was her enemy, wasn't it? Her punches faltered, doubt seeping into her heated blood. She let up enough that the witch lowered her arms from her protective position in front of her face.

Lily's heart shattered.

Sky-blue eyes opened in a face that was little more than mask of blood, and fire-red hair sticking to pale skin. A face she knew, knew so very well.

"Will you kill me, too?" Merle asked.

"Too?" A whisper, a broken sound.

Merle glanced to the side, and she followed her look, jerked when she saw the crumpled body of a male—Baz's lifeless eyes stared back at her.

She screamed as her world splintered.

Lily woke with a start and the strangled remnants of a scream stuck in her throat. Her pulse raced, her skin covered in a sheen of sweat, her soul stained with a darkness she couldn't shake.

Breathing so fast that white spots flitted across her vision, she thrashed, her eyes finding nothing familiar to hold onto when she opened them. A darkened room, a bed she didn't know, lingering images and feelings of a nightmare that seemed all too real.

The scent of autumn nights and wood fires filtered through the chaos in her mind at the same time as her hand landed on a warm body next to her. She ran her fingers over muscles, fine hair tickling her fingertips. A forearm. A wrist.

A hand grasping hers.

"Alek," she whispered.

"Shhh. Come here, Lilichka." His voice was drenched in sleep, the timbre a rough caress.

And she went. Without hesitation, she curled into him, buried her face in the curve of his neck, inhaled him until she was drunk on him, her heart relaxing on a sigh. His arms came around her, a protective embrace that felt so safe, so *right*.

"It's okay," he muttered, stroking her back. "You're okay. I'm here, *tsvetochek*."

The stranglehold of fear around her mind loosened. He kept petting her, anchoring her with touch, and she hadn't known how much she needed that physical connection until he enveloped her in his arms. Her breathing calmed.

Here, locked in his embrace, in the heat of whatever it was they shared, she could almost start to believe his words. That she was okay. That this new darkness inside her wouldn't devour everything that was good about her. Yes, she could almost believe him.

Almost.

CHAPTER 16

"**B**ut I'm hungry *now*."

At Lily's whine, Alek stifled a grin and ushered her to the front door. "It's just a few minutes. I promise it'll be worth it."

Halfway across the living room, she made an attempt to lunge toward the kitchen, so he caught her around the waist and dragged her farther.

She flailed in the direction of the fridge. "But there's actual, real food in there *right now*. I can't wait a few minutes."

"Yes, you can." He patted her butt and kept hauling her outside.

"Grant!" she cried with an air of overdramatization which caused carefree amusement to bubble up inside him. "You need to get a message to my people. I'm being kidnapped and denied food. Be a good boy and run for help!"

Alek threw a glance over his shoulder to see Grant curled

up on his blanket, eyes closed, his tail lifting and flagging down once in response to Lily's plea.

"Traitor," muttered Lily.

His heart light with laughter, Alek pulled her outside, locked the door, and led her down the sidewalk. "It's just two blocks."

The horizon was ablaze with the last brushes of the fiery sunset under the already darkened sky as they walked the short distance through his neighborhood. When he ascended the steps to a small two-story home, Lily followed him with a huge frown on her face.

"I thought you said we were going to eat at the place with the best food in town."

He shot her a grin and opened the front door. "This *has* the best food in town."

"But it's not a restaurant."

He saluted her as he held the door open. "Captain Obvious."

Her narrowed eyes promised retribution as she walked past him into a lovely but cluttered living room.

He had barely closed the door behind him when loud shrieks filled the room.

"Uncle Sasha!"

Two little demon missiles hit him straight on, one half his size, the other even smaller. Uttering an *oomph* at the impact for the benefit of his nephews, he doubled over and hugged both boys.

"Hey there, buddies." He ruffled first Jordan's, then Lucas's blond hair. "How are you doing?"

Jordan, the ten-year-old, his eyes the rich, dark brown of his mother's, started telling him in rapid-fire speed about everything he'd done since Alek saw him last week, while five-year-old Lucas kept tugging on Alek's pants leg. When Jordan paused his machine-gun account for a moment to inhale, Alek hunched down to Lucas's level and nodded at him.

"What about you?"

The kid's eyes—silver striated with gold—lit up. "I ate a worm."

"Is that right? How'd it taste?"

"Yucky." Lucas's face scrunched up in the most adorable way.

"But you ate another one right after," Jordan pointed out.

"To check if it's yucky, too." Lucas threw up his hands in a gesture that made Alek want to hug the little guy and never let go.

"Ever so inquisitive, that one." Dima came down the stairs into the living room, his 1.5-year old daughter Chloe on his hip and an indulgent look on his face. A face that was the mirror image of Alek's, his eyes the exact same shade of gold-rimmed silver.

"Did you give them sugar again?" Alek asked by way of greeting his twin, both Lucas and Jordan now dangling from Alek's arms, babbling about worms and bugs and tastes.

"If I had," Dima said, "you'd *know* it."

"They'd be hanging from the ceiling speaking in tongues?"

"Exactly."

"And it's a pain in the butt getting them down again." Coming from Tori, Dima's mate, who shuffled in from the kitchen at that moment, wiping her hands on a dish towel, heat from the cooking brushing color over her fair skin.

"Hey, Tori." Alek bent to give her a kiss on the cheek.

The female *pranagraha*, currently six months pregnant,

her blond hair done up in a haphazard ponytail, smiled and turned to Lily with a curious glint in her dark eyes. "You must be Lily. I'm Tori, and this is my mate, Dima."

Lily accepted Tori's hug with shocked stiffness, looking just a little overrun by the whole situation. Alek cringed. Maybe he should have warned her after all.

When Lily turned to Dima and held out her hand to him, he pulled her into a one-armed hug as well, still holding Chloe on his other arm. "No need to be formal here," he said as he patted her on the back. "After all, you'll be spending a lot of time here, bringing your kids over so they can play with their cousins—"

"*Tikho.*" Alek smacked his twin on the back of his head, careful not to touch Chloe in the process, whom he then plucked away from Dima.

Dima stepped back and held his palms up. "What? I'm just making conversation."

"Lily's a *friend*," Alek said through gritted teeth, glaring daggers at his brother, willing him to remember their earlier phone conversation when he told Dima about Lily. Not just about her transformation, but also how skittish she was, and his plan to court her without her noticing he was courting her. The last thing he needed was for Dima to drag up the mating issue in front of Lily. And right off the bat, to boot.

He'd figured it was a good idea to bring Lily along to meet his twin and family, drawing her in further by showing her the example of a happy *pranagraha* mating. He'd hoped it might help erode some of her commitment issues, give her a glimpse of what she and Alek could have together.

Seeing the glint of mischief in his brother's eyes, he was beginning to doubt the soundness of that decision.

"It's really nice to meet you, Lily," Tori said, breaking Alek's silent communication with his twin.

"Likewise."

"How are you feeling?" Alek asked Tori, while bouncing a giggling Chloe.

"Starting to get the beached-whale feeling." Tori patted the proud swell of her belly. "But other than that, I'm doing okay."

"I think you look just fine, baby," Dima said, curling his free arm around Tori's waist, regarding her with unadulterated affection.

"You're just saying that because we've got company." Tori's teasing smile belied her words.

"Yep." Dima's grin was wicked. "If we didn't, I'd show you just how fine I think you look."

"Ew, no kissing!" Jordan made retching sounds and ran off.

Lucas doubled the volume of his brother's fake puking and took off after him. On Alek's arm, Chloe made a noise mimicking the boys' sounds, though it was little more than an adorable cough.

Alek smiled at his niece. "And how are you tonight, princess?"

As always in the first few minutes she saw him, Chloe looked at him with wide gold eyes full of wonder. She poked his nose and said, "Daddy."

Inside his chest, his sturdy male heart didn't stand a chance, and melted in the blink of an eye. "Close, *solnishko*, but not quite. I'm Uncle Sasha. I just look exactly like your daddy."

They had this conversation every time he came over, and every time, Chloe would study him for a long moment, tilt her head, and then nod as if granting approval. "Sasa."

A pang of longing echoed through him, growing stronger with each visit. He wanted this. Kids, a family, a home. And there was only one female he could imagine sharing it with. He glanced at Lily, who stood next to him, staring at Chloe with what could only be described as a transfixed expression.

"Would you like to hold her?"

Lily startled. "What? Me?" A spark of panic lit up her aura. "I'm not really sure that's a good idea. I'm not the best at handling tiny people. You see, they're so tiny. And breakable."

"You'll do fine," he said, and held Chloe out to her.

Indigo eyes widening, Lily accepted the bundle of cute with stiff arms. Chloe immediately touched the parts of Lily's *tvaglakshana* visible above the cut of her shirt's neckline, brushing her little pudgy fingers over the swirling lines.

"Pwetty," she cooed.

Lily's aura flared with warmth.

Chloe looked up at Lily's face then, mouth open and gaze filled with the kind of honest admiration unique to toddlers. She reached up and almost touched Lily's eyes, if not for Lily's last-second flinching back. "Pwetty," she repeated.

A beautiful blush darkened the white of Lily's cheeks, before she caught herself. "You're quite the little charmer, missy."

"Yeah, she gets that from her dad," Tori said. "I need to get back to the stove, but I can take her off your hands if she bothers you."

"O-okay." Lily handed the toddler over to her mom with just a hint of hesitation.

"I'm gonna go check on the boys." Dima glanced upstairs, a decidedly worried expression on his face. "It's way too quiet up there."

He sprinted up the stairs while Tori waddled back into the kitchen, leaving Alek and Lily alone in the living room.

The blush still rosy on her cheeks, she turned to him. "You brought me here, to your family."

"Sure did."

A shadow passed through the radiant blue of her eyes. "Aren't you worried I'll betray them to the other witches?"

⚜

"No." ALEK SHOOK HIS HEAD, THE LINES OF HIS FACE RELAXED. "I know you wouldn't."

She sucked in air, her hands trembling as much as her insides. "Such trust."

Enough to bring her to the very heart of his life, to the one thing that meant everything to him. Even if he hadn't explained to her the sigils of his demon tattoo that stood for his commitment to family, she'd have known the depth of his love for Dima, his mate, and their kids by the look in his eyes when he interacted with them, the strength of affection in his aura.

He'd brought her here, showed her this private, treasured part of his life, placing such implicit trust in her that she'd keep the knowledge of them safe.

And right there and then she vowed that she would.

She'd once betrayed information under duress, when Aunt Isabel interrogated her in the wake of Merle's unsanctioned unleashing of Rhun. Never again would she surrender that way. The conviction of her commitment was an unflinching truth in her heart, that she'd rather suffer pain, have her body and mind broken, than break Alek's trust.

She marveled at this new feeling that unfurled inside her, the desire to honor this male's faith in her, to prove she was deserving of it. At the same time, she purposely ignored the small but growing part of her that craved that trust, that affection—wanted it *always*. A core of primal possessiveness, the deep-seated longing to have Alek continue looking at her with the kind of warmth that made cracks appear in the walls around her heart.

Right now, that warmth turned to heat as fire sparked in the silver-gold of his eyes, demon red and black taking over. The searing burn of his regard mirrored in the flare of his aura, he closed the distance between them until her breasts brushed his front, her nipples hardening at the promise of touch. His hands settled on her hips, pulled her to him as he lowered his head, bringing his lips so close to hers she wasn't sure where her breath ended and his began.

A breeze of chilly night air blew in as the front door opened.

Alek sighed and turned, and Lily peeked around him to look at the visitor. A younger version of the male who ignited wickedly addictive desire in her stepped inside, shrugging out of his jacket. When his eyes—more gold than silver, as far as she could tell from the distance—met hers, he gasped, his energy pattern betraying his excitement.

"Hi," the younger demon male said as he sidled closer, scooting around Alek and holding out his hand to her. "My name's Yuri. And you are?"

"Mine," Alek growled.

Lily snapped her head up to glare at Alek, the cave demon. She cleared her throat and narrowed her eyes.

To his credit, he recovered quickly. "My *friend*," he corrected, though she'd never heard anyone say that word with quite such a proprietary undertone.

"Lily," she said, shaking the hand of the very eager-looking young male.

"So you're unmated?" He beamed at her, still holding onto her hand.

"Umm..." She furtively tried to tug her hand back, but he held fast, rubbing the sensitive patch between her thumb and forefinger.

"You've got the softest skin," he said with a sigh.

It was so adorably cute, Lily didn't have the heart to tell him she'd feel like a cradle-robber if she even considered dating someone his age.

She didn't have to say anything, though, because the next moment Yuri was tucked into a headlock by a nicely muscled arm, which effectively broke the young male's hold on Lily's hand.

"As you might have guessed," Alek said, flexing his arm to increase the pressure when Yuri struggled, "this is my youngest brother. Good kid, but going a bit overboard in his pursuit of females." He waved his free hand. "He's newly transitioned, you know."

"I think he's trying to say something."

Alek peered down at his flailing brother and loosened his hold just enough for him to speak.

Yuri's eyes met hers as he hauled in a coughing breath. "Mate...with...me?"

Alek sighed and reinforced his chokehold. "Quit that." Smiling at Lily, he said, "Let's go see if Tori needs our help."

And with that he walked toward the kitchen, dragging a thrashing Yuri along with him.

"*Alek.*" Lily tried hard not to laugh.

He stopped and turned, a picture of innocence, if it wasn't for the cursing young male still choking under his arm. "What?"

"Will you let him go?" She grinned. "Please?"

He heaved a long-suffering sigh. "You're too soft, you know that?"

Shaking his head, he released Yuri, but not without tripping him so the young male landed sprawled on his back. "No trying to mate with her," he told him matter-of-factly, while he ushered Lily toward the kitchen.

She glanced behind her to make sure Yuri wasn't comatose. He was very much awake and glaring at Alek's back as if he wanted to tackle him, but when he caught Lily's eye, his face lit up like a struck match and he mouthed, *I love you.*

What was it with these males and their eagerness to mate?

⚶

LILY HADN'T HAD THIS MUCH FUN AT A FAMILY DINNER IN years.

Between the boys running around and winning tiny pieces of her heart...little Lucas bringing her pictures he'd drawn for her, his face showing a shy pride, and Jordan involving her in an ongoing discussion about all the things that made Harry Potter the best series ever...and the banter pinging back and forth between Alek and his brothers, she had the feeling the grin on her face could end up being permanent.

When Chloe, whose highchair sat next to Lily, kept handing her peas from her plate, her expression so earnest and stately as if she were granting Lily a royal honor, Lily's heart simply melted into a puddle at her feet.

"All right," she said to the tiny toddler, her voice quiet so she wouldn't disturb the conversation of the others, "you've done it. I'm completely convinced of your irresistible charm and superior state of adorableness. You can lay off the cute now, okay?"

Chloe blinked and held out a pea.

"Oh, you," she whispered, and graciously accepted the majestic offering.

"Lily," Dima said, and she sat up straight, hoping no one had witnessed her abject submission to the Toddler Powers of Charm, "has Sasha told you yet how he came to be scared spitless of spiders?"

"Spitless!" Lucas shouted and made noises to demonstrate what having no saliva would sound like.

"Shh, sweetie." Tori handed him another piece of cornbread. "Eat something."

"He hasn't," Lily drawled, pivoting slowly in her seat to face a disturbed-looking Alek.

"Oh, you're in for a treat." Dima clapped his hands, silver-gold eyes glittering with mischief. "Sasha, why don't you enlighten your future mate—uh, I mean *friend*. You tell the story so well."

"I don't know you," Alek growled, pointing his fork at his twin. "Why are you talking to me?"

"Fork fight!" Jordan launched himself half over the table, brandishing his own fork and clinking it against his uncle's.

"I wanna hear about the spiders," Lucas piped up.

"Sorry, can't," Alek shot back, parrying Jordan's fork attacks. "Busy fighting over here."

Lily couldn't keep her giggle in, and it spilled over, tumbled out, just like a feeling she'd been content to ignore slipped out of the cage she'd tried to cram it in. Her heart both soared and ached while she watched Alek chase his nephew around the table with a fork. This feeling...so bitter-sweet, so furtively consuming—so dangerous in its implication.

For if she allowed herself to follow it, would she lose herself on the way? This happy scene, this example of a loving family—it contrasted too starkly with memories of her own childhood, of how twisted love could become.

If she fell for Alek, if she gave in to the budding promise of a sweeping devotion, how could she know that it wouldn't someday turn her eyes as dull as her mom's, stifle her spirit like hers had been?

When you love someone, you make concessions. Her mom had said that to her, years and years ago, when Lily found her crying after another argument with her dad. *He's not bad,* Hazel would say. *He doesn't mean it.* Lily sat with her then, as she had so often before, and stroked her hair, feeling so help-less at her mom's pain.

She'd only ever seen her mom like this, had never known she could be any different until her father died. The woman who raised her—meek, pleading, cowering—was a stranger compared to her mother now, the suffocation of years of abuse lifted to allow her spirit to reemerge.

Love, Aunt Isabel spat when they talked about her parents one spring day, the sunny afternoon a stark relief to the darkness of the past. *She could have stopped him a thousand times over if she hadn't been so stupid for him. That's what love does to you, it makes a mockery of who you are. If you want to be smart, don't ever get married, don't ever depend on a man.* Isabel yanked a weed out of the earth. *You'll be happier, I promise.*

She'd never realized how much her aunt's words had steered her course in life—well, she'd never before stumbled upon a male who challenged those deeply ingrained beliefs. Considering how Aunt Isabel had ended up butchering the sanctity of the witch community's laws, had kidnapped Maeve and tortured her to gain access to her powers for the insane vision of wiping out all demons, maybe those lessons Lily had soaked up from her aunt didn't represent the truth Lily had believed them to be all those years?

"Are you okay?"

The soft question pulled her out of her swirling thoughts, and she blinked at Tori. The female *pranagraha* leaned closer to her from her seat next to Chloe's highchair, concern in her brown eyes.

"Uh, yeah." She cleared her throat, accepted another pea from Chloe. "Thanks. So, um, you and Dima, you've been mated for ten years?"

A radiant smile broke across Tori's face, and Lily could have sworn the room lit up as well. "Yes. Can't believe it's a decade already. Time flies by so fast."

And hasn't dulled your shine, Lily thought. While she watched Tori interact with her mate, with their kids, her aunt's words rang in her mind, only they had lost a little of their edge, and a lot of their glamor.

Love, as she'd witnessed tonight, didn't always rob a person of all will to fend for themselves. Sometimes, it turned up a person's light until it became a beacon of hope.

CHAPTER 17

A hot thrill shot through Drake's veins. He'd found her again.

Finally.

As soon as the sun set, he'd gone out searching the city for any trace of Lily and the male she'd been with. Too bad he hadn't caught the bastard's name, or he could have found them both much sooner. He wouldn't have had to waste hours upon hours quietly asking about anyone seeing a blond male *pranagraha* accompanied by a female *pranagraha* with long black hair. Digging for information like that without arousing suspicion and drawing too much attention to oneself was sadly undervalued.

He was pretty proud of himself, especially since he also managed to avoid getting caught by Seth and his guys, who were undoubtedly combing the town for him. By now, Seth would have figured out it was Drake who stole the vial, and he was coming after him with a vengeance, of that Drake was sure. Seth would want the vial back, or—once he realized Drake had used it—he'd want to claim the result.

And that, Drake could never allow.

He peeked around the corner of the railroad car he was hiding behind, checked on his female and the scum she was with. Luck was on his side tonight—she still wasn't mated. He sneered at the other male's weakness. That demon had to be a fucking sissy for not having claimed her yet. Well, his stupidity played into Drake's hands.

"We can check out one more spot before sunup," the weak-ass male said to Lily.

"All right." She followed the SOB toward an old sewer pipe, the nearest entrance to the tunnel system, which was, as usual, protected by demon wards that would drive both witch and human away with powerful compulsion.

Drake's heart raced, his hands shook. Though he'd hoped to find out where they holed up for the day, and to ambush them there when they were resting, he couldn't chance following them underground. Last night he'd lost them when they entered the tunnel system. He couldn't risk losing them again.

The chances of the male claiming Lily rose exponentially the more time she spent in his company. Drake couldn't waste another day. He had to act now, even if it meant going up against the other *pranagraha*, who—for all his failings to take charge and make Lily his—still possessed enough power to pose a real threat. Drake wasn't stupid enough to discount that danger.

He just had to be quick, strike fast and hard enough to incapacitate the other male so he could snatch Lily. Calculating the best angle from which to hit and still retain the element of surprise, he scanned the ground, picked up an old piece of rusted metal pipe the length of his forearm.

That should do the trick.

※

ALEK COULD SEE THE DEMON WARDS HIDING THE ENTRANCE TO the sewer pipe shimmer as they drew closer.

Scanning their surrounding for signs of movement, Alek heard the clink of a pebble on metal a split second before a shadow registered in the upper periphery of his vision. He whipped up his head at the same instant he barked for Lily to get down, and jumped to the side.

Not fast enough.

Pain exploded in his skull, reverberated down his spine, and the world blackened. Somewhere behind him, Lily screamed his name. His mind locked on to the sensation of the attacker's aura—demon, male, hot with rage—and he struck out in that direction. His fist connected with flesh and bone, and the other demon grunted. Light seeped back into his vision just as the attacker brought down his weapon again—and whacked Alek straight in the face.

The blow slammed him to the side, his head crashed against the edge of the railroad car, and everything went dark.

In the midst of the black fog around him, he fought for consciousness. Sounds of struggle registered, grew louder, clearer. *Lily.* With teeth-gritting stubbornness, he yanked himself out of the abyss of darkness, willed his body to function. He sucked in air, the metallic scent of blood heavy and consuming, and forced his eyes to open, his limbs to move.

A few feet away, the female who held his heart fought against the grip of another *pranagraha*. Alarm fired up his nerves, propelled him to stumble to his feet. The world swayed in and out of focus. *Fucking head wound.* He clenched his jaw, ignored the pounding pain in his head and staggered forward.

He was about to lunge at the other demon when Lily executed a series of martial arts moves that were beautiful in their efficiency—and sent the other *pranagraha* face-first onto the ground in a few seconds, with Lily on his back holding his left arm in a vicious hammerlock.

Alek grinned, deep satisfaction and grim pride at his female's fighting skills filling his chest. Yeah, their demon attacker made the fatal mistake of underestimating Lily's ability to defend herself, even without her witch magic. Served him right that he should eat dust for that alone.

"Is that the fucker who shot you?" Alek rasped as he staggered over to them, his mind still playing funny balance tricks on him. It required a Herculean effort to just walk straight.

"Sure is." Lily increased the pressure of the armlock, and the demon shrieked. She glanced at Alek while grinding her knee into the spot between the bastard's shoulder blades, sparks of fiery red dancing in her eyes. "Are you okay?"

He nodded, and a wave of nausea swamped him. "Just a scratch." Fuck if he was going to let that damn head wound get to him.

Lily narrowed her eyes at him. "I'll call you on your bullshit later. Right now, I have some questions to ask of *you*," she growled at the male in her grip. "How did you make the serum to turn me?"

"Like I'm just gonna tell you," the demon ground out.

Lily leaned down further, escalating the pressure of her hammerlock. "Do you *want* me to dislocate your shoulder?"

The *pranagraha* groaned. "Fuck you."

"So that's a yes, then?" She twisted his arm farther up his back.

White-hot pain spiked in the demon's aura, and he screamed.

Lily kept his arm in the tighter position. "*Talk.*"

"I don't know how the serum was made!"

Lily stilled, her eyes a storm of fire and night, her jaw clenched so tight the muscles flexed. "How could you not know?"

Alek sucked in air, realization a dawn of trepidation in his bones. "Because he wasn't the one to make it."

Whipping up her head, Lily stared at him. "What?"

Alek growled, went down on his haunches, grabbed the other *pranagraha's* hair and yanked his head back so he could look directly into the jerk's eyes. "Who are you working with?"

The demon spit on Alek's boots.

"Answer me or I'll snap your neck."

Brittle sounds fell from the other male's mouth, and it took Alek a second to realize he was laughing.

"They're gonna come after you," the fucker said, straining to look at Lily on his back. "Even if you kill me, they're gonna find you. They need more successfully turned females. You're too valuable for them to let you go."

Alek gritted his teeth. "Who?"

A tremor flashed through Lily's energy. Nostrils flaring, she twisted the demon's arm up again. "There are others like me?"

The *pranagraha* cried out and then laughed some more. "Did you think you were the only one?"

She gasped, her face losing all color. "The missing witches."

Rage a fire in his blood, Alek yanked on the demon's hair again. "One last time, you slimy piece of trash—who else is in on this?"

A whisper in the night…and then the air vibrated with magic. A ball of power slammed into Alek's back, making him keel over into Lily. He rolled with it, gritting his teeth against the explosion of pain across his shoulder blades, shielding Lily with his body.

"Run," he whispered in her ear. "To the sewer pipe. Tunnels."

She sprinted toward the entrance to the underground grid the second she and Alek rolled to a stop, and he ran after her an instant later. Another blow of magic missed her by a foot as she dashed away. He glanced back, darted sideways to evade the next spell thrown at him.

Three witches came running toward them from several yards away, active power a radiant glow around them in the dark of the night. One veered right in pursuit of the other *pranagraha*, who was hightailing it out of the rail yard at a breakneck pace.

The air crackled with more gathering witch magic. Alek focused ahead again, doubled his speed despite throbbing pain in his head threatening to make him keel over, his back burning where the first spell had hit him.

Lily had reached the sewer pipe, skidded inside through the shield of protective demon magic. He followed her a second later, dashed past her to the hidden trapdoor. As soon as the spell gave way under his touch, he cranked the handle, yanked the door open, and jumped in first to check for danger.

"All clear," he shouted up.

Lily hoisted herself down, pulling the door shut above

her. The clank echoed in the tunnel, sending the musty, earthy air swirling around them. The thick darkness was broken only by small lamps hung intermittently along the rough-hewn walls, providing enough light for most demon species' eyes.

He put his hand on Lily's lower back, nudged her forward. "Keep going."

Though it was highly unlikely that the witches could break through the wards, it wasn't impossible. The more distance he and Lily put between them and the witches the better. Plus, the tunnels really weren't the best place to hang out and take a break.

"We need to find a safe spot where we can stop for a moment," Lily said as they jogged down the tunnel.

"Are you injured?" He shot her an assessing look, worry twisting his stomach.

"No." Her eyes flared red in the dark. "You are. And don't you dare grumble at me now. We're going to stop somewhere, and I'm going to check you."

Warmth spread through his chest at her concern, at her determination to take care of him. Although he still snarled a bit. He did have a male reputation to uphold.

CHAPTER 18

"Wait a second." Lily gaped at the black velvet walls, which were drenched in atmospheric red lighting, while Alek closed the door to the stairway leading up from the tunnel. "Is this *Nine Circles*?"

"Yep."

"And it has its own connection to the underground grid?"

"Yep."

"That is so cool."

Alek grinned over his shoulder at her, the jarring flickers in his aura belying his nonchalant facade. That male had a dressing down coming, thinking he could pretend he wasn't hurt in front of her.

Approaching a demon waitress, Alek said something to her, and she nodded to her right. He steered Lily toward one of the more secluded corner booths, his hand on her lower back sending pleasant shivers to her core. The background music twined around her senses, the beat low, its rhythm seductive.

Pulling aside the heavy, blood-red curtain which shielded the booth from view, he led her inside. When the curtain fell back into place behind them, it was as if they were enclosed in a luscious cocoon of privacy. A low, ornately carved table made of darkest wood stood in front of a couch, its fabric a luxurious shade of gleaming dark red brocade. The throb of the music's rhythm filtered in through the curtains, hummed over her skin.

As soon as they sat on the couch, the curtain lifted to the side and the demon waitress entered the secluded booth. She placed a towel and a bowl of water on the table and left again.

"For your wounds?" Lily asked, eying the mass of red matting Alek's hair on one side, the bloody bruise on his cheek.

He nodded, then winced and grimaced.

When he reached out to the bowl, she slapped his hand away and dunked the towel in the hot water. "Let me." Scooting closer, her thigh pressing against his, she carefully dabbed at the wound on his face. "Aren't you worried about appearing injured in a bar full of demons?"

Dark blond lashes lowered down to his cheeks, and when he opened his eyes again, the silver in his irises was radiant. "Ava would never tolerate an attack on one of Arawn's people in here."

"Ava? The waitress?"

He shook his head, then apparently remembered that wasn't such a good idea, his jaw clenched in a hard line. "Ava's the succubus who owns *Nine Circles*."

"Succubus, huh?" Chest twisting with a hot, dark feeling that aggravated her in its irrationality, she wrung the washcloth hard over the bowl.

When she turned back to Alek, it was to see him with a decidedly pleased smile tugging at his mouth, his eyes glittering in the low light. "My dealings with Ava have always been business in nature." He curved his hand over her thigh, making her feel her heartbeat in low, low places. "Never pleasure."

The possessive satisfaction that filled her at that was even more irrational than her jealousy. Like she had a right to him.

But maybe I want to. The thought whispered through her mind, took root inside the cracks spreading through the wall around her heart, widening them.

Maybe...just *maybe* this wouldn't have to end. What if... she kept him after she turned back into a witch? He'd made it clear he wanted more—perhaps he was open to continuing their relationship, see where it took them. It didn't have to be the real deal right away, didn't mean they had to get married. If she didn't have the pressure of a deeper commitment looming over her, she could try to give this a chance.

"You shouldn't have lied to me about being injured," she said to him, using the washcloth to remove as much blood as possible from his hair. The wound now visible on his scalp turned out to be small, which didn't mean much. Head injuries bled like hell.

"Look who's talking, Ms. Shredded Soles."

She paused, slanted a glance at his face. "Touché."

He still had his hand on her thigh, was now drawing small, delicious circles with his fingers.

Turning to the table, she wrung out the washcloth, placed it next to the bowl. "How's your back?"

"Not hurting anymore." When she raised a skeptical

eyebrow, he added, "Truth. Whatever spell it was, it didn't leave any lasting damage."

"Hm." Deciding to believe him, she straddled his lap and leaned in, her hands on his chest.

He grasped her hips, squeezed. "Is this your way of nursing my wounds?" His breath was hot on her lips. "I like it."

Her unbound hair fell around their faces like a veil of midnight, locking them into sultry intimacy. He opened his mouth to her at the first brush of her lips on his, his tongue stroking hers, pleasure rippling through her at the wet, hot touch.

Her focus turned inside, and she found the glowing center of her life force inside her chest. Cradling the radiant energy, she pulled part of it up, pushed it out through her mouth and into his.

His grip on her hips tightened as he broke the kiss, jerked back. "Whoa. What's this?"

"Funny I should have to explain *prana* to you."

He narrowed his eyes. "Why are you trying to give me breath?"

"To speed up your healing. Doesn't a boost in your energy kick up your ability to self-repair?"

"Yes," he said slowly. "But—"

"I don't like seeing you with these." She gingerly touched the bruise on his cheek, grazed her fingers around the small wound on his head. Catching his eye, she made sure he saw she meant it when she said, "I want to take care of you."

She felt a flicker of some deep, entwining emotion in his aura as he apparently understood her reference to what he told her while he cleaned her injured feet. "I'll just need a little," he said a moment later, his voice having dropped to a timbre that brought up memories of her body tangled with his, skin-on-skin, hot and sweaty.

Breasts growing heavy and primed for touch, she leaned in again, took his mouth in a meeting of lips far beyond what was necessary for *prana* exchange. By now she'd realized that when he gave her breath, he'd done so with sneaky sensuality, and what should be considered an inappropriate overstepping of boundaries.

But somehow she couldn't scrounge up an ounce of indignation about it.

Flicking her tongue against his, using her teeth to nip at his lower lip, she deepened the kiss—and pushed her *prana* up and into him. The radiant force of life, its energy palpable heat in her throat and mouth, flowed into him as he accepted her gift.

He drew on her *prana*, and she felt the pull all the way down to her toes, leaving a crystalline path of prickling excitement in its wake. Her nerve endings fired up with pleasure, white-hot and consuming. Acting on the surging impulse that short-circuited her higher functions, she rolled her hips, pressed her aching core against the growing hardness in his jeans.

His arms locked around her. His aura pulsed and whirled while his energy twined with hers. She moaned into his mouth, rubbing herself harder against him. One of his hands cupped her breast, and she pushed against him, eager for more touch. He pulled up her shirt and the shelf bra of her camisole until the heat of his palm was on her breast, soothing some of the ache. His index finger and thumb tweaked her nipple.

She cried out against his lips, the pressure that was half-pleasure growing, growing, growing.

Breaking the kiss and the flow of *prana*, he drew back until he met her gaze with eyes of red and black. "I've had enough."

"I haven't," she shot back, her breathing ragged. "Not of you."

An approving growl rose from his throat, and he flicked his thumb over her nipple, kneaded her breast. "Good. Because I'm not done with you, either."

Desire and need for him coiled under her skin. But— "How are your wounds?"

"What wounds?" He leaned forward, closed his mouth over her nipple, and sucked.

Her thoughts scattered like dandelion fluff, a flash of pleasure arcing through her. She gripped his shoulders, her claws slicing out of her fingertips. When she regained a semblance of coherent thought, she pushed until he let go of her breast and kissed a trail up to her neck instead.

"I don't," she said on a panting breath, "want to—" Her sentence ended on a moan when he reached the spot behind her ear, his lips tickling skin that was surprisingly eroge-nous. "...when you're still injured," she finished after he'd lightly bitten her jaw.

"I'm healed enough for this." A kiss driven by passion and demand. "Believe me, stopping right now would hurt me far more."

She smiled at his sneaky verbal manipulation. But she'd take him at his word. Skimming her hands up under his T-shirt, she roamed the expanse of his chest with her palms, gave the flexing muscles of his abdomen that thorough exploration she'd been planning. She tugged at his belt buckle, her fingers making short work of it while she met his kisses with equal fervor. His belt undone, the button and zipper went next.

And before he could stop her, she'd slipped off his lap and between his legs, pulled down his boxers, her lips closing around his cock.

৩৵ও

ALEK'S EYES ROLLED BACK IN HIS HEAD AT THE INTENSE pleasure of feeling Lily's hot mouth swallow his dick.

"Hot damn, woman," he rasped out, his fingers tangling in her hair.

In response, she fluttered the tip of her tongue against the sensitive underside of his cock's head, then sucked on his shaft with vigor.

His breath stalled in his throat, heart pumping exquisite pleasure through his veins until he was all but consumed by it. *Holy hell.* That mouth of hers... His balls grew heavy, aching with need.

As much as he was on board with everything she was doing to him with her wickedly talented tongue, he had to redirect the action now. Tugging up her head with a gentle pull on her hair, he flipped her around to face away from him before she could voice her sure-to-come protest at being interrupted—again.

"I love your mouth on my cock," he muttered in her ear, placing her on the couch with her arms braced on the back-rest, her knees on the cushion, "but I love the feel of your pussy clenching around me even more."

A violent tremor of lust set off fireworks in her aura, and if he'd had any doubts about whether she liked dirty talk, her response laid them to rest. He reached around her, opened her jeans, and shoved them down to her knees along with her panties. The scent of her arousal—which had already curled around him before, tantalizing and eroding his ability to think—now hit him full-on, a feast for his senses.

He yanked her pants and panties from her knees to her ankles so he could spread her wider for him. The next second he had his mouth on the glistening wet, flushed center of her, lapping up the delicious evidence of her need for him. Lily uttered a throaty moan, her aura a wild tapestry of pleasure and passion. He gripped her hips to hold her in place, and ate her like a starved man would devour a sumptuous buffet.

"Oh gods, Alek—" The distinctive sound of claws ripping into fabric.

When she came, her orgasm lit up her energy pattern in an explosion of rapture.

He'd never seen, never felt, anything more beautiful.

And he never, ever wanted to let her go. He wanted her as his with a primal possessiveness that was raw, uncivilized, and unrelenting. The thought of watching her walk out of his life, of her seeking—finding—this kind of pleasure with another male, would drive him mad if he dwelled on it. So he didn't.

Instead, he focused all his attention, all his power, on drowning her in sexual ecstasy, on fulfilling her sensual needs until she glowed with satisfaction, on showing her, in the only way she allowed him right now, the depth of his determination to take care of her.

He finally stopped his uncompromising sensual assault after he lost count of her orgasms. Having shredded the backrest with her claws—Ava would shred *him* for that—Lily hung her head between her outstretched arms, breathing in quick, heavy pants, her legs trembling under his steady grip. He half-expected her to collapse any second, but then she threw a glance over her shoulder that was so unabashedly lascivious, it had his already aching cock harden impossibly further.

"Are you going to fuck me now, or what?"

Lust pulsed in his groin. "You really do enjoy talking dirty, don't you?" Not just hearing it, she had no compunction to shoot back some saucy words as well. Just one more thing he adored about her.

"Only when it's paired with action." She wiggled her hips suggestively.

And how could he pass on an invitation like that?

Renewing his grasp on her hips, he thrust into her. Ah, the feel of her, it all but shattered his mind. None of his previous lovers had this effect on him. He'd enjoyed them, but he'd been able to leave each and every female afterward without a second thought, their sexual encounters brief and singular as agreed upon, no strings attached, no follow-up. None of them had kept a hold on him—no one but Lily.

And that was what deepened every sensation, highlighted every touch, turned every caress into a permanent, cherished mark on his soul. It elevated the basic, pleasurable feeling of having a welcoming female underneath him into something that went far beyond the physical, an experience that left him bare in a way he'd never been. With anyone.

More than ever, he craved the culmination of that experience yet out of his reach, trembled with the need for it. The unyielding belief that he'd soon get to share it with Lily—

only ever her—was the one thing that soothed the voracious yearning.

He'd waited all this time. He could be patient a little while longer.

The bouquet of her feminine excitement thick in the air, he thrust into her heat, increased speed and force when she begged him for it until he pounded into her. A husky moan escaped her throat, and then her inner muscles clenched around him, squeezed his cock in a rhythm that had his mind blanking.

Still on the precipice—always one fucking step away from what he could sense would be devastating pleasure—he kept up his pace, shoving into her with the kind of power that made her aura scintillate and ripple until she climaxed again. Judging by the way she all but melted onto the couch, she was ready for him to finish.

It was probably too much to hope that he'd be able to fuck her into unconscious bliss a second time, so she'd miss the fact that he *wouldn't* finish—again.

He had to hold her up during her final orgasm, helping her ride out the pleasure and realizing she definitely couldn't go another round, so he gave her a few hard thrusts and withdrew. She collapsed in his arms, wheezing into the cushion.

Having stuffed his aching cock into his jeans—damn, that hurt—he sank onto the couch next to her, stroking her back, her hair, petting her down.

It was a solid five minutes later when she stirred. She sat up with the languidness of a well-pleasured female, her lids still heavy over eyes once again a deep indigo, and stood to pull up her jeans.

Would she notice?

A frown gathered on her forehead like a thunderhead. She studied the rock-hard erection easily discernible under his fly. "Did you not get off?"

Yep, she'd noticed.

He shook his head, so not looking forward to the impending conversation. In hindsight, he should have used condoms to disguise that little tidbit, but—the allure of feeling her in the most immediate, intimate way, without barriers, had kicked that idea out the window.

Lily blinked at him, her aura a still life of perplexity. "Why?"

Here we go. "Male *pranagrahas* can't come until they're mated."

◈

LILY'S MIND SCRAMBLED TO MAKE SENSE OF WHAT ALEK JUST said. "What the what?"

He let out a long exhale. "Our ability to climax is tied to mating status. The process of bonding to a female *pranagraha* unlocks that ability."

Dumbfounded, she looked back and forth between his face and the still-prominent bulge in his jeans. "But—you're obviously able to be aroused and...functional."

A flicker of mischief in his eyes. "Want me to show you again how functional?"

"Alek." She shoved her fingers through her hair, paced away from him, turned back. "But you've had sex before, right? How—?"

He leaned forward, resting his elbows on his knees. "I've been with females, yes. Most male *pranagrahas* gather some experience pre-mating, part of wanting to increase their eligibility as mates." One side of his mouth tipped up in a half-smile that had her stomach flutter. "*Pranagraha* females tend to favor males who know what they're doing in bed."

She kept on pacing, her hand on her forehead, her emotions a maelstrom of confusion. "So, you're twenty-eight, and you've had sex, but you've never had an orgasm?"

He simply raised a brow.

She stopped pacing. "But—but—" Her hands flailed wildly. "How have you *survived* until now?"

"Well," he drawled, "you know how they say you can't miss something you've never had?"

She nodded.

"It's bullshit." He gave her wry smile.

Processing that for a minute, she swallowed hard. "Aren't you…in pain a lot?"

"Nothing I can't deal with." He shrugged. "From what I've heard, we don't suffer from blue balls as much as others until after we're mated."

She shook her head, unable to believe what she was hearing. "This is so fucked up. How did you explain your inability to orgasm to the females you've been with?"

"Some were demons who knew and were okay with it." He leaned back. "With humans I used condoms and they didn't notice."

Pressing her lips together at the surge of irrational jealousy about any ex-lover he ever had, she started pacing again. Stupid. How could she be jealous of something that happened before her time?

"You wanted to know." Alek's voice was gentle, his eyes hard.

She paused and faced him fully, something dark boiling

up inside her. "So that's why you're so eager to mate? So you can get off?"

"What?" He sat up with a start, his aura flashing with anger. "Hell, no. Is that what you think of me? Have I given you the impression I only care about sex?"

Crossing her arms, she returned his hard stare, some anger of her own sizzling over her skin. "All I know is you haven't exactly been honest with me."

"I didn't lie to you."

"Maybe not, but you conveniently left out some vital information. Why didn't you tell me about this before?"

A muscle ticked in his jaw. "It never came up."

"Right," she said, her voice dripping with sarcasm. Unbidden, her eyes darted to his groin, and her unruly mind brought up tantalizing images of what *had* come up. Several times. Mouthwateringly so.

"Lilichka." Alek stood, walked over to her. "I want to mate because I want a family. I want a home, a female to call my own, kids, the whole thing. And you're the only one I want to have that with."

He cupped her face with both hands, his palms cradling her cheeks with heat and care. "You're the one for me. The first time I saw you—when you were still a witch—I forgot to breathe for a moment. I've never believed in love at first sight, but you…"

The look in his eyes blasted open the cracked wall around her heart, tore into her in a way that stole *her* breath.

"You just hit me," he rasped, his raw voice stroking along her senses, sinking into her. "Like a freight train. I couldn't stop thinking about you, craving you. You were the one bright spot during endless nights of watch duty. And now that I've felt you, now I know what it's like to be with you

—" He shook his head. "I don't ever want to let you go. I know I said I wouldn't push you, but—"

"Don't," she croaked, her throat raw, the heat of tears threatening at the back of her eyes. "Don't ask me again." Raising her hand, palm out, she took a step back, broke the gentle hold he had on her face. "Don't make me give you an answer that'll hurt us both."

"Lily." He reached for her, his eyes so forlorn, it broke her inside.

Shaking her head, she whispered, "I need some time to think. Away from you."

He stilled. "What do you mean?"

"I can't stay with you anymore."

Mind racing, heart a confused mess, she rubbed her temples. His revelation about male *pranagrahas* not being able to climax seemed like such a small, inconsequential piece of information, when in reality it had sucker-punched her in the guts. Up until now a fledgling hope had grown inside her, ready to unfurl its wings. The idea that maybe, maybe she could keep Alek without mating with him—that she could turn back into a witch and still hold on to this male who challenged so many of her beliefs—it had become stronger, made her dream and *yearn*.

Knowing he couldn't orgasm until mated blew that idea to smithereens. Because how could she keep him, continue any kind of romantic relationship with him when he'd never be able to have a fulfilled sex life with her? The impossibility of that scenario was a slap in her face.

Which meant the only way she could keep him was to stay demon and commit to a bond that would tie her to him for better or worse, in life and death. A decision she couldn't just make with a snap of her fingers, no matter how tempting, not when so much more than her heart would be affected by it.

She was the heir to the Murray family, next in line to become Elder witch, meant to carry on the blood and magic of her ancestors. Staying demon would break that line. Since Basil was a male without powers, there was no way of knowing if his future children would inherit the family's magic.

Time. She needed time to think and get her head—and heart—on straight, figure out how to deal with this.

"I don't think it's safe to go home yet," she muttered, more to herself than to him. "Or to Merle's. But maybe Rhun can ask Bahram—"

"The incubus?" Alek's energy darkened like an approaching storm cloud. "Fuck that." He whipped out his phone, started dialing. "Like I'm going to watch you move in with a fucking sex demon." The growl in his voice curled her toes, sent a pleasant shiver over her skin.

Her heart ached for having to forbid herself from reaching out to him. "Who are you calling?"

"Dima." His look slammed into her, red embers glowing in obsidian. "You'll stay with him."

CHAPTER 19

"So," Alek said, while he and Dima walked out of the club's back door into the dimly lit alley behind the building, directing the two human males whom they'd chosen as prey to follow them quietly. "How is Lily?"

He'd tried not to pester his brother with questions about her, even though he was going crazy wondering how she was doing. Several times over the course of the day he'd been close to calling her, his finger hovering over the call button. He'd typed ten texts, then deleted every one without ever sending it off.

She wanted space. And he'd hack off his own arm to give it to her.

Dima checked his phone. "Wow. You made it to one hour and three minutes before asking about her. Held up pretty well there, Sasha."

Alek glowered at him.

"She's..." Dima huffed out a breath. "She spent most of the day sleeping or holed up in the spare bedroom. Heard her on the phone a few times."

Probably talking to Merle or her family.

"She ate with us, but was quiet," Dima said, steering his human to punch his companion in the jaw, then let him draw the knife Dima had conveniently deposited in the guy's jacket, and ordered him to stab his buddy in the gut. "Last I saw her before I left, the boys had roped her into playing a video game."

Alek kept his hold on the mind of his own human during the staged fight, and then directed the jerk face to slash at Dima's human with the switchblade Alek had so graciously provided. And even though Alek's human already bled like a stuck pig, he did deliver what could later be read as a killing blow to his former partner in crime, his movements still coordinated thanks to Alek's mind control. Dima grabbed the collar of his prey and leaned in. The human's aura flared up, the glow almost blinding, and then his *prana* left his mouth as Dima extracted it with skill. His own energy now a radiant gold, Dima let go of the dead human, watched him slump to the ground.

Alek maintained a mental grip of steel around the remaining man's higher functions, and stepped up to slake his own hunger. The vile darkness in the human's mind assaulted him, the lack of empathy or compassion sending chills down his soul.

He and Dima had chosen these two by following the nauseating trail of their auras into the club. When they took control of their minds, the human males had been in the process of spiking the drink of a girl with a drug that would leave her unconscious and at the mercy of both men. They'd done this before, several times, and had never been caught. Judging by the festering evil spreading in their minds like the sickest sort of cancer, they were well on the way to escalating their MO from sexual assault to murder.

After Dima and Alek discarded the contaminated drink, they took the men outside, where they could feed in privacy. These scum would never be able to hurt this girl, or any other one, ever again.

Alek made it quick, feeling no desire whatsoever to stay in the man's mind any longer than necessary. Lifeless, the guy's body joined his friend's on the ground. To the authorities, it would seem as if they'd died of the wounds from their fight.

Turning his back on the two humans, Alek left the alley with Dima, making sure they remained in the shadows and unnoticed by passersby. They'd also taken care to slip into the minds of the people who saw them leaving the club with the two guys, had made sure no one remembered they had any contact with the now dead men.

"Did she say anything about me?" Alek asked his twin, hope and anxiety twisting his heart.

Dima cut him a glance that raised his hackles.

"What? What did she say?"

His brother shook his head, looking away. "You're so full of shit."

"The fuck?"

Skewering Alek with a look that practically drilled a hole in his brain, Dima stopped at a crossroads. "Why do you want to mate with her?"

"Because I love her, you dimwit."

"Yeah," Dima said, crossing the street when the light turned green, "I'm calling bullshit on that."

"Care to explain?" He ground his teeth together so hard, the pain shot straight through his skull.

"You don't really love her."

The only thing keeping Alek from smashing in Dima's face was that his twin was the person closest to him, who knew him best, who never sugar-coated his opinion. He might be an irreverent pain in the ass more often than not, yanking Alek's chain to the point that he wanted to throttle him, but when Dima delivered something that sounded like a dressing down? You *listened*. Because he never said stuff like that without reason.

So Alek took a deep breath, fought down the storm of emotions, and carefully relaxed his fists, which were itching to do some damage. "Go ahead. Enlighten me, brother."

"All those talks we had about her," Dima said, cutting through a small city park toward their trucks, "all I heard you say was how much you want her, how you need to court her so she'll mate with you. You go on and on about making her fall for you, making her yours, winning her heart, blah-di-bla-la-la." He waved a hand to illustrate his point.

Mustn't punch him, mustn't punch him, mustn't…

"What I'm missing in there—" his twin hopped over the low fence separating the green space from the parking lot, "—is any kind of acknowledgment of, or interest in, what *she* wants."

Alek paused before following Dima over the fence.

"You don't even see how self-centered your whole attitude is, do you?" Dima leaned against his car, arms crossed, stretching the leather jacket over his shoulders. "Have you ever, even once, considered that turning back into a witch is what she really needs? What she truly wants? You're pursuing her like a slobbering dog runs after a treat, without any care for her needs. That's not love. That's selfish infatuation."

Anger raced through his blood stream, his immediate reaction to reject Dima's accusation. But he knew better. After years of relying on his twin's advice and astute mind to help him analyze sticky situations, he'd learned to trust Dima's judgment and evaluation. Was he right this time, too? He swallowed hard.

"This thing with Lily..." his twin went on, "it can't work if you think of yourself first. Honestly, I can understand why she's reluctant to commit to you. You've shown no real concern for her needs and wants, and you've given her no reason to trust you on a deeper level. Why should she agree to bind herself to a lifetime with you, when your entire act so far has been about getting what *you* want?"

"Damn you..." Alek rasped, rubbing a hand over his face. Damn his twin for being so on point. Because Dima's words wouldn't hurt him like this if they didn't ring with a truth he couldn't deny.

"When you truly love someone," his brother said, his voice gentling, "you put their needs before your own. You care more about their happiness than your own." He pushed away from his car, walked over to him and put one hand on Alek's shoulder. "I want to see you successfully mated as much as you do, Sasha. But if you build a mating on selfish needs rather than true affection and consideration for your partner, it won't be a successful one. When you love someone, you want to ensure they're happy. You don't stand in the way of their happiness." He squeezed Alek's shoulder, gave him a hard look. "You don't sabotage their search for a way to turn back into a witch just because you want to keep them."

"Fuck you," he said, his heart cringing, the words holding no heat. He grasped Dima's shoulder in turn, touched his forehead to his twin's. "I hate it when you're right."

"I know." Dima clasped the nape of Alek's neck, squeezed twice. "It's what I live for."

◈

HUNGER COILED INSIDE LILY. DARK, VORACIOUS, UNRELENTING hunger.

Only this need for sustenance wasn't for food. At least, not the usual kind. She'd just eaten—a huge portion of the lasagna leftover from dinner—so she knew it wasn't her stomach sending those signals.

This kind of hunger was a full-body craving for energy—for *prana*.

She thought she'd still be good until tomorrow, but the breath she gave Alek last night apparently demanded replenishment right the fuck now. One look at the demon signs peeking out from under the top of her blouse—another borrow from Tori, and damn, but she'd have to pay her and Dima back for everything they'd given her already—confirmed her *prana* level was low again. Too low to last the night.

She had just finished folding laundry for Tori in the living room, while the boys were galloping up and down the stairs chasing each other with what looked like toy light sabers, and Tori was upstairs putting Chloe down for a nap when the front door opened and in strode Alek.

Her heart skipped a beat, the knot in her chest easing at the sight of him. She hadn't realized how much she missed him, despite everything. She was rising from the couch when the mirage faded, reality slapping her in the face.

She blinked, recognized the difference in his aura, how his hair was a little shorter. The way he held himself was different enough from the male who tugged at her heartstrings that anyone should notice after a few seconds.

"Hi, Dima," she said, trying not to let her disappointment show.

"Hey, there." He nodded at her then frowned. "You look antsy. Did the boys give you trouble?"

"Oh, no, not at all. It's just—"

Said boys came thundering down the stairs at that moment, having heard their father arrive. They launched themselves at him, raining down complaints about how the light saber fight had escalated over the question of whose turn it was to play with the coveted model of the Millennium Falcon.

"He hit me!"

"He broke my light saber!"

"Oy!" Dima shouted, effectively silencing both kids. His voice lowering to a pitch that was no less authoritative for being quiet, he said, "I want you both to sit down in different rooms and think about why you're mad at each other. I'll come collect you in five minutes, and I want each one of you to tell me what exactly happened, what each of you did, and how it made you feel. And I want you to think about how *either one* of you could have handled the situation in a way that would have made *both* of you happy. Now go."

There was some unintelligible grumbling and whining, but both Jordan and Lucas shuffled off upstairs.

"Impressive," Lily said.

"Parenting." Dima blew out a breath. "It's like a diplomat's job without the great pay." He shrugged, joy lighting up his eyes. "Then again, they *are* cute enough to eat, so I guess that makes up for it."

The front door opened, and Yuri breezed in. He went straight into the kitchen—waving at Dima and giving Lily a beaming smile—rummaged around the fridge, and came back into the living room with a huge sandwich he'd apparently found.

"What's up?" he asked while chewing.

"Lily was just about to tell me."

She heaved a sigh, rubbed her arm. "Well, it's just that I need *prana*, but I'm not—" Swallowing past the growing lump in her throat, she said, "I really don't want to kill again." The darkness inside her, it demanded to be fed, wanted *death*. Greater than that hunger, though, was the fear of giving into it. Could she do it alone? What if she didn't have the control yet?

"Plus," she added, shoving a hand into her hair, "I'm not sure it's a good idea to go out there to hunt when I'm the one who's being hunted by—oh, just the entire witch community, a psychotic *prana*-grouch, and apparently some other demons or who-the-hell-knows what, out to nab me because I'm a successful experiment of some sort."

"You know," Dima said, "I wish I could give you a boost, but I've got just about enough to feed Tori later. She can't make a kill while she's pregnant, so…"

"I'll give you *prana*." Yuri virtually bounced on the balls of his feet.

Lily eyed him. "Are you sure? I don't want to inconvenience you…" *And I don't know how I feel about taking breath from someone who's barely legal.* She inwardly grimaced and looked to Dima for help, but he'd taken out his phone and was busy typing on it.

Yuri skipped closer, his aura vibrating, his face eager. "I'd love to. It's no inconvenience at all."

"Um." She cleared her throat. "I don't know…"

Her mind kept bringing up images of the only male she'd ever want to share that special intimacy with. A pang of longing twisted her heart. It wasn't like she could just go ask Alek if he'd give her *prana*. Considering the way she snubbed him recently, it wouldn't be fair to ask it of him.

Can't have your cake and eat it too.

The dark hunger inside her coiled tighter, made her heart race, and sweat break out all over her. Her hands shook, light-headedness making her dizzy.

"Please," Yuri said, "let me help you. Accept my *pranada*."

Aw, damn, now he was looking at her with those earnest, adoring eyes…eyes that showed none of the maturity of his older brother, none of the power to make her knees wobble. She bit her lip.

Taking her hand, Yuri stepped closer. "You'll honor me."

The vicious hunger bit at her from inside her skin. "Well…okay…"

Yuri leaned toward her. Young as he was, he still topped her by several inches, so she had to crane her head back a little to look up at him. He cupped her face with one hand, warm and comforting, though not the least bit arousing. *As well it shouldn't be.* If she found him hot at all, she'd have *issues.*

She closed her eyes, the need to feed shredding her from the inside. Her lips parted. Yuri's body heat brushed her skin.

A bang, and then a gust of chilly night air blew against her back. Her eyes flew open just as a storm of pissed-off male yanked Yuri away from her. The next second, Alek hauled her into his arms, his breath a touch winded, as if he'd run here from a distance, his body hot and hard and devastatingly *perfect* against hers.

Eyes afire with sparks of red on black, he cradled her head with a gentleness at odds with the naked hunger that was so palpable it almost bit her skin. "I know you want space, and I'm trying to give you that, but fuck if I let anyone else feed you."

His mouth crashed down on hers, and then there was nothing but heat, brutal need, and a passion so stark, so consuming, it razed her down to her foundations. She grabbed on to his shoulders and gave as good as she got, devoured him as much as he did her.

When she felt the tingle of his *prana* on her lips, her tongue, she licked at him—and pulled. His life force flowed into her with a rush of invigorating warmth, spread out into every last cell of her body, setting her aflame. Pleasure a buzz in her blood, she pressed herself against him, wanting to wrap his heat and power around her.

She took all he offered, until he stepped away, his hands on her hips, breath heavy and fast.

Those eyes of fire and night met hers. "You need *prana*, you come to me."

And then he let her go and walked toward the door, leaving her shaking with a need that had nothing to do with *prana*, and everything with the male who'd just kissed the living daylights out of her. She felt the loss of his warmth, his touch, like a physical hurt.

Good gods, I have it bad.

"Alek..." she said on an impulse.

He paused, looked over his shoulder.

Her phone rang, making her wince.

"You should answer that," he said in a tone so quiet it stung her.

Breaking eye contact with Alek, she accepted the call from Merle. "Hey, what's up?"

"Lil, I have some good news and some... Okay, screw this, it's only bad news. Sorry."

Her heart hammered in her chest. "There will be no more seasons of *Portlandia*?"

A sigh on the other end of the line, carrying all the dejection of someone who'd tried until their mind bled—and failed. "We found the right spell to turn you back. It should work well, even without more detailed knowledge about the magic used..."

"Tell me the *but*." Her fingers numb from her death grip on her phone, Lily turned her back on the three male demons still in the same room, and walked over to the side window.

"We're missing one vital ingredient to brew the reversal potion."

A chill went down her spine on icy spider feet. "Don't tell me it's Donald Trump's toupee."

"I don't think he even wears one." Another sigh, the rustle of book pages. "It's a stone, a kind of crystal. It's called *nymphenstern*, and looks simple, but is, like, one of the rarest types of gem ever. So rare that humans don't even know about it. Apparently there's only one place it was ever found, a mountain in the German alps, and it was mined out completely by dwarves three hundred years ago. Only a couple *dozen* stones were ever in circulation, and the last documented one was used in a ritual some twenty years ago. All of us here have been digging around among our resources, but the collective knowledge of witches, demons, and every otherworld creature we've asked is that there's not a single unused *nymphenstern* left."

Lily trembled, inside and out. "What do you mean by unused?"

"The stone naturally holds some magical properties, but when it's used, those powers are drawn out of it, and the stone's color changes from pink to black." She paused, let out a heavy breath. "We need an unused one for the reversal potion."

Which meant that—

"I'm sorry, Lil. There's no way we can brew the potion to turn you back."

I'll never be a witch again. The shock, when it hit her, knocked the wind out of her, arrested her breath like the most expertly thrown solar plexus punch. She grabbed the window sill to steady herself when the floor wobbled. Or was it her legs that were wobbling? The room shrank in on her, and her vision pinpointed to the small scratch in the wall she was facing.

Somewhere on the periphery of her senses, the sound of her phone thudding to the carpeted floor registered. Merle's voice sounded frantic on the other end of the line. Inside her, the hollow that used to hold her witch magic throbbed with excruciating emptiness. Her fucking *soul* ached. If she thought it was bad after she'd been turned into a demon, it was nothing against the pure, unadulterated despair of knowing for sure that she'd lost her identity, had lost what had shaped her all her life.

And she'd never get it back now.

She'd been able to deal—with the generous help of Alek —with being a demon so far, because the buoyant hope of it being temporary had kept her afloat. What composure she had been able to maintain crumbled in the face of the stark reality that she'd remain a demon, the choice taken from her.

She'd have to live out the rest of her life as a *pranagraha* female, killing to survive. A demon, cut off from her family's bloodline, hunted by her former community. Since she couldn't turn back, she'd never be able to face Juneau and her followers in a fair trial, as a witch. They'd prosecute her as the demon she'd become, and no way would the verdict fall in her favor.

Never would she be able to walk among her peers again.

Heart splintering under the implications that just kept on rolling over her in a massive avalanche of loss, her mind locked on to the one thing she could hold on to, the one person whose presence in her life even now soothed the violent waves of despair in her. *Alek.* He'd been there for her all this time, had taken care of her even after she'd pushed him away.

Visceral need for him made her turn around, her heart already reaching out to him—to find him standing in the open door, his face set in harsh lines, his aura a maelstrom of patterns too complex, too rapidly swirling for her to decipher. He shook his head when she opened her mouth to speak.

"Don't," he rasped.

The next second he was gone, the door closing behind him.

<hr/>

ALEK'S HEART BEAT TRIPLE TIME WHILE HE JOGGED AWAY FROM Dima's house, leaving Lily as distraught as he'd ever seen her. His every impulse screamed at him to turn back, to do his damnedest to wipe that expression of despair and mourning from her face, to alleviate the pain she was feeling. To make her happy.

And yet, to accomplish that, he had to leave.

Because, while he stood there listening to what Merle told her on the phone—thanks to his demon hearing, he'd heard every word—as he watched all color and life drain from Lily's face, her aura flood with cold, cold shock, he understood what his twin had tried to tell him. *True love is caring about someone else's happiness more than your own.*

"I get it now, Dima," he muttered when he reached his driveway, hopped into his truck and started the engine.

Lily's happiness didn't lie with him. It hinged upon her turning back into a witch.

That was her heart's desire, the one thing she wanted, needed, more than anything else. He'd only realized *how* much it meant to her when the news she could never have it crushed her like a landslide. To watch her heart break right in front of him because she lost all hope for turning back— that had broken *his* heart.

Lily, his strong, resilient, bounce-back-swinging Lily, reduced to tears and crumbling dreams, her soul smashed by an inescapable alteration she didn't choose. His blood roared with anger at her pain, the need to make it better a pulse underneath his skin, driving him on.

For the first time in his life he truly understood the selflessness mentioned so often when people spoke of love. The desire to see Lily smile again, overwhelmed with joy at being able to turn back into a witch, the need to give her what she so desperately wanted, eclipsed the possessive urges inside him that pushed at him to swoop in, press his advantage, and make her mate with him. Now she knew she had to remain a demon, she'd probably agree. But it wouldn't make her happy, not the way regaining her identity as a witch would.

And so he'd fulfill her heart's desire, even if it broke him.

Because he knew where to find that fucking stone Merle talked about, and he was going to get it for Lily.

CHAPTER 20

The stench of fear permeated the air, so acrid it turned Drake's stomach. Never mind that it was his own.

Above him, the single bare bulb hung from the basement's ceiling, every now and then swinging with the vibrations of the people walking on the upper floor. Sometimes, when someone banged a door above, fine dust would drizzle down on his sweat-slick, blood-encrusted skin.

I'm fucked. That realization should have been a given when Seth's men grabbed him, but he'd held on to the sliver of hope that maybe he'd be able to escape later. He looked again at the magic-infused manacles shackling his arms and legs to the metal table. *Yeah, not very likely.*

The door to the basement opened, and warm light spilled in, before a shadow blocked the view of the hall beyond. The *pranagraha* male closed the door, and his heavy footsteps thudded on the stairs while he descended into the basement.

Stepping into the cone of light from the lone bulb, Seth gave Drake's shackled form a once-over, his blue eyes as cold as glacial ice.

"I see you've stopped struggling against the restraints. Smart." He turned his back on the table, and the clink of metal echoed in the dank room. "Perhaps you're ready to tell me what you did with the serum."

Drake craned his head to see what Seth was picking up from what looked like a small tray on a sideboard along the wall. "I don't know what you're talking about."

"Games." A flash of light glinted off a blade Seth raised to slide over the thumb of his other hand. Blood pooled along the small cut. He licked it off. "Thing is, Drake, *I* enjoy playing. Do you?"

A shiver started deep inside him, spreading outward to rattle the manacles around his wrists. "I didn't do anything. I swear."

"You know me," Seth said, facing the table again, the wicked sharp hunting knife still in his raised hand. "You know not to take me for a fool. You stole the serum. You ran away with it." He waved the blade nonchalantly. "Probably to use it on a witch without our sanction. Was it because you're an especially impatient idiot and didn't want to wait your turn, or is it perhaps that you wanted that particular witch for yourself, and didn't want to risk someone else winning the bid for her?"

Drake gritted his teeth to keep from answering, but of course Seth noticed.

"So that's it." Seth's cold smile sent frost into Drake's veins. "You covet a special witch. Tell me, have you used the serum on her already?"

"I'm not gonna tell you anything." If he did get out of here by some miracle, it wouldn't do to have blabbed about Lily. He could still claim her for himself.

"Oh, you'll talk." He lowered the knife to Drake's

exposed torso, hovering the blade over the soft flesh of his stomach. "Where to cut, where to cut...? Can't damage you too badly yet, or I won't get all the information out of you." He sliced a precise line over Drake's chest, stopping at his collarbone.

Pain fired along Drake's nerves, and he cried out.

"Did you use the serum on a witch?"

Panting, Drake pressed his lips together, refusing to answer.

"Let's try this again," Seth said in a voice so calm, he might as well have been talking about fixing a flat tire.

Again and again the blade cut into Drake's skin until the smell of blood saturated the air, his body crazed with pain from countless wounds.

"Fitting, don't you think," Seth said, as he wiped the hunting knife on a cloth, laid it back down on the tray and picked up a horror-inducing drill of some sort, "that you should bleed on the same table we used to drain the first witch. You should have seen it. Such potent magic, I could almost taste it on my tongue just by inhaling the air down here. Well," he added, turning back to the table, "the last of her blood's gone now, thanks to you." He flicked the terrifying drill with a finger, and muttered more to himself, "We'll need a new witch soon if we want more serum."

When Seth moved to apply the drill to Drake's already mangled arm, Drake yelled, "Stop! Please."

Seth halted, raising one eyebrow. "Did you use the serum?"

"Yes." His lips quivered, a bead of sweat ran down from his forehead.

"Was it successful?"

He nodded.

"Did you mate with her?"

"Yes. Yes, I did."

Ice-blue eyes narrowed. "I don't appreciate being lied to." Seth switched on the drill and bored into bloody flesh.

Drake's scream rended the air. "No!"

The drill stopped. Seth tilted his head. "No?"

Drake shook his head, tears streaming from the sides of his eyes. "I didn't. She's still available."

"Good." The beatific smile on Seth's face contrasted starkly with the blood on his hands. "I see we're getting somewhere. Tell me her name."

"No."

"Drake." Seth's tone was so gentle, almost loving. "Tell me her name, and I will pardon you for your transgression." He petted Drake's sweat-soaked hair, the drill casually hanging from his other hand. "You'll even be allowed to bid on her. Who knows, maybe you'll win?"

Heart thumping wildly against his ribs, he blinked against the tears pooling in his eyes. "Lily," he croaked. "Lily Murray."

"Ah, yes." Seth's eyes flashed with recognition. "An excellent choice. Young and strong. More fire than I'd prefer in a mate, but to each his own, hm?" He put the drill away. "Since you haven't mated with her yet, I assume she escaped your tender care. Where is she currently hiding?"

"I—I don't know for sure. She's with another *pranagraha*. Goes by Alek. I haven't found where he lives yet."

A flicker of anger in Seth's controlled aura. "You let her hook up with another male?" His eyes twitched before he caught himself. "No matter. We'll find her. Now—" He selected an axe from the tray. "Thank you for your cooperation, Drake."

Drake's heart stuttered. "Wait. You said—"

The bulb's yellowish light glinted on the sharp blade as Seth brought it smoothly down on Drake's neck.

CHAPTER 21

An audience with the Demon Lord always involved some form of humiliation. Like being forced to take the scenic lake route, and then showing up before Arawn dripping wet and chilled to the bone.

Alek waded out of the lake and trudged up onto the shore. Pausing for a moment, he shook his head, then peeled off his soaked tee and wrung it hard. Water hit the sand with a muffled splash. *Ten years.* Ten damn years of working for the son of a bitch, and he'd never figured out another way to reach Arawn's lair. And there were other ways. Those closer to the Demon Lord traveled back and forth without arriving soaking wet.

He eyed the crumpled, soggy lump in his hands and grimaced. He'd rather have the cool night air assaulting his bare skin than put that dripping wet T-shirt back on, but appearing topless before the Demon Lord was not an option. Not that Alek had any problem with showing some skin, no. Arawn simply liked to keep his supplicants uncomfortable.

Having to wear soaked clothing to an audience with him would accomplish that nicely. *Bastard.*

He gritted his teeth and pulled the tee back on. Turning to the vast expanse of water, he called, "Thanks, Kalista. I'll be back in a bit."

The nymph who'd taken him through the lake smiled while she swam in lazy circles, her pale skin luminescent in the moon light. "My pleasure. I will wait for you."

Her purr followed him as he set off down the path into the darkness of the forest, conscious of gazes on him, invisible in the dark, guards hidden in the shadows. They let him pass because he was one of Arawn's. Any unwelcome guest would meet a swift death if he dared set foot in the Demon Lord's inner dominion.

At a fork in the trodden path, he paused. Tilting his head to the side he called out, "Anyone kind enough to point me to His Grace?"

Arawn's home in the woods was spread out over winding trails, haunted groves, and an underground maze of tunnels and dens brimming with age-old magic. Unless Alek knew exactly where to find the enigmatic son of a bitch, he might wander for several nights.

"To your right," a female voice answered a second before a wolf shifter in human form emerged on silent feet from the shadows.

A mane of tight dark curls tumbled around a face of bronzed ebony, hazel eyes watching him with the kind of sharp intelligence that made Zaina one of Arawn's elite soldiers. Many had underestimated her in the past because of her gender and petite frame, as Alek had observed on more than one occasion. None of them would ever make that mistake again.

"He's in the clearing by the waterfall," she said, crossing her arms over her chest.

"Thanks." Alek nodded at her and took the path forking off to the right.

The quiet of the forest whispered over his skin as he moved through the trees, the chill of the air penetrating his soaked clothes, seeping into his bones. Well, at least it was September, and some summer warmth still lingered. He'd been summoned to an audience with Arawn in winter once, and his balls had stayed frozen for a good two days.

He now followed the faint dancing lights blinking in and out of sight several yards ahead, and, with the same caution one would use to navigate through the enclosure of a sleeping tiger, he stepped onto the clearing.

The sight that greeted him stopped him dead in his tracks. The Demon Lord stood on a grassy bank in front of a waterfall, illuminated by a slowly swirling swarm of fireflies —next to a grizzly bear the size of an SUV. The moment the bear spotted Alek, it let loose a rumbling growl that echoed in the clearing. The fireflies swirled faster in an uproar. Lips curling back from an impressive set of yellowed teeth, ears flattened against its head, the grizzly rose on its hind legs, its focus locked on Alek.

His heart pounded against his ribs. His muscles tensed to deny the instinct to turn and get the hell out of there. Demon he might be, but he wouldn't stand a chance against a grizzly weighing eight hundred-something pounds.

The bear, however, was not the most powerful predator in the clearing.

Arawn turned to the grizzly, laid his hand on the expanse of its chest, completely unconcerned about the destructive animal force in front of him. The bear stopped growling.

Digging his fingers into the mass of fur, Arawn spoke a word in an unknown language, his voice a rumble in the dark.

With a throaty huff, the grizzly dropped down on all fours again. The fireflies quieted and resumed their lazy swirling. As Arawn's hand stroked over the bear's back, the beast lowered its head and closed its eyes. The night was still for the span of a heartbeat.

An instant later, the grizzly turned and trotted away. The brush still rustled with its retreat when Arawn faced Alek. Always, he seemed to compress the air around him, as if he demanded more space than nature could grant him. Seeing the Demon King out in the open, under the promise of endless sky, was by far more preferable than meeting him in the confines of a room. Out here, there at least was enough air left to breathe.

Even though his build was massive, as if he'd been carved from the first elements that had seeded this world, his form was human still. Well, human enough to walk among people undetected for the wildness of his true nature, although even those not gifted with magic would sense he was *more*. The otherness that imbued all his forms—whether human or animal—would sneak past any ignorance, would leave a niggling sense of discomfort, an instinctual aware- ness of being in the presence of something one should run from. Fast.

"Aleksandr." He inclined his head just the slightest bit, taking in the soaked, dripping condition of Alek's clothes, before he raised his eyes again to pin Alek with the kind of unnerving stare that was the Demon Lord's look of relaxed indifference.

Alek immediately averted his eyes. A consuming rush of

heat infused his blood, centering in his stomach with a swirl of nausea as he went down on one knee against every instinct in his body, and bowed his head. "My lord." Underneath the skin on his fingertips, his claws itched to slide out. Just one slash. One well-aimed slash at the bastard's throat was all he craved.

Only it wouldn't be enough to kill him. And the attempt alone would cost Alek his life.

So he simply got to his feet again, careful not to look into Arawn's eyes. Those eyes of green and gray, of secrets lost in the woods. Others might lower their gaze out of deference. To Alek, it was born of hatred. He had no desire to make eye contact with the monster who had ripped a gaping hole in his family barely a decade ago.

"What brings you here?"

Alek cleared his throat. "I would like to ask you for something."

"Obviously. You would not be here unless you would have me grant you a favor of some kind." It was probably as close as the Demon Lord would come to saying, *Spit it out.*

Here we go. "There is something in your possession that I need." He knew, without a shadow of a doubt, that Arawn had the stone, or at least that he had it at some point, because Alek was the one who delivered it to him. The Demon Lord had sent him on a mission a couple of years back, to retrieve the gem from a fae in payment of a debt. He still remembered the feel of the crystal in his palm, its warmth due to the magic slumbering inside. Its pink color, which he now knew meant it remained unused.

A tilt of the head from Arawn, the movement anything but human. "And what would that be?"

"The *nymphenstern* I brought you a few years ago." He inhaled a heavy breath. "If it's still unused, that is."

The Demon Lord stilled, and the air seemed to freeze around him as well, the fireflies halted in their lazy flight path as if someone had pushed a universal *pause* button. When he spoke, his voice was rough silk over a blade. "Tell me why."

Alek's thoughts raced. How much information could he—should he—offer up to Arawn? If he told him about the witch turnings, it might open a can of worms. What if the Demon Lord decided the idea of transforming witches into *pranagrahas* was so awesome, he wanted to adopt that practice himself?

At first, Alek might have welcomed the fact that Lily had been turned—would still support it if it didn't threaten to break Lily—but the truth was, the whole project was a fundamental violation of the witch victims' identity, body, and integrity. If the knowledge of how to produce the serum fell into Arawn's hands, and he chose to carry it on himself, the consequences would devastate the witch community.

And because he knew it would devastate Lily as well, he struggled to find an explanation that would satisfy Arawn's curiosity without giving too much away.

"It is needed to heal my—" He did a mental double-take, unsure what to call Lily. *Girlfriend* didn't seem to express just how much she meant to him, and yet, *mate* didn't apply—yet, or maybe ever. "The female I love."

"What kind of illness could be cured by the magic of a *nymphenstern*?"

Like a dog with a bone. Just wouldn't let it go, would he? If he lied outright to Arawn's face, the Demon Lord would sniff it out immediately, so he tried to stay with the truth as far as possible. Keeping his aura tightly controlled lest it show the surge of irritation and impatience that racked him, he said in a deliberately bland voice, "Her condition is special and rare. There's a potion that can treat her, and one of the necessary ingredients is an unused *nymphenstern*."

"Who will brew the potion?"

Careful, careful. "I contracted a witch through an acquaintance." It wasn't unheard of for witches to do occasional magic for otherworld beings, sometimes covertly, as in case of dealing with demons, to avoid repercussions in the witch community.

Apparently satisfied with his answer, Arawn turned his back on Alek. A blatant display of the arrogance that lay upon him like an exquisitely tailored cloak—the Demon Lord was so sure of his superiority and power that he didn't even perceive Alek as a danger to him. No predator would turn his back on a real threat.

Alek breathed through his nose to calm himself, pushing down the rage heating his skin by sheer force of will. Soon he could leave.

"I will demand a price for the stone."

Naturally… "I'm aware of that, my lord."

Arawn prowled closer, moving with far too much grace for his powerful frame. The air around him shimmered, as if the fabric of the world itself couldn't decide whether he fit into this plane of existence at all. "Do you know why I assigned you the task of watch duty?"

"No, sire."

"Your term of service with me will soon come to a close."

Like I don't know. There was a countdown on his phone, and—just because he reveled in the physical act—he crossed out the days on the calendar on his fridge as well.

"I had thought," Arawn continued, "to avoid endangering your life with a risky task so close to the completion of your service."

Alek's head jerked back as if slapped. Mind scrambled, he stared at Arawn, speechless for a few seconds. A tingling, unbidden feeling spread in his chest—utterly misdirected, though. Had it been anyone else before him, Alek might have believed those words showed authentic consideration and...respect. But this was Arawn. The same Arawn whose hands were still stained with the blood of Alek's family.

Consideration, my ass.

Muscles sore from the tension, Alek bowed his head, disgust clawing him bloody on the inside. "Thank you for your thoughtfulness—" he bit back the insult that leapt to the tip of his tongue, yearning to be set free. "—my lord."

"You have always been one of my best enforcers, Aleksandr. You have not failed me once."

Only because I know what failing the Demon Lord would get me. Alek had enough self-control—though barely—to swallow that comment before it left his mouth.

"My price," Arawn said, his voice a rumble in the semi-dark of the fireflies' glow, "for giving you the *nymphenstern,* which is unused still, is the continuation of your service to me."

His heart stopped for a moment that seemed far too long, the gloom of night stretching its greedy hands to grab his soul, and pull it under. "For how much longer?" he rasped.

"Until death takes you."

His whole life, serving the one who murdered his parents. Shaking with an inner rage he had no means to vent, he raised his head, met eyes of deepest green and swirling shadows. *For Lily.* "I accept."

FOR WHAT FELT LIKE THE HUNDREDTH TIME THAT NIGHT, LILY called Alek's phone. Pacing in the spare bedroom Dima and Tori had so generously ceded to her, she listened to it ring and ring until the call rolled over to voice mail.

"Where are you?" she whispered, checking her texts. No reply from him.

What was going on? Had she pushed him away too often? He'd still come to her aid when she needed *prana*—Dima admitted later that he had tipped him off, assuming Alek would want to be the one to help her—but then he left without so much as a word while her world shattered to pieces around her.

Neither Dima nor Yuri had any idea where Alek had gone, since he hadn't told them a thing, either. Lily had been about to call Alek right after he left, when her phone rang, Merle checking in on her. She'd apparently been worried as hell when Lily dropped the phone before, and hadn't answered her frantic questions.

And best friend that Merle was, she'd drafted Rhun to track Lily, arriving on Dima's doorstep a little later with her demon mate in tow. All the while, she'd remained on the phone talking to Lily, giving her constant, unwavering emotional support. When Dima opened the door to let a worry-riddled Merle bustle inside, she immediately enfolded Lily in a bone-crushing hug. Tears flowing freely now, Lily allowed herself to feel the full force of the news Merle had given her, mourning the loss of her witch life in the arms of her best friend.

Coming to terms with the unalterable fact that she had to remain a demon for the rest of her life was...the hardest thing she'd ever done. Wait, no, scratch that. The more she thought about it, the more she realized she'd had to do many a thing that had rattled her far more, had left deeper scars in her soul. Like laying to rest all three of her cousins in close succession. Like watching her mom wither away under the relentless taunting of Lily's father, while Lily felt as helpless as if she didn't possess an ounce of magic. Like seeing the damage done to Maeve's psyche, her body, after the wisp of a girl came back from her abduction, and feeling so damn guilty by association because it was her aunt who had done it to Maeve.

So, yeah, accepting that she had to kill to make a living? Didn't seem like the worst compared to that. Especially since she figured she could choose other demons as her prey, those who truly breathed evil. Like those fuckers who had turned her and the other witches. And that unnerving, writhing darkness inside her, that vicious hunger for death and blood and breath...she'd harness that force, and direct it at those who had committed such despicable crimes, simply sucking the life out of them was not enough of a punishment.

Hadn't she already done the same thing when she was still a witch, taken out the lowest of the low demon scum to protect others?

She could deal with this, with the loss of her magic, her former life.

What stung her almost more, though, was the fear that she might also have lost the support—the passionate affection—of the demon who had managed to crack walls she believed to be unassailable. In all the time she spent with Alek, she hadn't wanted to get too close to him, and yet she'd basked in his attention, hadn't she?

Shaking her head at her own selfish complacency, her

muscles buzzing with the need to *do* something, to shake this feeling of helplessness and fatalism, she left the room and went downstairs. Merle and Rhun were sitting on the couch talking with Dima and Tori while the kids played on the floor.

Because both *pranagrahas* would have understandably been wary and defensive about a witch in their home, they accepted Merle's vow to keep their location secret probably only because of Rhun's presence. A witch married—mated— to a demon was a novel thing, and it spoke to the truth of Merle's assurance of safety.

All conversation stopped when Lily came downstairs, five sets of eyes trained on her, with far too much pity in them for Lily's taste. Impotent anger at the fate dealt her, at the ones who'd done this to her—and others—fired her blood, made her grit her teeth.

And speaking of the ones responsible for her predicament... "We need to find those motherf—" a glance at the children on the floor, their young ears eager and listening "—those incredibly inconsiderate and evil guys who did this."

"I agree." Merle's voice cracked with the strain of frustration. "The question is how. We have barely anything to go on."

Right after Alek brought her to Dima last night, Lily called and told Merle what they learned from the *pranagraha* who'd shot her. Merle had immediately started on a search for more information, with Rhun tapping his demon contacts for any rumors about a serum like that, or anyone planning to do something of the magnitude of turning witches into demons. They'd found nothing so far, not even the slightest hint that anything like this was in the works.

Whoever was behind this nefarious scheme had set the operation up with meticulous attention to remaining under the radar.

Lily met Merle's sky blue gaze. "Since we can't find them, we'll have to let them find us—or rather, me." Before Merle could interrupt, Lily raised a hand and went on, "They want me, we know that much. I can play bait. No, listen. Let them come get me, and then Rhun can track me to wherever they take me. That way, we'll at least have a shot at finding their base or more of these bast—um, misguided people—so we can grill them about where the other witches are being held."

Her heart cringed at the thought of any other witches forced into a life and identity they'd never chosen, isolated from their families and community—at the mercy of someone as cold, callous, and truly evil as the ones behind this operation surely had to be.

"If what that *pranagraha* told me is correct," Lily continued, "there's at least one other witch-turned-demon, and, Merle, I can't sit here doing nothing while I know one of us is out there, suffering gods-know-what and—" She broke off, her mind imagining way too vividly what might have happened to a turned witch among *pranagraha* males hellbent on mating.

Merle rose from the couch. "Lil…"

"It's the only way to find them right now, and you know it." She turned to Rhun, nodding at him. "You said you can track me by my demon energy signature. But they don't know that. Which means when they nab me they won't find anything on me that would tip them off that I have a rescue team standing by. They'll think themselves safe. And the whole thing can be quick. You guys will be right behind me, can storm their hideout as soon as they take me inside, and before they know it, we'll have them shut down. They won't even have enough time to do anything to me."

Merle rubbed her forehead, her face troubled. "I don't know, it still sounds risky..."

What followed was a back-and-forth argument about the danger of the mission, but Lily remained adamant, wouldn't back down. She had to get those witches—demons, she corrected with a wince—out, had to stop whoever was behind this from turning more of her kind.

In the end Merle and Rhun conceded. To increase the likelihood that she would be kidnapped, Rhun decided to have his contacts indulge in gossip in known demon hang-outs—especially those frequented by *pranagrahas*, thanks to tips from Dima and Yuri—with the express request for them to casually drop hints about where they'd seen a new female *pranagraha* named Lily who'd had a spat with her lover and apparently had to find a new hidey hole. Judging by how fast the otherworld grapevine usually worked, the information should reach the right ears before the night was over.

"All set," Rhun declared when he walked back into the living room, pocketing his phone. "Bahram says he got word out in the right places. If these *pranagrahas* are sharp enough to pull off a huge coup like this without so much as stirring the waters, they'll be well-connected enough to hear about it, fast."

Lily gave a grim nod. "Time to get started."

"I still don't like it." Merle folded her arms in front of her chest, her forehead set in unhappy lines. "What if someone other than those *pranagrahas* decides you'd make an easy target and wants to grab you?"

"That's a risk I'm willing to take."

Dima, who'd been mostly quiet during the initial discussion, and had only chimed in here and there, blew out a breath. "I'm sure Alek's gonna throw a fit when he finds out about this." Silver-gold eyes identical to the ones that made her heart flutter—and yet lacking the same effect—met hers, a hard glint in them. "He'd never let you go play bait."

"Well," she shot back with more bitterness than she wanted to show, "he's not here, is he?" Nodding at Rhun and Merle, she opened the front door. "Let's go."

They dropped her off a couple of blocks away from the demon bar Rhun and Merle had visited during Maeve's kidnapping, and Lily walked the rest of the way so she wouldn't be seen close to the bar in the company of a witch. Both Merle and Rhun would stalk her from the shadows, ready to pounce should things go horribly wrong. Hazel was on her way to join them. Two Elder witches and a demon should be enough to take on Lily's kidnappers, once they'd tracked her. Any group larger than that would draw too much attention from the otherworld community, as well as from other witches potentially patrolling the area.

After she entered the bar, chatted with the shifter bartender and the demon waitress for a bit, casually asking them about good places where she could hole up at sunrise, she hung out at a table nursing a drink for a while before making her way out again. The bar itself was a neutral ground for otherworld creatures, and the chance of her being abducted was low as long as she stayed inside. She'd lingered long enough to make sure patrons saw her, banking on someone passing along information, since some beings made their living dealing in intel. Given the rumors spread about her already, with hints that she'd show up here, word should have gotten around about where to find her.

She yanked open the heavy front door of the bar and stepped out, past the shifter—feline? He sure smelled like it —who guarded the entrance. The tall, muscled hunk of a man nodded at her, his eyes tracking her every movement while she descended the stairs to the sidewalk.

"Have a good night," she said and waved over her shoulder.

Senses alert, she ambled down the street. Magic lay heavy in the air, the demon wards meant to deter witches and humans from the vicinity of the bar. Her chest constricted with a sting at just another reminder of how her essential nature had changed. *Demon. I'm a demon.* Her mind still stumbled over that, not quite ready to fully embrace and process the fact she'd remain one for the rest of her life.

A blur of white shadows slithered around the corner ahead, and the blood froze in her veins. Shrouded in a white, tattered cloak that undulated in an invisible wind, a soul sucker demon came spider-crawling toward her. It kept creeping closer, until she could make out the rotting skin of its head half-hidden beneath the cowl of its cloak, the mouth perpetually gaping in its readiness to suck souls out of its victims, and eyes of swirling milky white. Finally shaking off her paralysis, she was about to run for the hills when it skulked past her.

Past her.

Because soul suckers only fed on humans, not other demons.

Her breath left her on a wave of relief that almost buckled her knees. Throwing a glance over her shoulder— the soul sucker entered the bar—she walked on. The street lay empty ahead of her, nothing else moving.

At least not overtly.

In the alley between two buildings across the street, there was a small flicker of movement, someone trying hard not to be seen.

All righty. Pretending not to notice, Lily continued on her way, also playing oblivious when she felt a presence following her from some distance behind. Her feigned cluelessness went so far that—*gasp*—she was *totally* surprised when someone grabbed her from behind.

Noting the trace of *pranagraha* in her attackers' auras, she held back some of her strength. She still put up a fight, since it would arouse suspicion if she was captured too easily, but her struggle was half-hearted enough that the three *pranagrahas*—they sure didn't fuck around, did they? Sending that many males against a single female—overpowered her quickly.

One of the brutes clapped a filthy, callused hand over her mouth so her screams wouldn't alert anyone nearby, and they dragged her behind a fence and into a courtyard where a van sat idling. Another of the males opened the back while the other two heaved her inside, never letting go of the grip they had on her wrists.

"Stuff a rag in her yap and search her," the black-haired male who'd opened the van—apparently the Leading Asshole—said as soon as he closed the door behind him.

One of the bastards gagged her with a piece of cloth he tied behind her head. What followed was a humiliating patdown of the sexual harassment sort, and she cataloged the faces of those two assholes while she had to lie there and take it. When Merle and the others took them all down, she'd make sure these two were hers to kill. And she'd use the drive to their base to think up fun, creative ways to deliver their death.

The brown-haired son of a bitch with a scar on his neck handed her phone over to Leading Asshole. "No sign of magical trackers on her."

Leading Asshole opened the door, threw out the phone, and then rapped on the division to the driver's cabin. "Let's go."

She gritted her teeth to suppress a growl. That phone had been new. *When I'm done with your lackeys,* she thought the moment the van started rolling, *you'll be next, fucker.*

CHAPTER 22

Shaking the water from his hair, Alek jogged back to his truck, the cool night air seeping through his soaked clothes, his wet skin. When he reached his vehicle, he set the *nymphenstern* on the pickup's bed, opened the tool box, and pulled out the towel and change of clothing he always kept there for visits to Arawn. With speedy efficiency he stripped, dried himself, and put on the fresh set of clothes.

Nymphenstern securely tucked in his jeans pocket, he hopped into the driver's seat and checked his phone, which he'd stored in the glove compartment for his audience with the Demon Lord. His heart jumped into his throat. There were several missed calls from Lily as well as Dima, and text messages from both, asking him where he was.

Lily's face before he left flashed through his mind, the utter despair, the tears glistening in her eyes, the hurt confusion when she saw him back out the door. She'd needed him, had reached out to him, not understanding what he had to do. And he couldn't explain it to her.

He hadn't been sure he'd be able to get the *nymphen-*

stern—unused, to boot—and the last thing he wanted was to get her hopes up, only to have to smash them again, should it turn out Arawn wouldn't give him the stone, or it had already been depleted. He'd just watched her heart break in front of him—he would not have been able to watch it a second time if he'd returned from Arawn empty-handed.

Now, he didn't hesitate before tapping the button to call her back. He listened to it ring, his mind scrambling for the right words to tell her the news. The call rolled over to voice mail. Frowning, he dialed again. No answer.

With a sinking feeling, he called Dima. He picked up on the second ring.

"Sasha, where the fu—" Dima cleared his throat. "—fudge are you?"

"Fudge!" Lucas shouted in the background.

"On my way back from Arawn. What's going on?"

"I could ask you the same thing. What the hedge were you doing, leaving like that? Did Arawn summon you?"

"Hedgehog!" Lucas sounded closer to the phone now. "Can we have fudge?"

"Later," Dima said. "Go play with your brother."

"I had to get something for Lily." Alek started the truck and maneuvered down the dirt forest road while holding the phone to his hear. He briefly explained the whole thing to Dima, whose laden exhale tickled all of Alek's warning senses. "Dima, what happened?"

What his twin told him raised not only the hair on his nape but his blood pressure as well. His grip on the phone so tight the device threatened to crack, he clenched his jaw and sucked in a deep breath through his nose. "And you didn't stop her?"

"Sorry," his brother drawled. "I was all out of rope to tie her up with."

His other hand gripped the steering wheel so tight, his knuckles whitened. "Where did they go?"

"You going to rush after her if I tell you?"

"Do I even have to answer that?"

A sigh on the other end of the line. "Fine. From what I heard, they planned it to go down near *Gehenna*."

"Thanks."

"Sasha," Dima said right before he wanted to disconnect the call.

"Yeah?"

"Don't get killed."

"I won't. After all, I still need to whip your ass for letting Lily get away."

❦

MERLE WATCHED A DARK BLUE VAN LEAVE THE FENCED courtyard where the *pranagrahas* had dragged Lily. Her muscles itched to run after her best friend, her magic tickling along her nerve endings, ready to strike.

She glanced at the demon crouching next to her, his dark aura a caress she felt deep in her soul. "Is she in there?"

Rhun nodded, a lock of his chestnut hair sliding onto his forehead. "Positive."

"Let's give them a head start while we wait for Hazel." It wouldn't do to tail the van right away. If the demons sniffed so much as a hint that they were followed, it would jeopardize the whole mission. She blew out a breath. "I *still* don't like this."

"I know." His warm hand on her nape, squeezing, comforting.

"What if they *hurt* her, Rhun?" Visions of Lily in pain flashed in her mind, of her suffering at the hands of these cruel bastards, her body beaten, broken, bloodied—images of another bruised and ruined body surfaced. Memories of a scene that was burnt into her retinas, would haunt her for the rest of her life.

"She's not Maeve," Rhun said, massaging her neck. "Lily knows how to fight, even without her witch magic. She's tougher than a bag of nails, and strong enough to handle this situation."

She arched a brow at her darling demon. "If I didn't know better, I'd think you actually like her."

"What I'm trying to say—" Rhun straightened, enunciating each word clearly. "—is that after a few minutes alone with her, these guys will probably throw her at us when we come in. Hey, we may even get some money from them for taking her back."

That earned him a hearty smack on his shoulder. He shot her a wicked grin that quickly melted as he cocked his head, as though listening.

"Hazel's coming," he said, nodding toward the other end of the alley they were using as their vantage point. Turning, he frowned. "And she's not alone."

And, sure enough, shortly after Hazel rounded the corner, another shape followed her. Merle rose from her crouch, her magic buzzing closer to the surface, before she recognized the man behind the other Elder witch.

"Basil."

Rhun stood as well. "I thought he was supposed to stay at the house."

At Merle's mention of her son's name, Hazel stopped and whirled around. "What are you doing here?" Agitated power pulsed around the older witch.

In the low light of the nearby street lamp, his hair shone like gold silk, a stark contrast to his hardening features. "I'm not going to sit at home doing nothing while you're out here fighting."

"Basil," Hazel said, her voice measured calm, "you don't have any magic, and you're slower and weaker than any of the demons we're going to fight. I won't have you walk into harm's way when you're so ill-equipped to face it."

A muscle feathered in his cheek. "I can fight. I've been on patrols with Lily and never had a problem holding my own."

"This is different." Hazel clenched her hands to fists.

"I can wield knives better than any of you, and with the bow and arrow, I can cover you from a distance, so I won't be in the thick of things."

Merle took in the quiver of arrows visible over his shoulder, and the bow Basil clutched in one hand. More than likely, he'd also strapped several knives and daggers in strategic places on his body.

Rhun leaned in, his breath hot and tingling at her ear, as he asked in a low voice, "He doesn't use firearms?"

She shook her head, the movement brushing her cheek against Rhun's lips, sending a thrill down her neck. "They don't work on him, either."

As one of the peculiarities of the magic that lived and breathed in witches and otherworld creatures, it somehow didn't *like* firearms. When a magical being tried to use a gun, the weapon simply didn't work—or worse, it backfired or exploded. If witches or otherworld beings wanted to use weaponry, they had to resort to pre-gunpowder arms. A small price to pay for the power that already pulsed in their blood.

"But he's human," Rhun muttered.

Shrugging, she whispered, "We've never fully figured out why, but we think maybe he still has enough magic in his blood to interfere with fire-powered weaponry."

"Hm."

Hazel stepped toward her son. "Go home. Please."

Basil glared at her, eyes hard. "She's my sister. I *will* be there to help her out."

Hazel's aura flickered with some strange emotion for a second, but then she caught herself and shook her head.

Merle cleared her throat before the other Elder witch could speak. "Let him come with us."

Her eyes met Basil's, and an understanding passed between them. Not too long ago, Merle had fought the same argument—stripped of her powers, weakened, and *human*, she'd gone toe-to-toe with Rhun about joining him to free her kidnapped sister.

Now she put a hand on Hazel's shoulder. "He deserves a part in this."

After a moment, the head of the Murray line gave a tight nod. "Stay as close as necessary for shooting range, and as far away as possible to avoid a close fight."

The tension leaked out of Basil's shoulders and he took a deep breath.

"Hi, man," Rhun said, "good to see you with us. But, hey, you should really have a doctor look at that. Or a healer witch."

Basil narrowed his eyes. "Look at what?"

"That..." Rhun gestured at Baz's head. "You know..." He winced. "Oh, wait—that's your face."

Merle put a hand on Basil's chest to stop him from lunging at Rhun. "Let's start tracking," she told her misbehaving demon through clenched teeth.

Rhun whirled toward the entrance of the alley, his aura snapping taut like a rope. "We've got company."

Power bucking inside her, tingling at her fingertips, she pivoted and assumed a fighting stance. Behind her, Hazel's magic crackled in the air, and the sound of an arrow being drawn whispered through the night.

Juneau Laroche slowly emerged from around the corner, flanked by four more witches, their magic drawn tight around them. Silver hair glinting in the lamplight, Juneau raised her chin. Slight of build, her movements betraying her age, she was nevertheless a force to be reckoned with. Her power drenched the air, filled every nook and cranny of the alley, slithered over Merle's skin.

"Hazel," Juneau said. "Merle." Ignoring the two males also present, the Elder witch continued her speech. "It's time to stop this foolishness. You've played your game long enough, and it's time for you to pay due respect to our laws and hand Lily over." Her deep green eyes narrowed. "I know you're harboring her somewhere, so don't pretend you're oblivious."

"Will you strike me, Juneau?" Hazel stepped forward, her move subtly shielding Basil. "I have broken no laws. Any aggressive action on your part would be an unsanctioned attack against a fellow witch—the same crime you're accusing my daughter of." Hazel turned to the witches flanking Juneau. "Thea, Catarina, Eva, Birgit—are you truly willing to violate our most sacred law?"

Catarina and Birgit exchanged a glance and shifted their weight, but Juneau's voice—booming at a volume at odds with her small stature—rang out, made both witches flinch and stand at attention again.

"Our laws," Juneau said, "do sanction action against those who hurt our community. Whether by harming one of our own—" her attention feathered from Hazel to Merle, then locked on to Rhun "—or by subverting our way of life and the traditions we live by." Her voice dropped to a harsh whisper, though it echoed in Merle's head like a shout. "We have been tolerant for far too long. These digressions cannot be allowed to continue, or they will destroy us. Demons are forged of evil, and there is nothing redeeming about any of them. We should not delude ourselves into thinking we can categorize them in shades of gray, when they are nothing but darkness."

"See," Rhun said to Juneau from his spot beside Merle, "this is what happens when you hold in your farts. All that gassy air bubbles up and fills your head, and then when you open your mouth to speak, instead of sensible words, all you utter are verbal farts." He made little bubbling sounds and wiggled his fingers in front of his mouth. "So, please, next time you feel like saying something, do us all the favor and just fart. Let it rip. It'll still be more palatable than your usual oral flatulence."

Rhun! Merle shrieked along their mental connection. *Are you batshit insane? You can't say that to the most powerful Elder witch.*

Come on, we're all thinking it. And someone needs to take her down a peg. Besides, I don't think she's the most powerful Elder anymore. He made a meaningful pause, stroked her along the glowing thread that was their mating bond, such pride behind the caress. *And Juneau knows it.*

She couldn't help the soft gasp that escaped her. *So you think that's what this is about?*

Those used to power tend to get testy when it slips away from them, Merle mine.

Juneau's magic grew into a buzzing crescendo, her eyes fixed on Rhun with a wild, murderous glint.

Gritting her teeth, Merle moved in front of her demon. "Hurt him, and I'll make your heart explode in your chest."

"If I were you, Juneau," Rhun said quietly, stepping beside her again. "I wouldn't doubt Merle can do it. Just ask Isabel. Oh—" One of his hands flew up to his mouth, his eyes widening in mock dismay. "That's right. She's dead."

Rhun, Merle growled mentally. *You're not helping.*

Well, she is beyond all help, little wi—

Rhun's voice in her head died as he sputtered blood, collapsing to the ground, Juneau's spell as silent as it was deadly.

"Rhun!" Merle threw a wave of power outward to cover them both as she sank to her knees next to her mate.

Around her, all hell broke loose, spells and arrows flying. She barely noticed. Pulling up a temporary wall of energy that would shield her and Rhun, she placed her hands on his body, sank her magic into him.

Don't leave me, Rhun, she whispered along the shared pathway between their minds, healing power pulsing into him, trying to repair whatever Juneau's spell had torn. *You can't leave me.*

Her plea was met with silence.

CHAPTER 23

They should be here by now.

Staring at the digital clock on the nightstand, Lily clenched her jaw, her heart pounding in her chest. Her hands and feet were tied, the rope also fastened to the headboard of the bed the brutes had thrown her on after dragging her into the house, so Lily had no way to get free. It had surprised her how normal the house seemed, with nice if bland-looking furniture straight out of a catalog, and a level of cleanliness suggesting that either whoever lived here had some OCD going on, or this was a model home in a new community.

She tried—again—to loosen her bonds. To no avail.

Honestly, where were Merle and the others? They shouldn't need this long to track her.

Sounds of movement in the hall. She snapped her head up, her body tensing for whatever—whoever—was coming. The door to the room opened, and two demons slipped inside—female demons.

Lily's jaw dropped when she recognized the two witches

who'd gone missing a few weeks back. Well, they weren't witches anymore. Turned like her, they had the unmistakable aura of *pranagrahas*, and the swirling signs of their demon markings adorned their upper arms and the skin above their necklines.

"Aveline," Lily whispered, meeting the eyes of the fair-haired, blue-eyed witch-turned-demon, youngest daughter of the Novak family. She just started college when she disappeared without a trace.

Lily's eyes darted to the other witch-turned-demon, whose normally brown complexion had taken on a pallor, as if she was suffering from some sickness. "Sarai."

Like Lily, Sarai had been next in line to inherit her family's magic, had been groomed since birth to one day become head of the Roth bloodline. With no siblings or cousins, that bloodline had now been severed.

Aveline's eyes shimmered as she stepped up to the bed and unfastened Lily's ties, her porcelain skin even paler than usual, echoing Sarai's loss of color. Both witches-turned-demons looked as miserable as withering plants denied sunlight.

As soon as her hands were free, Lily pulled the younger female into a hug. She'd never been close to either Aveline or Sarai, since their families were only loosely connected within the witch community, but what had happened to all three of them now forged a bond that lay heavy among them, regret and anger at a destiny none of them had chosen.

Aveline exhaled a shuddering breath and turned away, sniffing, while Lily hugged Sarai, too. No words. There were no words for the magnitude of this crime.

When they separated, Lily swallowed past the lump in her throat. "Are there any others? Like us?"

Sarai shook her head. "Just the three of us. They had more in the beginning, but they died when they injected them with an earlier version of the serum." A muscle twitched in her jaw. "Apparently it took them a few tries to get the dose right."

The other missing witches... So the locator spells for them had failed because they'd already been dead. She closed her eyes for a second. "Merle and my mom are coming to get us out of here. They should be here any minute. We should start getting ready to kill these fuckers and bail."

Aveline and Sarai exchanged a glance that raised the hair on Lily's neck.

"What?" she asked, her heart thundering.

"We're—" Aveline began then broke off, her throat working as she swallowed hard. Her aura oscillated with shame and fear.

"Mated," Sarai finished. Her sea-green eyes held a hard glint. "They made each of us mate with one of them. If we kill them—"

"You'll die, too," Lily rasped.

Mouth in a grim line, Sarai nodded, her mahogany curls bobbing. "And if we run, they'll find us through the mating bond. We're fucked for life, Lily. Because the greatest part of all this? Mated females need *prana* from their partners every night."

Lily frowned. "Wait. So you don't have to kill?"

"Oh, we do. This nice little tidbit is just in addition to our need to take someone's life force. Once mated, females need to sample their partner's *prana*. But not by breath or blood."

"How...?"

A bitter hardness twisted Sarai's features, the intensity of it hinting at the answer even before the other witch-turned-demon spoke. "Wanna guess what else besides breath or blood carries *prana*?"

Lily's hands fisted, her stomach roiling with a combustible mix of nausea and fury. "You have to have sex with them."

Aveline whimpered and turned away.

Muscles twitched in Sarai's cheeks, her energy pattern a contained storm of hatred. "So even if we locked them up instead of killing them to keep us alive, we'd have to go to them. Every. Damn. Night."

Lily's breath left her on a hollow sound of horror, her heart heavy, so heavy at the two lives ruined. She was struggling for something to say just as the door flew open and in strode Asshole Leader from the van.

Aveline flinched and visibly shrank in on herself, and even without confirmation, Lily knew the black-haired bastard was Aveline's mate. His ice-blue eyes darted to each of them, then locked onto the petite witch-turned-demon cowering against the wall. His upper lip peeled away from his teeth as he stalked toward her, grabbed her hair, and slapped her. Aveline yelped and closed her eyes, her small frame trembling as much as her aura.

"You were supposed to get her ready," the male demon snarled, "not hold a happy-sappy reunion."

Red-hot rage slamming down over her vision, Lily lunged at the bastard. She got one good kick in before pain sliced across her side, making her jump back. Blood—her blood—coated the dagger Asshole Leader was pointing at her. Another *pranagraha* had entered the room, restraining a fuming Sarai.

One side of Asshole Leader's mouth tipped up as he held

the blade in one hand, his other still gripping Aveline's hair, making her wince. "I don't mind etching a few new markings into your skin," he said to Lily, his voice as cold as his eyes. "But I'd rather have you intact for the ceremony, so your future mate can enjoy you unspoiled."

Lily's stomach dropped to her feet. *Oh, hell no.* If those sick fuckers thought they could mate her off like that, they were dumber than a sack of dirt. She glanced at the digital clock, and dread curdled her blood.

Where are you, Merle?

⚅⚄

THE SOUNDS OF FIGHTING REACHED ALEK BEFORE HE EVEN MADE it to *Gehenna.* Two blocks from the demon bar, the night sky was lit up with magic, power cracking the air like lightning. Invisible and undetectable to humans, for otherworld creatures this kind of power display had the same effect as a cacophony of human noise had on forest animals—they scurried away in utter terror.

And sure enough, the area around the fight was so blatantly devoid of any otherworld creature presence, it almost felt forsaken.

Alek parked his truck a street away and jogged closer, peeked around the corner into the midst of what appeared to be...a battle between witches? Merle, Hazel, and Basil faced off against Juneau Laroche and two other witches, using parked cars and recessed doorways as cover while they hurled spells at each other. Two more witches lay unmoving on the street and sidewalk, an arrow protruding from the chest of one of them.

Well, hell. Fight to the death it was, then.

Given the lethal nature of the conflict and the time ticking away for Lily, he felt no remorse when he sprinted with his demon speed to the nearest of Juneau's witches—who'd just shot a spell at Merle from the shadow of a van—and snapped her neck like a twig. She crumpled to the pavement.

While he avoided the witch's spell with a duck-and-roll, Merle spotted him behind the van. She gave him a grim nod and shot to her feet again, throwing out some form of short-lived shield to block an incoming charm.

"You're down to two, Juneau," she yelled as she dove for cover in a doorway. "Stop this fucking madness before more of us have to die."

Silence echoed between the houses, all spells and arrows halted. Still, power hung in the air, palpable and thick as humid summer heat. It pulsed and crackled, and Alek could taste the charge with every breath he took. If he didn't have a stake in this conflict, he'd have fled like all the other other-world creatures.

"You will pay for their deaths." Juneau's voice, a terrifying whisper magnified and creeping along the pavement, the walls, raising all the hairs on his body.

Peeking out from behind the van, he caught a glimpse of Juneau and the remaining witch running away.

"Their blood is on *your* hands," Merle yelled after them, stepping out of the doorway. Hands clenched so tight her knuckles flashed white, she added in a hoarse whisper, "I didn't start this insane fight. I never wanted any of this."

Tears glistened in her eyes as she looked at the fallen witches. Inhaling a shuddering breath, she walked to the nearest one, closed the dead woman's eyes, and muttered a prayer with her hand over the witch's heart.

"Travel well," she whispered, her hand shaking as she pulled it back and stood. "Hazel?" she asked as she wiped her eyes.

"I've got them." The other Elder witch approached the second of the fallen.

Merle nodded and turned to Alek. "You here to help us with Lily?"

"Yes."

"We have a problem."

Gesturing for both Hazel and Basil to stand down as Alek emerged from behind the van, she briefly explained who he was, then beckoned him to follow as she jogged to the mouth of an alley a few yards back. There, behind a dumpster, she crouched next to the slumped form of Rhun, stroking his hair away from his face.

"He won't wake up," she said, her voice cracking. "I've healed all his injuries as far as I could detect them, and I keep trying to nudge him mentally, but he's just...shut off."

And with him, the only way to find Lily.

CHAPTER 24

Forced into a glittering black and red nightmare of a dress that was as tacky as it was ridiculous, Lily walked down the hall in front of Seth, otherwise known as Leading Asshole, her hands tied again, this time behind her back.

"Tell me," she said, flicking a glance over her shoulder and indicating the hideous dress, "did you ask Madonna's permission before you raided her 80s wardrobe?"

He shoved her, making her stumble and crash down face-first on the carpeted floor. It still hurt like hell, since she couldn't break her fall with her hands, and the recent wound from when he'd slashed her with his dagger started stinging again. *Motherfucker.* She should have kept her mouth shut, but when it came to sadistic bastards like him, she couldn't resist the compulsion to poke at him.

"How's your side?" he asked with a saccharine smile while she struggled to her feet again, the process clumsy and humiliating with her hands still bound behind her back.

"Peachy," she said when she faced him again. "How's your lip?"

His glacier-colored eyes narrowed on her as he licked the bloody cut on his lower lip where her knee had connected while she fought against putting on this pathetic excuse for a dress. She'd lost, but so had his lip. She grinned with grim satisfaction.

"Move it," he snapped, and pushed her forward.

He led her down a sweeping staircase into a foyer and the lofty living room next to it. High windows covered with heavy dark blue drapes dominated two walls, and elegant black leather furniture filled the room—as well as a veritable horde of *pranagrahas* who mingled on said furniture. There had to be at least a dozen demons in here, and their eyes followed her every move with the unnerving hunger of starved animals.

Fear pricked her rage-hardened composure, and she had to struggle to keep it from showing in her aura. Merle and the others would be here any minute. All she had to do was stall as long as possible. And fight like a lunatic if they tried to force her into a mating.

I can do this. Deep breath in, long breath out. From what she'd pieced together, females had to actually *agree* to a mating, and she'd rather bleed to death than hand her freedom over to one of these Neanderthals.

Seth-with-the-busted-lip hauled her to a stop in front of the crowd of demons, his grip on her arm tight enough to make her clench her teeth to keep from whimpering.

"Gentlemen," he intoned, "without further ado, I present to you our newest addition, the lovely Lily. A bit prickly, no doubt, but all the more enticing a challenge for the right male. Hours of fun bringing her to heel. Bids start at five hundred thousand dollars."

She whipped her head around to glare at Leading Asshole. They were *auctioning* her? Just when she'd thought they couldn't sink any lower...

Males shouted their bids, the room heating with rising testosterone and bitter competition. Where the fuck did they even get the amounts of money they were bidding? Did they use their mind tricks to embezzle those funds from humans? Locking her knees so she wouldn't fidget and shift her weight under the force of the *pranagrahas'* stares, she watched while more and more demons dropped out of the auction, leaving only two, both with hints of cruelty in their eyes that soured her insides.

"Five million," Seth-with-a-death-wish called out. "Do you want to up to six, Jaxton?"

The male in question nodded, gray eyes fixed on her. He looked close to drooling. *Ew.*

"Six million. Greg?"

Jaw clenched hard, Greg shook his head, his nostrils flaring.

"Sold for six million dollars to Jaxton." Seth-on-the-highway-to-hell clapped his hands, a radiant smile on his face that she wanted to wipe off. With sandpaper. "Jaxton, my man, come claim your prize."

Lily's lip curled when the burly male stepped up to her, already stripping her with his roaming eyes. She barely heard Leading Asshole's pep talk to the rest of the desperately underfucked males, yammering on about how they'd soon get their turn with the next batch of witches, most of her attention on the nauseating demon who'd bought her.

Bought her, like a piece of flesh. Which was all she was to him and the others, of course.

Jaxton grabbed her face and squeezed, leaning in until his acrid breath fanned against her mouth and nose. "Submit to me now, and I'll go easy on you."

She gritted her teeth so hard, her body tensed all the way down to her toes. "Let me go now, and I won't bite off your fingers," she ground out.

He sneered but didn't release her. "Feisty."

"Stupid," she shot back—and wrenched her head to the side so fast she broke his hold and snapped back to his hand before he could withdraw. Her teeth clamped down on his knuckles with all the force of her demon power, cutting through tendon, sinew, muscle and joints.

Howling, he punched her in the side of her head. The blow knocked her back and—to her glowing delight— helped her rip off his phalanges. Blood sprayed on her face as she stumbled to keep her balance. Jaxton clasped his ruined right hand with his left, his teeth bared at her. She spit the two digits she'd bitten off onto the floor and grinned, savoring the taste of his blood in her mouth.

Seth-with-an-ego-problem grabbed her around her neck, his claws slicing out to prick her skin. "What the fuck do you think you're doing?"

"Snacking," she choked out, her hands reflexively struggling against the ties. "I get bitey when I'm not fed."

Jaxton growled at her, his eyes promising a lifetime of torture.

A muscle ticked in Seth-suffering-from-halitosis's jaw. "Let's cut this short."

He dragged her down the hall into a bedroom at the back of the house, and threw her on the floor. The laceration in her side screamed bloody murder as she crashed down, and she gingerly rolled to a sitting position. Jaxton strode into the room, bandaging his wounded hand.

"Aveline!" Seth bellowed.

Oh, no. Dread icing her blood in chilly foreboding, Lily stared at the door. A minute later, the wispy witch-turned-demon appeared, chewing on her nails, green eyes wide. She dropped her hand the second Leading Asshole focused on her.

"Close the door," he said in voice that was all the more horrifying for how calm it was.

Aveline hurried to comply, her aura betraying her terror. Seth struck her the moment she turned back. Crying out, she slammed against the closed door.

"No!" Lily struggled against her bonds, staggered to her feet.

Jaxton clamped his good hand around her neck and squeezed, holding her back when she wanted to launch herself at Leading Asshole.

Seth-will-soon-burn-in-hell hit Aveline again, so hard the door rattled. Sobbing, she raised her arms to shield her head and curled into herself. Fury burned through Lily with the force of a razing firestorm. Baring her teeth, she snarled at him, her powerlessness corrosive acid in her veins.

Seth unsheathed his dagger with a whisper of sound that made her heart stutter. Grabbing a fistful of Aveline's hair, he made as if to slice her back open.

"Stop!" Lily writhed in Jaxton's grip. "Please."

A cold look from Seth, not a hint of compunction or mercy on his face, in his aura. "Are you willing to comply?"

Lily glanced at the trembling form of Aveline, and her heart lurched to her feet. If she'd wondered before how anyone could be forced into a mating, she had her answer now. If it had been only her, she'd have fought and endured and suffered rather than agree. She could take pain.

But Aveline...she swallowed hard, her throat dry as desert sand. Hot tears pricked at the back of her eyes. She couldn't watch Aveline be tortured in front of her.

"Please don't hurt her," she whispered.

He twirled the dagger in his hand, the sharp blade catching the light. "I won't if you're cooperative. Will you be a good girl and accept Jaxton as your mate?"

She slumped in Jaxton's hold. "Yes."

ALEK PACED THE LENGTH OF THE ALLEY, BACK AND FORTH, BACK and forth. Anxiety skittered across his nerves, his skin taut with the pressure of time ticking away. Time Lily didn't have much more of. He punched the dumpster, the material bending with a metallic groan under the force of his blow.

"Keep it down, will you?"

At the slurred male voice—not Basil's—Alek whipped around.

Rhun was heaving himself into a more upright position, his face a mask of pain. "Some people have a headache the size of Africa, and would appreciate it if you didn't demon-handle the dumpsters."

"Rhun!" Merle practically jumped him.

"The same goes for squealing, little witch," he choked out around her tight hug. But his arms closed around her, and he turned his face into her hair, inhaling deeply. Some of the pain left his face, his aura. He looked at peace.

A pang of longing in Alek's chest, his thoughts returning

to the raven-haired female with indigo eyes who'd stolen his heart, his soul. To the bitter fact that, even when they freed her from the *pranagraha* bastards who held her, he'd never have with her what Rhun had with Merle. Lily would never look at him in quite that way.

The *nymphenstern* lay heavy in his jeans pocket. He'd give her that, at least. If she couldn't find her happiness with him, he'd help her achieve it without him.

"Can you track her?" he asked Rhun, who was getting to his feet.

The other demon closed his eyes, his aura turning inward. "Yes," he said after a moment, opening his eyes again, which were now a glowing a pale green. He jerked his head toward the other end of the alley. "That way."

Merle, Hazel, and Rhun got into Merle's car, while Basil opted to ride with Alek in his truck. They'd been on the road for a few minutes, Alek making sure he followed the other vehicle closely, when Basil spoke up.

"So you're with my sister." Tension twined into his words.

"I was wondering when you'd ask me about that."

Basil gave him a silent glance heavy with meaning.

Taking a deep breath, Alek said, "If by *with her*, you mean love her until I'd give my own hide to save her, then yes. If by *with her*, you mean involved in a committed relationship, then no. I'd love to, but your sister is very clear on her boundaries, and being with me is not what will make her happy." He took out the *nymphenstern* from his pocket. "So I got her this."

Basil sucked in a breath then exhaled through his teeth. "How did you get that?"

He pocketed it again. "Doesn't matter. What matters is

that she'll be able to turn back, and then I won't be any of your—or her—concern anymore."

"So you'll just give her the stone and leave?"

His jaw locked. "Yes."

Silence stretched between them. Then, "Are you sure that's what she wants?"

He shot a look at Basil. The other male stared out of the side window, his face half-hidden and unreadable. His aura —hard to decipher for a human energy pattern—didn't give much more away either.

"I'm positive," Alek said. "I watched her fall apart when Merle told her she wouldn't be able to turn back."

"Doesn't mean turning back is more important to her than staying with you." Eyes of rich brown met his. "Just a tip—if you still want her, don't just drop off the stone and leave. Give her the choice, but let her know how much you still want her. She'll need that reassurance."

Considering the tight bond between the twin siblings, Alek didn't doubt the accuracy of Basil's assessment. But— "Why are you helping me? Shouldn't you want your sister to turn back into a witch?"

"If I only cared about our bloodline's continuity, yeah." He shrugged. "But that's not the only factor here. And I don't think it's the most important. We've talked on the phone a lot, Lily and I." A sideways glance from those eyes that almost…almost carried a hint at something more than human. Did he inherit some witch magic, after all? "The way she talks about you… I've never heard her sound like that about any other guy she's been with."

The biting jealousy at the thought of Lily in the arms of any other male didn't care that it lay in the past. Alek fought the feeling down, his hands squeezing the steering wheel as a sad substitute for the necks of the males who came before him.

"I think," Basil slowly said, as if coming to terms with voicing an unpopular truth, "you would be good for her."

"If she'll let me," he murmured.

"What do you know about our parents' relationship?"

He frowned at the change of subject. "Not much. Your father died a few years back."

Basil snorted. "He didn't just die. Aunt Isabel killed him."

"What?" He whipped his head around to stare at Lily's twin.

"Well, it was never proven, and she didn't admit it, but everybody knew. Just like everybody knows why she did it."

Everybody in the witch community, it seemed. None of this had leaked outside. "Tell me."

"He was an insecure, controlling ass, insanely jealous, and he verbally abused our mom for years." His bitter tone left no doubt Basil had little love for his late father, and didn't mourn his death. "He never lifted a finger to hurt her physically, but he smothered her in every other way he could. He controlled every step she took, to the point that she couldn't leave the house or make a phone call without his permission."

"But your mother—"

"Given her powers as a witch, she could have easily put a stop to his taunting and control issues. But for whatever reason, she never stood up to him. Aunt Isabel said..." A heavy sigh. "They argued sometimes, Isabel and Mom, when our father wasn't home. Always, Isabel would lambaste our mom for letting him treat her like that. And always, Mom would tell her to stand down, making excuses for his behavior. When Isabel threatened to put an end to it herself, Mom would get uncharacteristically furious. Isabel accused her of having become docile with foolish love." His fingers drummed on the passenger side door. "Our mom never challenged that accusation."

Pieces clicked together in Alek's head, and he exhaled on a sigh of understanding. "That's what Lily fears. She thinks that's what love will do to her." His voice turned hoarse. "I thought she was just afraid of getting stuck in a lifelong relationship. But she's scared that if she allows herself to love fully, she'll become so enamored and submissive that she won't *want* to fight back against abuse."

Basil's mouth was a grim line. "It's all she's ever known of romantic love."

He rubbed a hand over his face. "Well, fuck me."

"No, thanks," Basil shot back drily.

He couldn't help snorting a laugh but sobered quickly. "How do I make her lose that twisted idea of love?"

"I'm not sure it's something *you* can do. But at least you can point her to it." Basil looked at him again. "I don't think she's even aware of all of this. Took me some time to piece it together, too."

Alek's deep breath didn't help ease the ache in his chest. "Thanks."

"Least I can do," Basil said, not looking at him, flicking some invisible lint off his pants. "Since you saved my life and all."

"No need to mention it again," he said, and gave him a curt nod.

Merle's car in front of them slowed and pulled over to park on the side of the street. Alek followed suit, his pulse a wild tick in the grip he had on the steering wheel. They'd entered a well-kept, expensive-as-shit-looking neighborhood with sprawling houses on huge properties. If they started a bloody fight here, the place would be swarming with human cops in no time.

He told Merle as much when they all exited the vehicles.

"Don't worry about that," the petite, ginger-haired witch said while Alek loaded himself up with the knives he stored in his truck, and strapped a short sword to his back. At his raised brows, she explained, "I'll throw a fogging charm around the area. Won't make us invisible, but it'll discombobulate any human minds in the vicinity so they won't react to us." She bounced a little on her feet, grinned at Rhun, and added in a low voice, "I've been wanting to use *discombobulate* in a sentence for so long."

"Of course you have," the *bluotezzer* demon said with an indulgent smile.

"I'll help you with the charm." Hazel stepped forward. "What's the perimeter?"

Rhun inclined his head at a house a few yards down. "From what I can tell, she's in there."

Dark eyes hard, Hazel nodded. She and Merle conferred about how far to cast the circle of the charm, and then went to work. Magic shimmered in the night like a desert mirage, only to disappear as soon as the charm snapped into place.

"Let's hope the jerks in there didn't see that," Merle said, residual power glowing around her.

Rhun shrugged. "They'll know soon enough that we're here."

Merle turned to Basil. "Set up your vantage point on the other side of the street. Kill every demon who runs outside."

Both Rhun and Alek cleared their throats.

Merle rolled her eyes. "Present company excepted, of course."

"Oh, I don't know about that," Basil said, giving Rhun the side-eye as he stroked the arrow he was nocking.

"Enough." Hazel nodded at Merle. "We split up, you and Rhun take the front, and Alek and I are going in from the back."

Merle's sky-blue eyes glittered. "Let's go."

CHAPTER 25

"Lily, no." Aveline cowered against the door, her face tear-streaked. "I'm not worth it. Don't let—" Seth's raised arm silenced her without even striking.

Trembling, Lily met Aveline's red-rimmed eyes. And saw something she hadn't noticed before. There was steel in that emerald green, a courage Lily hadn't reckoned with—no one had reckoned with, judging by how carelessly Seth turned his back on Aveline, his focus on Lily.

Away from a threat he'd clearly underestimated.

It showed in the surprise in his icy eyes when Aveline wrenched the dagger from his hand. In the moment of shock when his features slackened after the young witch-turned-demon slit her own throat. In his gasp when she managed to slice through both femoral arteries on her thighs as well before she collapsed. Her blood gushed onto the floor, ruby red on the white carpet.

Seth blanched, his aura wavering. He sputtered something incoherent and fell to his knees. Groping toward Aveline, he fumbled to put pressure on her wounds, red seeping over his shaking hands. His efforts were in vain. She made sure she'd bleed out in seconds by cutting so many vital arteries. With a gurgle, he crashed face-first onto the ground, his life force snuffed out like a candle.

It had all happened within a few heartbeats, too fast for Lily to stop her, or for Jaxton to jump forward. His energy pattern shocked still as his body, he loomed next to Lily, as dumbfounded into silent paralysis as she was.

She found her senses with a gasp. Aveline had died for her. Lily couldn't stop to mourn her, linger in her shocked sorrow, or Aveline's death would have been in vain.

Wrestling her mind into lethal focus before Jaxton regained his composure, she dropped to her knees, twisted her bound arms and slashed across the back of his calf with her claws. Falling back, she immediately kicked into the knee of his other leg. Vital muscles cut and one knee smashed, he went down with a scream.

She scrambled to her feet and ran over to Aveline's body. The wet carpet squished underneath her bare soles, making her wince. *Warm.* The blood was still warm. Gritting her teeth against the nausea bubbling up her throat, she crouched down, twisted and grabbed the dagger. Her heart pounded against her ribs while she used the blade to saw the rope around her wrists. Thank the gods Seth-rotting-in-hell had tied her hands with enough give for her to reach the rope with the blade. She couldn't have done it with her claws alone.

"You bitch," Jaxton bellowed, creeping toward her. His legs were useless, so he had to do it in Army-crawl style, which slowed him down a little. Enough for her to cut the ties?

Sweat beaded on her temples, rolled down her neck. One

part of the rope severed, but the tie still held. *Dammit.* The coarse material chafed the skin on her wrists as she furiously sawed with the dagger.

Jaxton kept shouting for the other *pranagrahas* to come. Commotion erupted in the hallway, more yells, and the sound of people running. *Shit, shit, shit.*

"I'll whip the skin off you," Jaxton growled.

He was three feet away.

More rope gave way. The tie held.

Two feet.

She doubled her speed.

One foot. He reached for her.

The blade cut through the last bit of rope, slicing her lower back with the force she put on it. Not that she cared. With a roar of bloodied rage, she struck out. The dagger embedded in Jaxton's right eye. He twitched once, then flopped down lifeless. His aura flickered out.

Breathing heavily, she rose from her crouch, her knees, shins and feet coated in Aveline's cooling blood. She spit on Seth-in-death's prone body and turned to the door just as it flew open, and a male *pranagraha* barreled in.

She had her dagger at his throat before he even spotted her. About to slash across his carotid artery, she paused—the scent of autumn nights and wood fires wrapped around her, his energy a welcome, familiar caress.

"Lilichka."

Gasping, she dropped the blade, threw herself against him. "Alek."

Her heart cracked wide open at the sight of him, the feel of his arms wrapping around her, his scent sinking into her every pore.

"You came for me," she whispered against his chest,

breathing him in as if this was the last time she'd ever be able to soak up his essence.

He kissed her hair. "Always, *tsvetochek*." He surveyed the carnage in the room, one eyebrow rising. "Although I can see you've done a great job on your own."

Darkness settled on her soul. "I couldn't have done it without Aveline. She—killed herself. To take away their leverage over me. To kill the leader." She nodded toward Seth's body. "Fucker was her mate."

Face a mask of unforgiving hardness, Alek brushed a lock of hair from her face. "I'm sorry about your friend."

Throat tight, she nodded. "We need to find Sarai—the other one."

୭୫୭

THE SOUNDS OF FIGHTING IN THE HOUSE GREW LOUDER AS ALEK and Lily filed into the hall, keeping to the walls, peeking around corners. Adrenaline thundering in his blood, Alek tightened his grip on the short sword he'd drawn.

There was so much he had to say to Lily, not the least of which was explaining the *nymphenstern*. But it would have to wait.

Up ahead, Hazel was in pursuit of a fleeing *pranagraha*, magic crackling around her. She'd run out of sight before he could tell her he'd found Lily.

"Let's keep going," Lily said, when he turned to run after Hazel. "We have to get Sarai out first."

Having checked the downstairs, they crossed the ruined living room, overturned furniture and drapes smoking from whatever spell had singed them, and ran up the stairs. More signs of fighting greeted them here in the hall, daggers impaled in the wall, shattered picture frames, stains of still-sizzling power on the carpet. They both made sure to give those marks a wide berth as they stalked forward.

In one of the bedrooms they encountered a closed door, probably to an adjoining bathroom. Alek silently gestured for Lily to stand to the side before he took a step back and kicked the door in. A metal rod swung toward him, and he ducked barely in time to avoid getting his skull smashed by the irate female *pranagraha* hiding in the bathroom.

"Sarai," Lily shouted as she skidded into the door. "He's okay! He's with me!"

The witch-turned-demon didn't relax from her fighting stance, the shower curtain rod she'd apparently broken off the wall still raised above her head while her eyes darted between Alek and Lily.

"Long story, hard to explain," Lily panted, "but trust me, he's on our side. Merle and my mom are here, let's go."

Sarai lowered her makeshift weapon, her throat working on a hard swallow. "My mate," she bit out. "If they kill him..."

"Can you find him? Through the bond?

Sarai nodded, her aura tinged with grim bitterness.

"Then we'll capture him and take him with us. We'll figure something out, Sarai."

Alek took the front, following Sarai's directions from behind him, while Lily brought up the rear. When agitated male voices and shuffles sounded from a room they were approaching, Sarai shook her head.

"Not in there," she whispered.

"Let's leave them to my mom and the others," Lily said in an equally quiet voice, gesturing for them to move on.

Back on the ground floor, Alek was almost past a closed

door when Sarai tapped him on the shoulder, signaling him to stop. She glanced at the door and nodded.

Basement, she mouthed.

Handing two of his knives to Sarai, he indicated Lily should cover his back. His heart pounded a feral rhythm when he tried the door. It opened toward him without resistance. The light from the hall fell on a set of narrow stairs leading down into darkness. Staying close to the wall, muscles primed to evade any attack, he descended.

The tang of blood and sweat and tears slammed into him, and he tensed. His eyes—adjusting to the gloom within seconds—scanned the room for Sarai's mate. He could make out the rough details of a table with shackles—empty—cabinets and counters, and what looked like lab equipment, before something snatched at his legs.

Losing his balance, he tumbled down the rest of the stairs, caught a glimpse of the tripwire that had waylaid him. *Sneaky little fucker.* He crashed down hard on his shoulder at the bottom, while Lily yelled for him from the hall. Footsteps pounded on the stairs as she and Sarai ran down.

He barely had time to register that. A soft, whirring sound ignited all his primal warning instincts, and he rolled to the side just as a long blade came down on him. The sword still sliced open his lower back, and he bit back a scream at the blinding pain. He gritted his teeth, ducked and blocked another strike with his own short sword, then whirled and lunged at the fucker's midsection while he was in upswing.

Heart in her throat, dagger clutched tight in her hand, Lily rushed down the stairs. Even after the second it took her eyes to adjust to the darkness, all she could see was a blur of shapes and shadows as Alek fought the other *pranagraha*.

Grunts and growls, the metallic scent of fresh blood, the clang of blade on blade. She tried so hard to track their movements, to discern an individual form, until her eyes actually *hurt*. If she jumped in now, she might end up causing more damage to Alek than to the other guy. Her muscles vibrated, her skin abuzz from forcing herself to stand still.

The muffled sound of a blow, followed by a thump.

Then Alek's voice— "I've got him."

Oh, thank fuck. She sprinted to where he stood over the collapsed body of the *pranagraha*.

"Is he—"

"Alive," Alek croaked, his breathing labored. "Just knocked out."

Sarai knelt at the male's side, yanking his arms back to tie them with a piece of rope she'd acquired the gods knew where.

Lily stroked Alek's face, the stubble on his jaw and cheek a welcome abrasion against her skin. "I was scared for you for a minute."

His eyes glittered, his aura tightly controlled. "Yeah?"

"Yeah." She stepped closer, his heat burning her through their clothes.

There was so much she wanted to say to him about those nascent feelings she'd denied until now, those tender affections she'd thought she could keep small, but which had grown into something with a potential that still scared the shit out of her. She stood on a precipice, an abyss gaping between her and what beckoned her, tugged at her so hard it hurt. All she had to do was jump.

If only the abyss didn't loom quite so large, so dark, making her heart stutter, her courage falter. If only she could be sure she wouldn't fall...

Later. She could figure all this out later, once they'd made it out of this hell house after crushing the bastards, their operation ground into dust. When she had a minute away from fearing for her life and snarling at kidnapping assholes, then she could face this darker, more consuming fear.

"I'm glad you're okay," she said to the demon who held more of her heart than he knew, because she couldn't yet tell him, not with the abyss still looming.

Alek exhaled on a shuddering breath, the tight leash of control he had on his aura slipping, and that was when she felt the sticky warmth of blood where her other hand rested on his side.

"Alek...you're injured." A hoarse whisper, some base part of her already understanding with predatory instincts what her mind rejected.

More cracks in the facade of his energy pattern, betraying the ravaging agony beneath, the ebbing flow of life. "Just a scratch," he rasped.

And fell to his knees.

The world spun out of focus. Thoughts derailing, she sank down next to him, her shaking hands pulling up the soaked black shirt—to reveal a gash in his side that went so deep she could see his internal organs. An injury that would have already killed a human.

"You—you can heal this, can't you? Alek? You can heal this. Tell me you can."

A strangled breath that sounded too much like a gurgle.

He slumped forward. There was another wound she hadn't noticed at first under the angry red coating his torso, another slash, this one curving from his other side to his back, deep, so terrifyingly deep.

"No," she whispered, and turned him as gently as she could.

Bending forward, she grabbed his face with both hands and covered his mouth with hers. Tasting blood on her tongue—*his* blood—she gathered up her *prana*, pushed it into him. Feebly, he drew it in, his pull little more than a tug. *Not enough.* He wasn't taking enough.

"Sarai!" She straightened, twisted around to the witch-turned-demon, who stood staring at the scene, her face ashen, eyes stricken with shock. "Run and find my mom or Merle, and get them here *fast.*"

Sarai nodded and sprinted off.

His wounds were so fucking deep and gaping, she didn't even know where to begin to stanch the bleeding. She tried anyway, slicing up his shirt with her claws to produce a makeshift compress. Bunching up one under his back, she applied the other to the slash in his side.

"Alek." She turned back to his too-pale face while keeping pressure on the compress with her knee. The smears of red her hands left on his jaw and cheeks were stark against the white skin. He felt cold to the touch, absent the heat that used to brush her like the most decadent sensual caress. "You can't leave me. You hear? Don't leave me. Stay. Hold on."

His breathing was too shallow.

"Help's on the way." She stroked his hair, tainting it with blood as well. Her hands shook so hard she wobbled his head where she touched him, so she made fists, forced her muscles to lock. "You just need to hold on until someone gets here."

Her voice was paper-thin. One more word and it would tear, she was sure. But she needed to talk to him, to keep him awake and holding on. Any Elder witch could heal wounds this vicious, this fatal, at least to the point where they would mend on their own. But none could rekindle the spark of life once snuffed out.

"Alek," she said on a sob, her voice breaking.

Those eyes of gold-rimmed silver fluttered shut. The glow of life around him dimmed.

"No." She grabbed his face again, not caring anymore that her trembling hands shook him.

All those things she'd wanted to say, everything that was in her heart—he'd never know. He'd die without knowing her love, because she'd been afraid to fall.

CHAPTER 26

"Alek. Look at me." Her vision swam, her throat raw. His aura had faded to all but an ember.

She stroked his cheeks, her lips trembling. "I love you. I'll mate with you, *prana*-griffin style and all. I'll fucking mate with you. But only if you hold on."

Her breath hurt, going in, going out, from her aching throat all the way down to her chest, to the epicenter of a pain so cutting it might annihilate her.

"*Please*," she whispered.

His lips parted. Silver-gold shimmered as he opened his eyes just a slit. Breath rattling in his throat, he met her anguished stare. "Holding…on."

She choked on a sob of relief. Her fingers tender on his skin, she caressed his jaw, his temples.

Raising his hand, he touched her lips. "Tell me…" he rasped. "Need to…hear…again… *Please*."

It could have been teasing, or cheeky, his request for her to repeat what he'd been waiting all this time to hear—but for the last word. There was nothing but naked vulnerability in his tone, in the furious need in his eyes. Pride, it was such a monstrous thing sometimes, and right now, he'd stripped himself of it completely, had ripped himself as deep and as open as the wounds on his back and side.

And her heart finally understood what she'd rationally known all along. That maybe, taking that leap across the abyss wasn't quite as daunting when you realize you're not jumping alone.

"I love you," she whispered, and meant it with every fiber of her being. "I love you so much it scares me."

"I know." A hoarse sound in the dark, and then his voice faded into a whisper as well, as if he'd lost the strength to use his vocal cords. "Won't ever let you...become a shadow...of yourself."

A shudder went through him. His hand fell to his side.

"No. Alek. No!" Darkness closed in around her. Her claws sliced out, pricked his skin where she held his head. "Stay!"

Footsteps thundered on the stairs. A familiar energy brushed up against her, and then her mom knelt on his other side, her hands on his skin. Magic surged, a bright glow illuminating the gloom in the basement, in Lily's heart. Not letting go of his face, she watched while her mom shoved power into him. The air buzzed with the magic that was worked into this world, that Hazel tapped in order to supplement her own powers.

"By the magic of my line," her mom intoned, "I call upon the Powers That Be..."

Lily had seen it a thousand times, had practiced it herself for most of her life, but she'd never witnessed the intricate spell work of witch magic as if looking on from the outside. Never seen it through the eyes of a demon.

Hazel's chant rose in the darkness.

What was broken shall be mended
What has torn be merged once more
Flesh and blood and life unended
Twine together at the core...

Such filigreed beauty, the way Hazel wove words into power, an embroidery of sound stitched into the fabric of this world, luminous threads of magic, breath, and life. Lily had never realized what a gift it was, this kind of power.

Under her hands, his skin regained warmth. His eyelids twitched but didn't open, his life force growing from a minuscule spark to something akin to a glow. Heart galloping in her chest, she gingerly pulled aside the compress on his abdominal wound. What had gaped so horrifyingly before was now a minor cut, the bleeding stopped. She glanced at her mom.

Sweat glistened on Hazel's forehead, her dark brown eyes glazed as if focused inward. Her hands trembled when she withdrew them from Alek's body. The magic in the air around her quieted, as if dissolving on a breath.

Lily almost didn't dare ask, the question not more than a whisper. "Will he live?"

"Yes." She'd never heard her mom's voice sound so drained, so utterly exhausted. Weariness settled on the Elder witch's shoulders like a cloak, pressing her down.

Lily grasped her mom's hand, squeezed, her chest tight. She knew the price for this kind of powerful spell work. Soon the Powers That Be would demand Hazel pay for the magic she'd drawn from the world, for nothing was given free. "Thank you, Mom."

For the first time since Lily had been turned into a demon, her mother met her eyes, a world of change between them. The lines in her face were more pronounced, carved deeper by sorrow and worry, and filled with age in the time Lily hadn't seen her.

"I'm sorry," Lily croaked. "Mom, I'm so sorry." Tears spilled over, ran down her cheeks, hot and guilty.

"My baby," Hazel whispered, then drew her into a hug over Alek's body.

Her mother's warmth enfolded her, soothed parts of her soul that had been sliced and splintered, mended them with a power so different from what she'd used on Alek, and yet no less potent. *Love*, Lily thought, *is a magic all its own.*

Sobbing into her mom's shoulder, she released all the anger, shame, grief, and shattered hope, found a calm place beneath, a place that let her *breathe*.

"What I did to Baz..." she began after they finally separated.

"...is something you should release. It's past time you let it go." Her mom's eyes shimmered with moisture. "Enough now, Lily. You've apologized enough for something that was not your fault."

She was silent for a moment. "I'll miss it," she said quietly. "Being a witch."

"I know." Hazel caressed her cheek, face soft with wistfulness. "But you'll be fine, honey. You always have been, always will be. Being a witch does not define you." She tapped Lily's chest. "This here does."

Lily sniffed. "My bountiful bosom?"

Her mom huffed a small laugh. "Your heart, silly. Who you are in here doesn't change, no matter what species you are."

"Thank you, Mom." She swallowed hard, trying not to let her voice break again. "Maybe—maybe Basil's kids can carry on the line."

Something flickered in the dark of her mom's gaze, there and gone so quickly, it might have been a trick of the light. "We'll see, baby."

CHAPTER 27

S ounds and light filtered through the darkness blanketing Alek's mind. His thoughts disentangling from a web of images and sensations, he became aware of his current surroundings. A pillow beneath his head, a mattress underneath his back, a soft sheet covering him.

And two warm bodies pressed against his own.

Eyes flying open to semi-darkness, he looked to his legs, where Grant snored softly, snuggled up to him. Alek turned his head, silky black curls brushing against his jaw. The scent of lush flowers and rain teased his nose, let him draw in a breath that threatened to burst his lungs.

Lily.

Her head resting on his shoulder, hands tucked between their bodies, she lay curled against him, one leg thrown over his. Eyes closed, her black lashes fanned out over her cheeks. Even though he hated to disturb her sleep, he couldn't help brushing a lock of her midnight hair from her face, his fingers lingering on skin so soft, it was a caress to touch it.

His heart expanded, filled to the brim with tenderness.

"You're awake," she murmured a second before she opened her luminous indigo eyes, meeting his in the gloom of the bedroom.

"How long was I out?" Even to his own ears, his voice scraped the bottom of a gravel pit. *Yikes.*

But Lily's lips curved up ever so slightly, her aura shimmering with appreciation. "Sexy."

"If I'd known you'd find a fucked-up voice so attractive, I would have made sure I was knocked out more often."

The smile on her lips died, her eyes taking on a haunted sheen, and he could have kicked himself for putting that look on her face. "You've been unconscious for the rest of the night and the following day. It's night now."

He'd guessed as much from his active demon senses and the quality of the light. "Tell me the rest of what happened."

The sheet slid down as she sat up, revealing a simple black tank top. "What do you remember?"

"The sword fight, pain...your eyes in the dark..." He brushed his thumb over her cheek.

Turning into his caress for a second, she then cleared her throat. "Well, my mom got there just in time and healed you, at least to the point where your body can do the rest. Rhun and Basil helped carry you out, and I told them to bring you here. Grant and I have been holed up with you for the day. He hasn't left your side." Her face softened while she leaned over to stroke the dog.

He smiled at his beloved companion of fifteen years. "Thanks, buddy," he said softly.

Grant's ears twitched, and though his eyes remained closed, his tail thumped once.

"What about the other *pranagrahas*?" he asked, looking back at Lily.

"All dead or accounted for." Grim satisfaction laced her words. "From what Sarai told us, and what we've gotten out of the fucker she was forced to mate, the whole thing was Seth's—Aveline's dead mate's—idea. He solicited like-minded *pranagraha* males who were looking for mates, they snatched the first witch—Marianne—and bled her dry, then mixed her blood with that of a *pranagraha* and did some fucked-up, crazy lab stuff with it that's basically dark blood magic on steroids. The result was the serum. They had to adjust the recipe twice, since the next two witches they kidnapped died after being injected." Her eyes glittered with fury.

So many lives lost... He twined his fingers with hers, stroked his thumb over the soft patch of skin between her thumb and index finger. "Bastards are dead now," he said, his voice rough due to more than his long unconsciousness. "They can't ever do that shit again."

"Yeah. No one can. Except for Sarai's bastard of a mate, who's locked up tight in our dungeon, none of them survived to tell the tale, and the house with the lab equipment is less than rubble."

He raised his brows. "You burned it down?"

"Not us." A line creased her forehead. "My mom and Merle were still clearing the perimeter after we'd gotten out when the whole building was wiped out as if someone had detonated a specifically targeted, very contained nuclear bomb. My mom said they didn't see anyone come or go, but the razed ground fumes with ancient magic as she's never felt it."

"Strange." While a part of him wanted to further explore that particular piece of information, he remembered something else. "What about Juneau and her witches?"

"Yeah, that." She sighed, picked at a bit of fluff on the sheet. "It's been quiet, but it's only a matter of time before she makes her next offensive move. She's rallying her forces, so to speak. She called an impromptu Elder meeting without my mom and Merle, and basically declared them traitors and insurgents. About half of the Elders are backing her, but the other half followed Elaine—she's head of the Donovan family—when she called Juneau a warmongering bitch and walked out of the meeting. Elaine went to my mom and told her. She's siding with us, as are the other Elders and their families who walked out of the meeting." She gave him a sad little smile. "The witch community has broken apart."

"Not just over you," he said, squeezing her hand. "From what you and Merle said the other night, this has been a long time coming. It's about more than your turning and what you did."

"I know." A whisper laced with grief. "It still pains me."

"So," he said after a moment, because he wanted to erase the hurt and sadness in her aura, needed to know the answer to the question in his heart. "I had a kind of interesting dream."

"Did you, now?"

"Mhm." He watched her closely. "I dreamed that as I lay dying, you said you loved me and promised you'd mate with me."

Color flooded her face. Intriguing, when she so rarely blushed. "That was real," she whispered.

His heart made a somersault in his chest. "Before I ask you if you want to keep that promise," he said, laying a finger on her lips when she was about to speak up, "I need you to see something."

Shoving his hand underneath the sheet, he wanted to

pull the *nymphenstern* out of his pocket—only to find himself sans jeans. Sans anything, really, the sheet rustling over his naked hips and legs.

Lily shot him a wicked grin, her attention on his hand that had patted his groin. "Oh, I've already seen that, but hey, I'd always love to take another, more *thorough* look."

His pulse thundered so loud, he barely noticed her quipping. "Where are my pants?"

"Ah, well." Her brows furrowed, and she bit her lip. "There was so much blood on them, they were beyond saving."

His eyes widened. "You threw them out?"

"Uh, yeah. Did you want to donate them? I don't think Goodwill would take—oy, are you even healed enough to jump up like that?"

He'd leapt off the bed and was on his way to the kitchen, hopping into a pair of sweat pants he'd snatched off his bedroom floor. His side and back twinged a little with every move, but nothing he couldn't handle. Breath unsteady, he rummaged through the trash. No jeans in sight.

He was about to dash outside to go through the garbage bin, when Lily's voice halted him.

"Looking for something?" It was the lilt in her tone that tipped him off.

He turned slowly on his heels, faced a saucy little demon with a knowing smile.

"You found the stone, didn't you?" he asked.

With a nod, she came closer. She wore nothing but a pair of black panties with her tank top, her long legs a visual delight as she stepped up to him. Raven curls tumbling about her shoulders, she tilted her head back to look into his eyes.

"Where is it?"

"With my mom and Merle. They're brewing the reversal potion."

The pain was instantaneous, lancing his heart, shattering the last shreds of hope. He couldn't breathe, his chest locked far more viciously than after the solar plexus hit she'd landed early in their courtship. Jaw clenched so tight he popped a muscle, he nodded, and turned away.

He didn't want her to see him break. Her happiness truly was more important than his own, and if this was what made her happy...

"Alek." Her quiet voice, threading around his shattering soul. Her hand on his arm, warm, comforting. "It's not for me."

"What?" He glanced at her over his shoulder.

"The potion..." Brilliant indigo eyes met his. "They're not brewing it for me."

Understanding rushed into him, knocking the stalled breath out of his lungs as he fully faced her. "The other witch-turned-demon. The one we got out."

"Sarai." She nodded, her lashes trembling. "She'll be free again."

"And what about you?"

"I don't need it." A whisper, a promise. "I don't want it." A vow.

"I thought," he said, his throat so dry it hurt, "turning back was your heart's desire."

"I thought so too." She rested her hand on his chest, over his thundering heartbeat. "It was what I should have wanted, what was logical. But you—" Her claws sliced out, pricked his skin in the most thrilling caress. "You blindsided me. In the best of ways. I never wanted any of the things you offered me—love, family, forever—but not because I didn't truly desire them. I was too scared to let myself want them." Her breath hitched. "I'm still scared."

He threaded his fingers through her hair, stroked behind her ear, down to the spot that made her shiver so adorably. "But...?"

Her throat worked on a swallow. "There's this poem I once read," she said softly, lowering her eyes, "by Erin Hanson. I didn't get it, not until recently. Not until..." She sucked in air. "Well. It says,

> *There is freedom waiting for you,*
> *On the breezes of the sky,*
> *And you ask 'What if I fall?'*
> *Oh but my darling, What if you fly?"*

Those candescent indigo eyes met his again, the full weight of her beauty hitting him hard. "When you lay dying...I realized I'd rather try, and fail, than never experience what it could be like to take that leap of faith and be with you. I want to believe that I can fly, more than I fear to fall. I want to have a lifetime with you."

"Lilichka," he murmured, his other hand cradling her face as well, with the tender knowledge that he was holding the most precious thing in his life. "You're the reason my heart beats. If you fall, I'll catch you. Always." Leaning in, he kissed her nose, her lips, the barest brush of breath on breath. "I won't ever let you become complacent, or meek." He smiled against her mouth. "I love your spunk too much, you know."

She exhaled on a soft laugh, her aura wrapping around

him with such glowing love, he wanted to savor this moment forever.

"I love you," he said in between kisses that were hot, frantic, stirring embers of lust. "Mate with me."

Looping her arms around his neck, she bit his lower lip, licked over the sting. "Yes." Her teeth grazed his tongue, her fingers playing with the hair on his nape. "How?"

Blood having rushed enthusiastically south, he could barely form more than one-word sentences himself. She was his magnet, his hands unable to separate from her skin, stroking underneath her tank top, to the swell of her breasts, her hardened nipples. A sound of pure pleasure from his female—*his*—and it all but disintegrated his thoughts.

"Alek," she breathed.

"Hm?" His lips on her throat, her scent sinking into him.

"How?" Her claws nicking the skin on his shoulders, a thrilling incentive. "Need...to know...oh!"

He'd slid his fingers into her panties, found her intimate folds, which were already wet with her desire. She moaned and bit his neck, shuddering against him as he brought her to an unexpected climax.

He withdrew his hand, licked his fingers under her transfixed gaze. "You were saying?"

Her lashes lowered and rose over eyes that were fireworks of red and black. "Tell me what I need to do," she said, her voice deliciously languorous.

Taking a deep breath to bring his racing pulse under control and focus, he stepped back, grabbed her hand, and tugged at her to follow him to his bedroom.

"We need to exchange *prana*," he said as he lay down on the mattress, pulling her on top of him.

She went willingly, straddling his hips, the heat of her

core pressing against the erection straining against his pants. He whipped his errant thoughts into shape so he could continue his instruction.

Palms on her thighs, he said, "Only this time, it needs to go further. An exchange of both blood and breath. I drink a little of yours, you drink a little of mine, we breathe into each other—and you'll feel a tug. That's the bond trying to form." His thumbs stroked over the inside of her thighs, up to the seams of her panties.

Her breath hitched, her aura shimmering like the most beautiful kaleidoscope.

"It won't snap into place unless you want it," he said, reining in his lust to finish his explanation. "That's what's needed for a mating. Blood, breath—"

"—and desire." She shifted her position, pressing a little harder against his aching cock. "Well, there won't be an issue with the last part."

A corner of his mouth twitched up, and he slid his hands up to her hips, cradled her waist. "Ready?"

Biting her lower lip, she nodded. He took one hand off her waist, pushed out a claw, and sliced a shallow cut over his heart. Blood welled out of the thin slash, the scent of iron tickling his nose. Holding his gaze, she leaned down, her hands on his shoulders, and licked at the gash.

A grin took over his face. "You do need a little more."

One of her brows cocked up, and she grinned back. Closing her mouth over the cut, she sucked. A groan escaped him at the thrilling sensation of pleasure rolling all the way down to his balls. His dick twitched against her hot center, and he growled.

"I need to feel you," he said, ripping through the fabric of her panties with his claws. He yanked the annoying barrier from between their bodies, and after a few more slashes and some quick acrobatics, his pants rained down around them in shreds. He flipped them both before she could so much as squeak.

"Alek!" she cried out as he entered her in one smooth thrust.

Sensing her full, willing participation also evident in the deep streaks of pleasure in her aura, he wanted nothing more than to pump into her until she shattered around him. Still, he paused and asked, his lips on her throat. "Stop?"

"*Never.*" The word, its meaning, reverberated through them both, touched places in him parched for her love. "You just surprised me."

He grinned and bit her earlobe. "Well, that's good, then. Gotta keep you on your toes."

"Mhm." Eyes sparking with fiery red on midnight, she lifted one hand to her throat, cut a line into the soft skin below her chin, careful not to nick her artery. "Your turn."

Not hesitating a second, he licked up the blood that was running down to the back of her neck, then closed his lips around the cut, and drew her essence into him. Her inner muscles clenched around him in rhythm with his pulls, and he rocked into her, the combined sensation of her heat around his cock and her *prana* flowing into him driving him mad with ecstasy.

And it was only the beginning.

He licked over the shallow wound on her throat, still moving inside her, and kissed his way up to her mouth.

"Breath," she whispered against his lips.

"Breath," he answered, and took her mouth in a bruising kiss. "Take mine first."

While their tongues tangled, she rolled her hips against

his, meeting each of his thrusts, her hands on his ass, claws digging in. The nick of pain ratcheted up his arousal, and he pumped faster, harder. Despite the lust hijacking his brain, he managed to gather his *prana*, pull it up, and push it into her with his breath.

She jerked when it hit her. Moaning deep in her throat, she drew it in, her aura bursting on a flash of pleasure. Her body undulated underneath him, against him, while she came, and he made sure to increase her enjoyment with long, hard thrusts.

She broke their kiss, panting against his mouth. "Now you." Her hand slid up his back, to his chest and up to his face, her fingers tender on his jaw. "I want to feel you come inside me."

Hell, yeah. He licked over her lower lip, sucked on it, and she opened to him with eagerness, an aphrodisiac all on its own. When she pushed her *prana* into him, it was liquid lust, and he drank as if dying of thirst.

Then...a tug, a pull, a tenuous bond that snapped taut and strong between his heart and hers. The pleasure that had been building inside him, the buzzing pressure of mounting excitement, was released with a force that would have toppled him if he'd been standing. His climax raged through him, a storm of potent pleasure, breath and life, and just a little death.

He understood, for the first time ever, why the French called it *la petite mort*.

Rocking into her with the last spasms of orgasm, savoring the feel of sweet satisfaction finally achieved, he laid his forehead against hers, his breath heavy, unsteady. Their new bond a glowing force between them, she enfolded him with her arms, her fingers stroking through his hair.

When she spoke, it was an intimate murmur, and he felt the love behind her words resonate along the mating bond. "How'd you like it?"

He raised his head, met eyes of relaxed indigo, the color so deep, so rich, it was inhuman. "I want to do this for the rest of my life."

Her laugh filled his heart with sunshine.

"No, I'm serious." He shifted his hips, his cock growing hard again inside her. "I'm sorry, but you'll never be able to leave this bed again. Or this room."

She pursed her lips, her face alight with laughter. "We'll have to eat sometime." But she rolled her pelvis in response to his languid thrusts, her claws drawing tantalizing lines down his back.

"All right." He gripped her leg, opened her wider for him. "The kitchen table is sturdy enough."

She gasped as he changed his angle. "The couch looks comfy."

"Well," he said, pleasure a buzz in his blood, "I guess I can make do." He kissed her hard, his heart too full with everything he felt for her. "As long as I have you."

A cascade of love along the precious bond between their souls. "Forever."

EPILOGUE

"Bye, Uncle Sasha! Bye, Aunt Lily!" The door closed, shutting off the kids' voices and their frantic waves.

Cool night air stroked over Lily's skin as she and Alek descended the front steps to the sidewalk. Twining her fingers with Alek's, she stole a glance at her mate—*mate*—and smiled, her heart ready to burst. She'd never get used to this feeling.

"So," she said, "how *did* you get to be scared of spiders? You never told me the story."

He shot her a look from behind narrowed eyes, the silver in them catching the moonlight. "Won't let it go, will you?"

"Like a dog with a bone. Now spill."

He grumbled something incoherent, and she nudged him with her elbow.

"Come on, Mr. *Prana*-grump."

"*Pranagraha.*" His smile made her belly flutter on fairy wings. "What's my incentive to tell you?"

"Hm, how about this?" Rising on her toes, she brought her lips to his ear and whispered her idea of a good reward.

He missed a step, straightened, and cleared his throat. "Okay, so Dima and I were nine, and—"

He broke off the same second she felt it, too. A disturbance in the air, not witch magic, but something darker, older, with a bite to it that raised the hairs on her neck and arms. Heart in her throat, she halted next to Alek while they both looked at his driveway—where a man leaned against the hood of Alek's truck.

Not a man, no. Even without ever having seen him before, Lily recognized Arawn at once. There was no mistaking that casual air of arrogance, the way he seemed to gather the night around him, power pouring off him like invisible steam.

Clad in black pants and a dress shirt of the same color, his arms crossed in front of his massive chest, he tilted his head, regarding them with eyes that whispered of magic steeped in time.

He shouldn't be able to stand where he did—her mom and Merle had both come by and cast wards around the perimeter of Alek's house, including his driveway, for added protection against other witches—and beings as insidious as Arawn.

The fact he was propped so casually against Alek's truck *within* the still-active wards spoke of more than a deliberate display of power.

It signaled, just as deliberately, that his power had *grown*, when not too long ago, he hadn't been able to breach Merle's wards.

"My lord," Alek rasped, releasing her hand to go down on one knee.

A pang in her chest at the knowledge he needed to continue calling him that because of her. In the hours of intimate tangling following their mating, he told her how he'd traded in his freedom for her chance to turn back. Even though she hadn't needed it—his sacrifice was forever etched in her heart.

"Aleksandr," Arawn said, his voice quiet thunder. Those dark eyes—not brown, but rather shadowed green, from what she could tell at this distance—found her and studied her from head to toe. "Lily Murray."

Unsure of whether she was also supposed to bend her knee for the Demon Lord—and loath to do it—she remained standing and settled on bowing her head to Arawn.

Alek rose to his feet, subtly shifting until he stood a little in front of her. "To what do I owe the honor of your visit, sire?"

"I wanted to extend my congratulations on your mating." The light of the street lamps should have glinted off Arawn's ebony hair, but instead it seemed to vanish within the black, as if sucked away.

"Thank you," Alek ground out.

"I see whatever ailed your beloved has been cured." Those shrewd eyes met hers, and she had to look away, the contact was so intense. He cocked his head in a quintessentially predatory way. "Or maybe not."

Beside her, Alek tensed, and though his aura was controlled, she felt his fear slither along the mating bond.

"And maybe," the Demon Lord went on, pushing off Alek's truck to saunter toward the flower beds beside the driveway, "the stone was used to cure another of the same rare condition..." He touched a rose with his index finger, the flower wilting underneath his caress. His voice dropped to a rumble. "One that should have never come to pass."

Lily held her breath, her pulse a staccato beat in her head.

Arawn straightened and faced them again. "It has come to my attention that death nearly took you recently, Aleksandr."

"Yes, my lord."

"Do try not to get killed after hours." Forest green eyes alight with an inner fire, Arawn prowled closer. "I would hate to lose a soldier I have just invested in."

Alek held himself rigid, his face a mask of neutrality. "Understood."

"Do you?" A soft question, his eyes assessing, almost... thoughtful. "Your father," he said, his voice a low murmur, "made a deal with me, and broke it. Despite knowing I would take his life. When I had him brought before me, he tried to bargain for his life. Do you know what he offered me?"

"No, sire." Alek's jaw clenched so hard, all of the muscles in his face hardened into a marble likeness. His bitterness trickled through the mating bond.

"Your mother, and every one of his children, to do with as I wished."

Lily's heart cringed, her pain echoed by Alek's through the connection they shared.

"I declined," Arawn said. "But I offered him mercy. Which he repaid by stealing information from me and selling it to settle his debts." Darkness pooled around him, clinging to his broad shoulders, vibrating along his arms and legs.

To cross the Demon Lord twice...*no one* ever survived such stupidity.

"Why are you telling me this now?" Alek ground out through clenched teeth.

"Since you will spend more time in my service," Arawn answered, "I thought it fitting you should know the truth."

And heed the subtle warning in it, too, no doubt.

Stepping closer to Alek, Lily twined her fingers with his again, leaning a little of her weight into his side. A reminder, a comfort, a promise. *I'm here with you, always.*

Alek's aura didn't flicker, didn't betray a single emotion, but a rush of love and heat flowed toward her along their bond.

"As a gift to your mating," Arawn said, waving a hand.

Power rose in the air, as if drawn from the earth and the space between, and on a whisper of the world that was half whimper, magic such as she'd never experienced threaded through the existing witch wards, fortifying them into a shimmering wall around Alek's property.

"Report to me a week from now for your next assignment." The Demon Lord inclined his head. "Until then, enjoy your mate." Lips curving into a half-smile that chilled her blood, Arawn turned, his hands in his pockets, and strolled down the sidewalk, courting shadows wherever he passed.

It was only when his dark shape had vanished that Alek exhaled on a breath that sounded like it held the weight of the world. Tension leaking from his muscles, he pulled her forward, through the fortified wards that prickled over her skin, into his house. He closed the door with a sigh, keeping his palm on the wood, his head hanging.

Brushing away the dark blond hair that had fallen into his face, she kissed his forehead, his nose, his lips. He responded, tunneling his fingers through her hair, turning her so her back met the door, his kiss that of a male in need of salvation.

"If I didn't know better," she said when they broke apart to breathe, "I'd say he...cares about you. In his own, disturbed—and disturbing—way."

Caging her in with his forearms braced on either side of her head, his eyes fixed on her lips, he quietly said, "It doesn't make it okay."

"No." It would never soothe the ache in his heart for the loss he'd suffered, but maybe—

"I still hate him for taking my mother's life. But..." A deep sigh, a shudder along their most intimate connection. "I get why he couldn't let my father live. It makes a sick sort of sense when you consider who—and what—Arawn is."

And that was the crux of it. Beings like the Demon Lord didn't rise to—and hold on to—power by having mercy thrown back in their face.

"The demons who are his, the ones he keeps in line," she said, stroking that hair of dark, burnished gold, "he wouldn't be able to control them if his punishments seemed weak."

He nodded, his fingers light while they glided over her skin, mapping the contours of her face. "He's still a jerk."

"But you're not his," she whispered, turning her head to kiss his palm. "You're mine."

A smile slid onto his lips, mirrored in the sunshine along their bond, eyes of gold-rimmed silver meeting hers. "I think," he murmured against her mouth, "I've been neglecting my duties as your mate for tonight." His smile turned wicked, stirring heat and hunger in her core. "You look like you need *prana*."

Laughing, she met his kiss, flinging her legs around his waist. "Well, this door looks sturdy enough."

He broke the kiss, laid his forehead against hers, his eyes closed. "I love you, *bahishprana*."

"*Bahishprana*?" She stroked his neck, played with the soft hair on his nape. "What does that mean?"

Eyes shimmering with brilliant silver-gold met hers. "Literally, it's external breath or life. But among our kind, it's used for the one thing that is closest to our hearts, the person who holds our *prana*, our life."

The smile on her face echoed the one blooming inside her. "I'm your breath outside your body."

He laughed. "Simply put."

"Fitting," she whispered. "Since you're my heart."

The kiss he gave her then lit up her soul, her very own beacon of hope.

ॐ

Thank you for reading *To Win a Demon's Love!*
If you'd love more of my writing, sign up for my newsletter to receive my novella *To Caress a Demon's Soul* for free, and to be notified of new releases, and get more newsletter-exclusive goodies in the future.
My newsletter is low-volume and won't spam your inbox.
I'll never share your information, not even with my demons.
You can unsubscribe at any time.
Sign up here: www.nadinemutas.com/newsletter

ॐ

If you enjoyed Alek and Lily's story, consider leaving a review on your favorite store or on Goodreads. Reviews are great to help other readers find the books they'll love, and to support your favorite authors.

You're also welcome to contact me via email:

nadine@nadinemutas.com

I love to hear from readers!

Books in the *Love and Magic* series by Nadine Mutas:

Novels:

To Seduce a Witch's Heart (Love and Magic, #1)

To Win a Demon's Love (Love and Magic, #2)

To Stir a Fae's Passion (Love and Magic, #3)

To Enthrall the Demon Lord (Love and Magic, #4)

Novellas:

To Caress a Demon's Soul (Love and Magic, #1.5) **Sign up for my newsletter to receive this novella as a free read!**

ABOUT THE AUTHOR

Polyglot Nadine Mutas has always loved tangling with words, whether in her native tongue German or in any of the other languages she's acquired over the years. The more challenging, the better, she thought, and thus she studied the languages of South Asia and Japan. She worked at a translation agency for a short while, putting to use her knowledge of English, French, Spanish, Japanese, and Hindi.

Before long, though, her lifelong passion for books and words eventually drove her to give voice to those story ideas floating around in her brain (which have kept her up at night and absent-minded at inopportune times). She now writes paranormal romances with wickedly sensual heroes and the fiery heroines who tame them. Her debut novel, *To Seduce a Witch's Heart* (first published as *Blood, Pain, and Pleasure*), won the Golden Quill Award 2016 for Paranormal Romance, the Published Maggie Award 2016 for Fantasy/Paranormal Romance, and was a finalist in the PRISM contest for Dark Paranormal and Best First Book, as well as nominated for the Passionate Plume award 2016 for Paranormal Romance Novels & Novellas. It also won several awards for excellence in unpublished romance.

She currently resides in California with her college sweetheart, beloved little demon spawn, and two black cats hellbent on cuddling her to death (Clarification: Both her husband and kid prefer her alive. The cats, she's not so sure about.)

Nadine Mutas is a proud member of the Romance Writers of America (RWA) and the Silicon Valley Romance Writers of America (SVRWA), the Rose City Romance Writers (RCRW), as well as the Fantasy, Futuristic & Paranormal chapter of the RWA (FF&PRW).

Connect with Nadine:

www.nadinemutas.com
nadine@nadinemutas.com

81594970R00195

Made in the USA
Lexington, KY
17 February 2018